Roses in Red Wax

The Darnalay Castle Series Book 1

Louise Mayberry

Louise Mayberry

Roses in Red Wax by Louise Mayberry

1st Edition. March, 2023

Copyright © 2023 by Louise Mayberry
Editor: Isabelle Felix
Cover art: by Hallie Zillman

Ebook ISBN: 79-8-9876378-0-7
Paperback ISBN: 979-8-9876378-1-4

Roses in Red Wax takes place against the backdrop of two very real historical events: The Scottish "Radical War" of 1820 and the Highland Clearance. That said, this novel is a work of fiction. Any resemblance to specific events or persons, living or dead, is entirely coincidental.

To Stanley,

who makes it all possible.

PROLOGUE

DARNALAY CASTLE, NORTHEAST SCOTLAND
JUNE 1818

"MARRY ME, JANIE." His smile was as bright as the sun itself.

"But—"

"I spoke to the laird."

She stared at him, disbelieving. "You spoke . . . *to my father?*"

"Aye." Kendric twined his fingers with hers.

"And he agreed?"

"Gave me his blessing." He'd been picking strawberries. She could smell their sweetness on his breath, the damp earth on his hands.

This was real.

Joy welled inside her, cautious at first, then surging, bubbling up, spilling over. She laughed, then wiped away the tears and pressed her forehead against his, looking deep into his beloved hazel eyes. "We're to be married. *Married*."

"Weel . . ." His eyes were dancing. "That depends, dinna it?"

"Depends on what?" Had Father set some sort of condition? A test they must pass?

"The laird was very clear. You must say aye."

She laughed. "Aye. *Aye.*" She could see their future unfolding before them, beautiful beyond comprehension.

He shouted his happiness to the sky, then drew her out of the shade of the pear tree she'd been thinning and into the sun, spinning her round till her feet left the ground and he was her only point of focus in a swirl of color and sound—*grass and birdsong, trees and sky, golden sunshine and wind*—then he pulled her close. The outside world fell away, and there was only him. His warmth. His constancy. His love.

This was where she belonged, where she would be, for the rest of her life.

"Janie." He drew away, his eyes suddenly serious. "Life with me . . . It willna be as grand as you're used to in the castle."

She reached out to stroke his cheek, this beautiful boy, now a man, who she'd loved as long as she could remember. The other half of her heart. "Doesna matter. I'll have you."

He led her to the most ancient tree in her father's orchard, a wine apple planted by her great-great-grandfather. Its gnarled limbs extended nearly to the ground, creating a secret chamber of leaves and branches, a world unto itself. As children, it had been one of their favorite places to play. Now, it was where they came to escape. To be alone, together.

A cloud dimmed the sun. Jane met Ken's eyes, and a shadow passed between them—so brief she barely registered it. Then the world was bright again. Ken smiled and squeezed her hand as together they ducked under the outstretched branches.

They gave themselves to each other that strawberry-scented afternoon, in the dappled sunlight under her great-great-grandfather's apple tree, their bodies consecrating the pledge their lips had just made.

ONE

GLASGOW, MARCH 1820

JANE PULLED THE HOOD of her cloak tighter as she hurried up the steps to the Sommerbells' townhouse. Not that it made any difference. The icy wind cut through the thick woolen fabric, chilling her to the bone. She shivered. With this weather, was it any wonder her dear friend's tree was dying?

Except it wasn't just the cold, was it? It was *her*. In the end, everything Jane cared for died.

No matter, she was numb to it now.

She stood, looking at the door. She could still turn around, go back home, give some excuse for not answering Cynthia's note— But, no, she couldn't. She must face what lay ahead, even if the tree *was* dead. She owed her friend that much.

She lifted her hand and knocked, seeing but not feeling her gloved knuckles as they struck the hard oaken door. It opened. She stepped inside and was surrounded by sudden warmth.

"Good afternoon, Miss Stuart." Thomas, the Sommerbells' footman, reached for her cloak. "Mrs. Sommerbell's in the—"

"Jane! Is that you?" Cynthia's distressed voice came from above. "Do come up!"

Jane handed Thomas her bonnet, then climbed the stairs to the sitting room. Her fingers began the painful ache that comes between numbness and warmth.

Cynthia was perched on the sofa in front of the fire. As Jane entered, she hastily put a mark in the book she'd been reading, then sprang up and crossed the room, beckoning for Jane to follow.

"Come see. Oh my dear, I think I've killed it." Cynthia hovered over the potted lemon tree before the window. Jane hurried over, relieved to see the leaves were still dark green and glossy. Certainly it wasn't dead, or dying. But instead of clinging to the branches, the lemons, small and green in their immaturity, were scattered on the floor. Lost. All twenty-two of them.

"The last one fell just a half hour ago." Cynthia stared at the little tree sorrowfully.

"Did you move it?" Jane removed her gloves, sinking to her knees to examine the tree.

"Yes." Cynthia stood back to allow Jane room. "When the weather shifted. It got so cold . . . I brought it closer to the fire." She paused, then added hurriedly. "But I moved it back as soon as I noticed the lemons dropping."

That was the cause. It could have withstood the cold, but the dramatic shift in temperature would have been too much for the sensitive tree. Cynthia wasn't to blame, though. Jane hadn't warned her of that.

"The tree itself is unharmed." Jane sat back on her heels, forcing an optimistic tone. "We'll just have to try again next year."

Her body felt weighty, lifeless, as if she herself were wilting. Why had she allowed this silly little tree to mean something to her? She'd fertilized it, hand-pollinated the blossoms, placed it just so in the brightest part of the room . . . she'd *cared* for it, when she knew perfectly well that such feelings only led to pain.

"Douglas, of course, was elated," Cynthia said dryly.

Cynthia's husband had informed them, in his most professorial tone, that fruiting a lemon tree in a Glasgow townhouse was impossible. Cynthia had tried for years to prove him wrong, and this year with Jane's help, she'd almost done it. Almost.

"What a week it's been." Cynthia knelt down to pick up the lemons, cradling them in her skirt. "First, Douglas' brother. Now this."

"His brother's arrived?" Jane's chest tightened. She'd totally forgotten Cynthia's brother-in-law was due for a visit. He'd recently acquired property in Glasgow—spinning mills—and was coming from Northumberland to inspect them. Cynthia had been looking forward to it. Apparently, the brothers had drifted apart in recent years and she was hoping this visit would repair their goodwill.

Cynthia shook her head sadly. "He's had an accident. A bad one."

"Oh." A wave of relief—*she wouldn't have to meet this stranger after all*—was subsumed quickly by guilt. *The man's hurt.* "His visit's delayed then?"

Cynthia shook her head. "Our nephew's coming in his stead. I expect him this afternoon, in fact." She straightened up and dumped the lemons on a side table. "I do hope you'll stay for a bit. Warm yourself."

Jane forced a smile, trying to ignore the sudden roar of her pulse, the heat rising on her face. This nonsensical fear of meeting new people was thoroughly irritating. *There's nothing to be afraid of.* She could allow herself a moment of warmth before she trudged the mile and a half back to her own cold house. Certainly, she would leave before this nephew arrived.

"It *is* cold." She forced herself to rise, then walked to the fire, reaching her hands as close to the flames as she dared. Coal was a resource to be tightly rationed in her own home, making the heat feel all the more luxurious.

Outside of the small rented house she shared with her brother, the Sommerbells' sitting room was the only place in Glasgow where Jane felt truly at ease, even, in short stretches, like the girl she'd been *before* ... before Ken died, and life started to unravel. The room was decorated in muted browns and greens. Botanical prints filled the walls—copies of illustrations from Mr. Sommerbell's books. The furniture had been chosen for comfort rather than style, and the pillows were mismatched yet plentiful. Bookshelves lined two of the walls. A large vase filled with dried lavender rested on an end table.

Jane had met Cynthia Sommerbell the autumn before, underneath an enormous quince tree in the University Botanical Gardens. She'd been rolling bits of the leaf mould that covered the ground between her fingers, pondering exactly what mixture had been used to fertilize such a beautiful tree, when Cynthia approached, drawing her into conversation. The gardens were officially closed to non-students—and hence to women in general—but Mrs. Sommerbell was the wife of the Regius Professor of Botany on an errand to see her husband. Jane had no allowable reason to be there, but after three months in Glasgow, she hadn't been able to bear another afternoon alone. Cam had described the gardens to her, and the prospect of time amongst fruit trees, even if they weren't *her* fruit trees, was too tempting to resist. She'd sneaked in.

Cynthia seemed to instinctively know that this sad, solitary girl needed a friend, and she'd invited Jane to tea. Jane surprised herself by accepting.

She'd been so sure the visit would be a humiliating disaster, but the older woman never pressed for the details of her past—she simply accepted Jane for who she was—and her weekly visits with Cynthia, and occasionally Douglas Sommerbell, had come to be one of the few pleasures of her life in Glasgow.

Annabel, the maid, brought in tea and a platter of scones. "Shall I take them?" She gestured to the lemons.

"Yes. Thank you." Cynthia watched sorrowfully as the maid piled the immature fruit onto a tray, then took her leave. As soon as the door clicked shut, her attention shifted back to Jane. "Well." She crossed the room toward the fireplace. "I've had enough melancholy for one day." She forced a smile. "Let's drink tea and forget our worries, shall we?" She resumed her seat on the sofa and began to pour.

Jane checked the clock. "I really don't want to impose. If your nephew's coming—"

"Nonsense. Percy won't arrive for hours." Cynthia stirred two spoons of sugar into a cup of steaming tea, exactly as Jane liked it. "Just one cup, then you can go."

"Well." Jane sighed. "If I must. . ." She settled on the sofa next to her friend, letting herself sink into the soft warmth. "Just one cup, though."

"Of course." Cynthia smiled and handed Jane her tea. "Now, let's see. Your new maid's started, yes? How are you getting on?"

Jane breathed in the fragrant steam. "I still feel useless, though it *is* a relief to have someone to talk to when Cameron's at school."

Employing a household servant had seemed a frivolous expense given their limited funds, but after Jane had injured her back lugging water for her bath, her brother had insisted, and at a certain point, she knew from experience that arguing with Cameron was pointless.

"I know what you mean. I'd go mad without Annabel and Thomas when Douglas is away." Cynthia poured milk into her own tea. "He'll be home shortly, by the way. To see Percy." She raised her brows meaningfully. "And to gloat."

Percy. That must be the nephew's name. Jane's eyes wandered to the clock once more. She really should leave, though she hadn't drunk any of her tea. She took a large sip, forcing herself to swallow the scalding liquid.

"I do hope you'll meet him while he's here. Percy, I mean." Cynthia was oblivious to Jane's discomfort. "He's just returned from the Continent. I'm sure he'll have interesting tales to tell . . . and you're of an age, I believe."

Jane willed the muscles in her face into a polite smile. She took another sip of tea, her mind racing to find another topic of conversation.

Her eyes fell on the book Cynthia had been reading.

"Did you finish the book you were reading last week? The American one?"

"*The Black Vampyre?*" Cynthia's eyes widened in mock horror.

"Yes. That one." Jane laughed. "How was it?"

"Delightfully gory. Amusing in parts . . . but disappointing. I'd rather hoped the author would use the opportunity to denounce slavery, but alas, he did not. In the end, the slave boy turned vampyre was killed, and the slave-master was cured of his vampyrism and lived a long and happy life." Cynthia shrugged. "I suppose it's too much to hope for, to have one's political beliefs reflected in novels. You're welcome to read it if you'd like."

Jane shuddered. "No, thank you." She'd never seen the appeal in the horrific gothic novels Cynthia was so fond of. "What's this one?" She gestured toward the book Cynthia had been reading.

"A new travelogue by Sir Hoare." She handed the book to Jane.

A Tour through Italy and Sicily. Jane ran her fingers over the soft brown leather. "'Tis a good day to be reading of a warm climate." She gave the book back. "Is it good?"

"Too much musty old history for my taste." Cynthia opened the book to where she'd left her mark. "I read this just before you came, though. He's describing an island just off Naples." She read aloud, "*Even in this sultry season the whole island exhibits the most lively verdure. The air is pure and elastic.*" She looked up with a wistful smile. "Reminds me of summer days when I was a girl, though I suppose Northumberland can hardly be described as *sultry.*"

A flicker of homesickness sparked inside Jane. The air was never pure, nor elastic in Glasgow. But in Darnalay— *No.* She would not think of Darnalay.

"Oh, and you'll like this." Cynthia turned back a page, two pages, scanning with her finger. "Here." She read aloud again, "*Near Ischia and toward Testaccio, the vines are trained to lofty poplar trees: but the grapes grown using this—*"

She was cut off by the appearance of Thomas at the door. "Your nephew has arrived, ma'am."

Jane's eyes flew to the clock, then the door. The anxiety that had been roiling in her stomach turned to full-fledged panic.

<hr />

Hell and the devil—he couldn't feel his bloody fingers.

Percy was supposed to be en route with Beau to Greece, where Mediterranean warmth, sublime scenery, and a luscious woman awaited. Instead, due to his father's mishap with a horse, he found himself in this freezing, dirty little Scottish city with nothing to look forward to but tedious meetings with solicitors and even more tedious inspections of his father's mills.

He would never have come at all, had decided not to come, in fact, but then Mother had cried. She'd begged him to do it—*for her sake*. The fact that Percy didn't know the first thing about his father's business interests, and cared even less, was beside the point. The mills had just been purchased, and according to Mother, it was imperative that someone from the family inspect the new holdings. She'd added a stern reminder that it was his father's wealth that gave Percy the ability to travel and live well. A trip to Glasgow was a small price to pay.

He knew better. The only reason his father gave him an allowance large enough to fund his travels was because Mother pleaded his case. He owed *her*, not his father, so of course he couldn't say no.

As soon as he'd assented, she'd launched into the litany of musts. He *must* tie his cravat in a barrel knot. *Must* tame his hair into respectability. *Must* leave the riding boots for riding and instead wear those detestable buckle shoes with the pointy toes. *Must* wear the stiff woolen trousers and *not* his comfortable buckskin. She'd even purchased him a walking stick, and a new hat that was too tall and made him look disturbingly like Father.

Damnation.

He'd spent the bulk of the day in his hotel room, lying in bed and drinking terrible coffee. He couldn't even find the inspiration to pick up his guitar. It just sat there in the corner, glaring at him, demanding to know why they were in this cold, drafty inn where there was no hope of staying in tune, when they were supposed to be playing wine-fueled harmonies to voluptuous Mediterranean beauties. He wouldn't have ventured out at all, but this call to his aunt and uncle's house had been another one of Mother's *musts*, so he'd come. Reluctantly.

The room was warm, at least. Two women sat on a sofa near the fire, drinking tea. He hadn't seen his aunt in over ten years, but he recognized her almost white blond hair and warm smile. He had no idea who the other could be—young, auburn hair, heavy lidded eyes, full lips. Her cheeks were flushed, likely due to her seat near the fire. His eyes lingered on her lips as she drew them into a tight yet polite smile. *Like a satin ribbon tied into a lush pink bow.* She did not meet his eyes.

"Percy. My dear boy." Cynthia rose from her chair and crossed the room.

He forced his gaze away from the stranger's lips and greeted his aunt with a bow. "Aunt Cynthia. It's a pleasure to see you again." He tried to keep the irony out of his voice. His memory told him that his aunt was a lovely person. Nothing about this situation was her doing.

"May I present Miss Jane Stuart. Miss Stuart, my nephew, Mr. Percival Sommerbell."

Miss Stuart reluctantly divested herself of her teacup and stood to dip a small curtsey. "I'm pleased to make your acquaintance, Mr. Sommerbell." Her voice was a breathy alto, like a bow drawn ever so lightly over the stings of a viola. He could feel her attention like a shaft of warm sunlight as it moved from his shoes to his trousers, his coat, his cravat, and finally, *finally* his face.

Their eyes met, and everything else blurred.

Her eyes were the dark blue-grey of a summer storm cloud, the type of cloud that made one think to look for a rainbow. But there were no rainbows there now, no joy, no warmth. Only a deep, guarded pool of sadness that drew him in, and down. He felt a moment of vertigo. He was drowning, unable to surface, gasping for air.

She took a sharp breath, turned her head, and the moment was over.

He needed his guitar. Needed to play the music behind the perfect sadness of her eyes.

"The pleasure is mine," he replied. She did not offer her hand, but he took it anyway, brushing his lips over her bare knuckles, willing her to look at him again. Her cheeks took on a deeper shade of pink, but her gaze stayed stubbornly stuck to the floor.

His aunt cleared her throat. "You must be chilled. Come, join us by the fire."

He seated himself on the opposite side of the hearth from Miss Stuart. She stared into the flames, ignoring him.

"Help yourself to a scone, dear. How do you take your tea? I'm not sure if it matters to you, but the sugar's from India, *not* the West Indies." His aunt looked at him pointedly.

So, Aunt Cynthia was an abolitionist, abstaining from sugar produced using slave labor. Percy nodded his approval. "I appreciate the sentiment, and the source, but no sugar for me. Just tea."

Miss Stuart's breasts stretched the fabric of her dress . . .

"I shall remember that." His aunt poured and passed him a cup and saucer. "It does seem like something an aunt should know about her nephew, does it not?"

Her lips were incredible.

"Dear Percy, how you have grown. Truly, I would not have recognized you if we'd passed on the street. How long has it been?"

But he must play the respectable nephew. At least for now.

"Since Cybil's wedding, nearly twelve years ago."

"Twelve years . . ." His aunt sighed, then suddenly seemed to remember the reason for his visit. "How is your father? Recovering more quickly than the doctors predicted I hope?"

In point of fact, his father was *not* recovering quickly, or at all. Since being thrown from a particularly jumpy young mare, Percy's father had lost the ability to move any part of his body below his neck. There had been no signs of improvement in the two weeks since the accident, and the doctors had soberly informed them that *if* James Sommerbell survived, he would, in all likelihood, remain paralyzed for the rest of his life.

But Percy was in no mood to share that news with his aunt today.

"He's the same. The doctors continue to predict a possible recovery, but so far, we've not seen it."

His aunt sighed. "And how's your mother?"

"As well as one could expect. She insists on caring for him, night and day. She's tired." Tired wasn't the word for it. It was something beyond that, an exhaustion so intense he no longer recognized his bright, whimsical mother in the unsmiling face and blank staring eyes of the woman who refused to leave Father's bedside. Percy had begged her to hire a nurse, but instead she'd looked at him with those liquid brown eyes and asked him to go to Glasgow.

"Poor Martha. I'm sure it's a great comfort to have you and Cybil." His aunt put her hand on his arm. "I do wish you'd stay with us instead of that hotel. I'd feel so much better knowing you were under our roof."

Coming to Glasgow was one thing, staying in his aunt and uncle's home entirely another. He'd be damned if he would have all his movements watched, even by his well-meaning aunt—*especially* by his well-meaning aunt. He was pondering a polite yet evasive reply when Douglas Sommerbell breezed into the room.

"Percy, my dear boy. You've arrived." Percy rose as his uncle crossed the room toward them. "Any news of my brother? Has he improved?"

"Good afternoon, Uncle. I'm afraid not. As far as I know, he's the same."

----◆◇◆----

Jane was still recovering from the wave of nerves that had crashed into her upon her introduction to Percy Sommerbell. She'd done tolerably well, until his dark eyes had caught hers, and if that weren't torture enough, he'd *kissed her hand*.

She'd been left trembling, barely able to lower herself to the sofa. Thankfully, the Sommerbells were too absorbed in their own conversation to make any attempt to draw her into it. She wouldn't have responded if they had. All she could do was stare into the fire, desperately trying to steady herself.

There was nothing outwardly frightening about the younger Mr. Sommerbell. He was slightly built, graceful. His hair was a jet-black mess, the same style she'd seen on fashionable young men in Glasgow. His eyes were framed with dramatically arched brows, his mouth held in a perpetual impish quirk. Jane supposed some might find him handsome in a self-important, roguish kind of way. But the way he kept stealing glances at her now when no one was looking, trying to catch her eye—it was infuriating, and terrifying, and entirely inappropriate.

A potent mixture of annoyance and fear surged through her. Enough.

"I must be going." She stood abruptly, pulling her gloves on. "Cameron will be home soon. I'll need to make sure the maid is settled, in the kitchen. She's new. She may need— some instruction." It was a feeble excuse, and poorly stated, but all she could manage in the moment.

"Of course." Cynthia shot her a concerned look. "I hope you and Cameron will come for dinner next week. I'm sure Percy would enjoy meeting a young man his own age while he's in town." She winked at her nephew. "We can't expect him to spend all his time in the company of us old folks." Mr. Sommerbell didn't seem to notice his aunt's quip. His eyes remained fixed on Jane.

"I'm sure Cameron would be pleased to accept," Jane replied. She herself would not be coming.

She crossed toward the door in a hasty retreat.

"Oh. Stay a moment." Douglas Sommerbell jumped from his chair and strode to the large desk that dominated one corner of the room. "I have something . . ."

He rifled through some papers and came away with a thin book. Jane instantly recognized the green binding and gold gilt lettering. It was the newest edition of the Royal Botanical Society's regular periodical.

"There's an article in there somewhere by an American fellow who grafted a French shoot onto wild crabapple stock. He claims the tree grew true to the scion but retained the hardiness of the crab. I'm thinking of trying something similar. I'd be interested to hear your thoughts."

She accepted the journal, breathing in the scent of fresh ink. She would spend her evening devouring every last word.

"Oh, and Miss Stuart," Douglas Sommerbell continued, a twinkle in his eye. "About that lemon tree . . . You should know, I *told* her not to move it." He raised a brow and his eyes moved to his wife, who simply sighed and rolled her eyes.

Jane attempted a smile. She never wanted to speak, or think, of that lemon tree again. "Thank you." She accepted the journal. "I'll return it next week." Then she turned and made her escape.

Back on the street, she gulped great lungfuls of fresh, cool air. Odd, just thirty minutes ago, this same air had been numbingly cold. The instant Cynthia's nephew had entered the room, the townhouse had ceased to be cozy and had turned stiflingly hot.

TWO

ONCE AGAIN, PERCY WAS alone in his hotel room, the weak coffee of the morning replaced by excellent whiskey. He'd discarded his shoes, cravat, coat, and waistcoat the moment he walked through the door, and now he sat cross-legged on the plush carpet, staring at the fire.

His aunt had insisted he stay for dinner, but he'd excused himself directly afterward, claiming fatigue from his journey. It was true. He *was* tired, but not from traveling. It was the kind of exhaustion that came after a performance, as if he'd been onstage all evening, playing the part of the dutiful nephew. The distraught, loving son.

In point of fact, Percy did *not* love his father. Perhaps there had been something between them when he was a boy, before James had purchased the first factory and they moved to Grislow Park. Father had more time then. He'd taught Percy to ride, played nursery games, taken him on rambles in the country. But then he'd started amassing his fortune. Within the span of five years, James Sommerbell had transformed himself from a sheep farmer's son to a wealthy industrialist, and he'd disappeared almost entirely from his son's life, preferring instead to spend his time at his office, or socializing with other men of business.

The few real conversations they'd had in recent years had been cold at best, hostile at worst. According to James, his son was a profligate. A brainless fool, lost in a world of dreams that could only lead to ruin and degeneracy. But the truth of the matter was that Percy's father was nothing but a cold, unfeeling churl—living a life devoid of beauty and joy, intent only on making money for money's sake.

Percy wasn't glad, exactly, that his father lay on what very well might be his deathbed, but the bulk of his concern was for Mother. Dear, sweet Mother, who for reasons unimaginable, was still in love with her husband. She would be shattered by the loss.

And there *was* something else, just out of sight, buried in the far reaches of Percy's mind—and though he tried to keep it there, every so often it flickered to the fore. If Father died, Percy would inherit everything. The factories, the estates, they would all be his. Just the thought made his stomach churn. It was unthinkable. Surely, Father would recover, at least enough to run his own affairs.

Percy tossed back the rest of his drink, allowing the whisky to overwealm his senses and drive the uninvited thoughts away.

He rose and went to the sideboard to pour another drink. Supposedly, this was the finest hotel in Glasgow. Per Mother's direction, he'd rented a suite of rooms that befit a wealthy young man of business. It was expensively furnished, with plush carpet lining the floors and a huge bed made up with the finest of linens. There was a sitting room, and a room for bathing and dressing complete with a large copper tub. A fire roared in the hearth. But despite all that, the lodgings felt barren and cold. Maybe it was because he kept comparing it to the Grecian villa where he was *supposed* to be, warmed by the Mediterranean sun and the lush heat of the woman who awaited him there, Alessia, the same courtesan who'd helped make his year in Italy so pleasant. Beau was likely there by now, content in the arms of his companion, Paulo. Or more probably he was with Paulo and Alessia both.

Devil take him.

Percy settled again by the fire, full glass in hand. The vision of sensual pleasure sent his mind wandering back to the woman he'd met at his aunt and uncle's house. *Jane Stuart.* He rolled the name around in his mind as the whisky rolled in his glass. A liaison would certainly make this trip more bearable. *Someone to warm that huge bed . . .* He needed to devise a way to see her again. Alone.

Who was she anyway? He'd casually asked his aunt about her during dinner and had been told that she and her brother had recently moved to Glasgow, that her brother was a medical student at the university, and that Miss Stuart had an interest and talent as an orchardist. But caring for fruit trees seemed an odd hobby for a beautiful young woman especially given the fact she lived in an inhospitable city with no orchard to tend. She must have lived in the country before coming to Glasgow.

But who *was* she? She spoke with a refined, delicate lilt, not the thick brogue of the Scottish country folk, and she carried herself proudly and formally, as if she came from the upper classes. Yet her clothing was plain, almost poor.

When he'd pressed for more, his aunt had given him an uncharacteristically stern raise of her brows and firmly changed the subject.

He swirled the amber liquid in his glass and gazed at the reflected firelight, turning the pieces of the alluring puzzle that was Jane Stuart over in his mind, remembering the impossible lushness of her lips, her eyes. There was such sadness there. Such depth.

The mystery of the beautiful girl with tragedy in her eyes.

His eyes wandered to his guitar, still sitting lonely in the corner. He swallowed the last of his drink, the familiar heat of inspiration melding with the burn of the whiskey.

His instrument had been sitting too long. It was horribly out of tune, and it took some time to get all six wound metal strings into alignment. Once he did, the music came quickly and easily. Mauro, his Italian friend and teacher, had introduced him to these new strings. Silver wound around silk. They made a world of difference, with their powerful, crisp sound— like playing vibrant color, rather than the mellowed shade of the gut strings Percy had used before. Mauro taught him many beautiful pieces composed for the guitar, but what he liked most about this instrument was the ease with which one could simply play, allowing the music to come of its own volition, letting feeling rather than thought take over. He'd never gotten the same satisfaction from the violin or the pianoforte.

What came this night was a sweet, haunting melody in a minor key. A tempest of notes. Music as stormy as Jane Stuart's eyes, as sensual as her pink satin lips. Melody that flowed like her unbound auburn hair.

He drank whisky and played, losing himself in the music just as he had lost himself in her eyes. The song built in intensity, and he found his arousal following suit. Imagining those lips locked with his, her blue eyes dark with desire, her legs wrapped around him as he thrust inside her, her silky hair cascading onto his skin . . . Desire finally overwhelmed him, and he stopped playing to find his own release.

———— •◦• ————

After a comfortably mundane dinner with Cam, Jane retreated to her room with the journal Mr. Sommerbell had lent her. On any other night, she would have been riveted by the article in front of her—she'd savor the words, like the honey candy the cook at Darnalay, Mrs. Brodie, used to make each Christmas—but on *this* night she found herself reading the same passage over and over without registering any meaning:

. . . extensive trials of our new method of combining scion wood from malus domestica 'Bonne Hotture' *with root stock of* malus coronaria *using vegetative propagation techniques . . .*

The words blurred as her mind wandered again to Percy Sommerbell. His expressive brown eyes unflinchingly boring into hers. The way he conveyed his interest with a playful smirk. She had no desire to get to know, or even occupy her mind with, this maddening nephew of the Sommerbells, but somehow, no matter how many times she drew her attention back to the words in front of her, her thoughts kept sliding back to him.

She finally gave up trying and readied herself for bed. After several hours of staring at the intricate web of cracks on the ceiling, she found a fitful sleep.

———◆———

The next few days dragged, just as they had for the last nine months. But something had changed. Since that afternoon in Cynthia's sitting room with the tree . . . and the nephew, it had become harder—impossible even—to find that comfortable numbness, where anything could be tolerated and nothing mattered. Despite all her efforts, her mind stubbornly returned to those twenty-two little lemons, and, even more disturbingly, to *him*. And she *felt* things. Things she thought she'd rid herself of for good.

Of course it didn't help that there was nothing of substance to *do* here. She yearned for something, *anything* to distract herself from her thoughts. At home in Darnalay, there had always been something to occupy oneself with—working in the orchards, walking in the forest, visiting her friends in the village. In poor weather, there was the wealth of books in Father's library, the companionship of her family and the staff in the castle. And, of course, there was Kendric . . .

But she couldn't let her mind wander there. It was too painful, too raw.

On Saturday, Cori came home from the market with a bunch of lamb's ear lettuce, the earliest of spring greens. Jane *should* have felt anticipation. The arrival of those crisp, velvety leaves meant winter was finally over. But, instead, she'd felt that all too familiar tightening in her chest, and she'd bolted, barely making it to the safety of her room before she lost all control and the tears came, hot and ugly, streaming down her cheeks. The last time she'd gathered lamb's lettuce had been with Ken, the spring before he died. The spring they realized their love was no longer that of children, but something more. She hadn't felt his loss so acutely in months, years even—so why did it hurt so badly now?

But of course she knew why, because as she lay on her bed, wracked with grief, her thoughts had suddenly shifted from the image of her beloved working next to her in the garden, smiling at her in the misty Highland morning . . . to him. Percy Sommerbell. His arrogant smirk. The stifling heat of his gaze. It was *his* fault. Somehow, he'd dredged this up in her, and even worse, she'd allowed him to do it. And then her tears were no longer those of sadness, or grieving for what should have been, but of guilt, and anger.

She found some relief in Cori's companionship. The maid had been forced to leave her homeland when her family had been evicted from their land, and she missed Ireland desperately. She often prattled on and on about the life she'd lost—her parents and siblings, the animals her family kept, the fields they tended, her friends. Jane felt for the girl, truly, and it *was* nice to have someone else in the house, but as much as she'd detested the quiet before Cori arrived, the constant chatter grew just as tiresome. In truth, she was jealous of this girl who had nothing to hide, no deaths to grieve, and the knowledge of her jealousy, such an ugly emotion, only added to Jane's disgust at herself.

Of course, Cam came home each evening as well, but conversation with him was brief at best. He barely had time to eat before he went back to his studies, then fell into bed.

On Monday, the expected invitation came:

27th March.

MY DEAR JANE

I hope you and Cameron will join us for dinner on Wednesday this week.

Our nephew will be in attendance. He has agreed to play his guitar! Douglas says to tell you that he is very much looking forward to hearing your thoughts on the periodical he lent you Thursday last, particularly your opinion of the "viability of the vegetative propagation method described therein." I haven't the faintest idea what that means, but I've no doubt you do. He also says not to worry about returning it just yet if you are not finished with it. Come at seven, we eat at eight. I remain

Your devoted friend

CYNTHIA SOMMERBELL

Jane decided not to tell her brother about the invitation. If he knew, he would pressure her to go. Better he remain ignorant of the whole thing.

She would write an apologetic reply, give some reason they couldn't attend, and that would be that.

But then Cameron came home early from the university. He'd misplaced a sheaf of notes—an important sheaf of notes—and he proceeded to rifle through every bit of paper in the house, leaving a trail of scattered letters and bills and shopping lists behind him.

She was straightening a stack of papers he'd just strewn about the desk when he strode in, the invitation in hand.

"This was in the kitchen, near the stove. *Almost as if it was meant to be burned.*" His eyebrows rose accusingly. "We've been invited to a dinner party. At the Sommerbells'."

Confound it. She felt like a little girl, caught in a lie.

Jane shrugged, feigning indifference. "You can go if you like."

"We'll both go." He was cheerfully resolute.

"I'm not going."

"Why not?"

"I . . . I dinna want to." She sounded petulant, even to her own ears.

"*Jane.*" He'd perfected that annoyingly aristocratic tone that reminded her so much of Father—his *earl voice* they used to call it. "'Tis only a dinner party. With friends. Surely, you—"

"*I'm. Not. Going.*" She graced him with her highest-and-mightiest older sister glare.

He changed tack, giving her a wry smile and sad shake of his head. "And what would Mama say, turning down an invitation from a friend, a *close* friend, for no reason?" His voice rose, and he wagged a finger at her. "It's just not *polite*, Jane. A lady would never be so *inconsiderate* of her friends." Apparently, impersonating Father's most aggravating tone wasn't enough for Cam this evening. He also had to conjure Mama's most abrasive scolding voice. When she didn't smile or laugh, he changed tack again. Softening into his concerned, younger brother guise. He put his hand her arm. "You visit the Sommerbells' every week. How's this any different?"

Jane glared at her brother. This was precisely why she hadn't wanted Cameron to know of the invitation, because now . . . now he wouldn't leave her be until she told him the truth.

"Their nephew will be there," she snapped. "I met him last week, and he's . . . 'twas dreadful. I'm sorry, Cameron."

His eyes narrowed. "Did he say something indecent? I'll talk to Mr. Sommerbell and make sure—"

"No." Cynthia's nephew hadn't done anything wrong. Not exactly. "It's just, with strangers . . . I get nervous they'll ask about us, where we're from. I get hot, and shaky, and . . . and I *hate* it." She couldn't disguise the quaking in her voice. What a milksop she'd become.

"All the more reason to go." Cameron paused, raising his brows and donning an obnoxiously superior expression. "'Twas hard for me, too, at first. But I got used to it. You will too, but you have to *try*." His lips quirked into a slight smile. "Nobody cares about our past anyway. It's the past."

"Cameron. I'm not. Going." But she was wavering.

"What if I promise to distract the nephew? Make sure you arnna left on your own with him?" Jane just glared at him, so he tried the only weapon left in his arsenal—the wide eyes and sweet tone that had gotten him everything he'd asked for as a boy. "C'mon, Janie. You can do this."

She sighed, partly in resignation, but mostly in annoyance. He was right. But it didn't stop the sick feeling in the pit of her stomach every time she thought about herself at that blasted dinner party.

"All right. But Cam, I swear. If you leave me alone with him, I willna ever forgive you."

THREE

PERCY WAS THE FIRST to arrive on Wednesday evening. The footman showed him to the sitting room, where his uncle stood, alone, gazing out the window and looking uncomfortable in his formal attire. Douglas Sommerbell had the same dark eyes and wiry black hair as both Percy and his father, but the similarities ended there. Percy's uncle had the build of a laborer, well-muscled, and solid with calloused hands and a face lined by many hours spent out of doors. Percy was more like Father, light-footed and lean, built for agility and speed, though James had long ago grown soft and paunchy from years sitting behind a desk.

Percy's mother kept up a frequent correspondence with Aunt Cynthia—they'd been friends as girls—but Percy could count on one hand the number of times he'd seen his uncle. As children, James and Douglas had been inseparable, at least that's the story Mother told, but as an adult, Percy's father had never made a priority of seeing his brother. James didn't understand Douglas' love of the natural world, nor his contentment with the middle-class wages of an academic. The lack of understanding, Percy guessed, was mutual.

Douglas turned toward him. "Welcome, my boy. What's that you're carrying?"

"Good evening, Uncle." Percy set the instrument down. "My guitar. Aunt Cynthia asked me to bring it."

"Ah." His uncle glanced warily at the door, then walked to the desk and carefully moved a stack of books, revealing a decanter and two tumblers hidden behind. "I've been saving this for the right occasion. A little indulgence from the last time I was in London. It's French. Very fine." He offered a glass.

Percy did not hesitate. "Yes, please."

His uncle poured. "Drink up, before my wife comes down. She's of the opinion that spirits should wait until after dinner. I don't agree, but I *do* prefer to stay on her good side." He shot Percy a wink.

An excellent example of why Percy would never marry. Why should a man have to sneak a drink in his own house?

"Not a problem, sir." He grinned and lifted his glass in salute before downing half of it in one swallow. Drinking good brandy so quickly was a waste, but he was in need of fortification this evening and it did the trick.

He'd been sitting in an office all week, listening to Father's solicitors' drone on and on about this account and that account, yards of thread produced, material costs, labor costs, profits, losses, taxes, imports, markets... It was incredibly dull. Percy's mind inevitably strayed, but instead of meandering aimlessly as his thoughts would have in the past, in the lecture halls of Durham and Oxford, they made a consistent and efficient beeline toward one subject in particular—Miss Jane Stuart.

He could conjure only three features with any detail, her lips, her hair, and the color and depth of her eyes. But these three features had become an obsession, impossibly alluring, constantly distracting. He'd begun to wonder if what he thought were memories of her were, in fact, distortions of the truth, memories of memories, amplified and idealized by his restless mind. Tonight would be a test. If the attraction was real, the seduction would begin. He'd have her in a week. If the reality of her broke the enchantment, then so be it. Maybe he'd go looking elsewhere in Glasgow, maybe he wouldn't.

"Have you thought of what you'll do?" Douglas' question jolted Percy back to the present.

"Sir?"

"If my brother were to be overcome by his injuries. It seems quite possible, does it not?"

Hell. Percy took another drink, slowly this time, searching for a response that would end this topic of conversation, and quickly.

"Even if he doesn't recover fully, he'll be able to manage his affairs with the help of his secretary." That sounded reasonable.

"You haven't answered the question." His uncle gave a stern look. "You'll have much to manage if your father passes on. You'd do well to settle down. Find a wife. Start a family."

Percy winced. "I have no wish to marry, sir." *Ever*.

Douglas retrieved the empty glasses, pushing them and the decanter into the shadows in the back of the desk. "A family serves as an anchor in life, my boy. They'd be a comfort to you." He replaced the stack of books. "You'll need an heir, your mother will want grandchildren."

An anchor indeed. Tying him down. Pulling him under. Drowning him.

"Cybil could give Mother grandchildren."

Five years after her marriage, a love match supposedly, his strong-willed, iron-hearted sister had shown up on their parent's doorstep in the middle of the night, with tears in her eyes and a bruise on her face. She'd not set foot in her husband's house since, but she was still locked in the prison of marriage, and she would remain so *until death do us part.*

Douglas raised his eyebrows. "You and I both know your sister will have no children. Not all marriages are like hers, lad. Marrying Cynthia was the best thing I ever did."

Percy opened his mouth to answer, then exhaled a sigh of relief when, as if on cue, Cynthia Sommerbell swept into the room. The breath caught in his throat when Miss Stuart entered right behind her with a young man who must be her brother in tow.

"Look who was coming up just as I came down!" Cynthia's cheeks were flushed. She beamed at him. "Percy. My dear, you look wonderful."

As directed, he'd donned formal attire. His cravat was tied into a perfectly elegant waterfall, his coat was pressed, the buckles on his pointy toed shoes gleamed in the candlelight. His hair was still wild, but that was the fashion, convenient as it was. He was not quite up to Mother's standards, but he was less than comfortable. He'd put in an effort.

"You didn't forget your instrument?" his aunt asked.

"No, I did not forget my instrument."

His eyes drifted to the woman standing behind his aunt.

She was dressed simply in dark blue, a grey satin sash tied at her waist. Capped sleeves and white gloves hid her arms from view, but her low neckline revealed a long elegant neck, the creamy skin of her chest, and the sweet, full curve of her breasts. A silver pendant hung just below her throat, and her auburn hair was swept up into a simple chignon.

Uncomplicated, uncontrived beauty.

Their eyes met for a split second, then she turned away, her cheeks suddenly stained pink.

A wave of excitement washed over him. She was everything he remembered and more. She would need pursuing, most women did. But the pursuit was half the fun, and in the end, he had no doubt she would enjoy the liaison every bit as much as he would.

He waited for the brother and sister to greet the older Sommerbells, then crossed the room for an introduction.

"Percy. I'm sure you remember Miss Stuart. This is her brother Cameron."

Percy nodded politely. Jane's brother looked pleasant enough. Warm smile, same coloring as his sister, but with brown eyes and lighter, red-streaked hair.

How will he react to his sister taking a lover?

Percy turned to Jane and offered his most innocently seductive smile. "It's a pleasure to see you again, Miss Stuart. I've been looking forward to it all week."

Her cheeks flushed even pinker, but her focus remained somewhere just below his eyes. The bridge of his nose? She kept her hands clasped behind her back.

She was nervous. He must mean something to her.

"Good evening, Mr. Sommerbell." She'd only gotten as far as the b in *bell* before she turned her back on him, pulling his uncle into conversation. "I've brought your magazine back. The American techniques seem worth trialing. I think it would be best to start with a scion from British stock, though. Perhaps one of the new varieties developed by Mr. Knight, paired with the stock of a wild Scottish crab . . ."

The brother, Cameron, stepped into the space vacated by his sister, shielding Jane from Percy's view.

"'Tis a pleasure to meet you, Mr. Sommerbell. I understand your father owns a number of spinning mills in Glasgow?"

The whole thing seemed too choreographed to be happenstance, but no matter. Nothing worth winning was won easily, and this was a game Percy never lost.

———◇———

Dessert was lemon posset, an English concoction of cream and lemon. It was served in memory of the small lemons that had been lost, Cynthia had declared, and though Jane still found herself smarting from their loss, it was entirely refreshing. As different as could be from the heavy Scottish desserts she was accustomed to. Mrs. Brodie's cranachans and clootie dumplings were delicious, but they weighed one down. This posset, in contrast, was as light as air. She felt refreshed, buoyant, as if she might float away. Of course, it was possible the two glasses of wine had something to do with it, combined with the sweet satisfaction of successfully avoiding Percy Sommerbell all evening.

She was scraping the bottom of her glass, looking for any last morsels of flavor, when Cynthia set her napkin on the table and suggested everyone retire to the sitting room.

"We'll finally hear this guitar of yours," she said, addressing her nephew brightly.

"Yes, you will." Mr. Sommerbell gave his aunt a sardonic smile—mocking her enthusiasm. Jane fought the urge to roll her eyes, though thankfully, Cynthia didn't seem to notice her nephew's rudeness.

The company rose and filtered out, but Jane found herself lingering at the table, indulging in a moment of pleasant quietude. She twirled the wine glass between her fingers, absently watching the candlelight as it flashed over each flat edge of crystal.

Their plan had worked seamlessly. She'd absorbed herself in conversations that, by design, did not involve the younger Mr. Sommerbell. She'd discussed grafting and propagation techniques with his uncle, then at dinner consulted at length with Cynthia about the best way to split household duties between herself and her new maid. Through it all, her brother had kept his promise and held Mr. Sommerbell in constant conversation. Cameron, being Cameron, had no trouble charming the man, and within ten minutes, he and Cynthia's nephew were laughing like old friends.

Three times, she'd looked up to find Mr. Sommerbell's dark eyes fixed on her, and three times, she'd ignored the flush of heat that washed over her, fearlessly met his gaze, then turned her back.

A satisfied sigh left her lips as she set the glass down and picked up her gloves, sliding one on, then the other.

"Miss Stuart."

Her pleasant warmth became a hot, prickly flush. He was standing just inside the door, staring at her.

"Mr. Sommerbell. Did you forget something?"

"Perhaps. My plectrum. 'Twas in my pocket, but it seems to have gone missing. I can't play without it." She hardly breathed as he strode into the room and made an exaggerated show of looking—on the table, the chair where he'd been sitting, *under* the table. Each place he looked just a tiny bit closer to where she sat.

She swallowed. She'd come this far. She would not let fear get the better of her now. "Are you sure you *want* to play, Mr. Sommerbell?" she asked lightly. He looked up at her questioningly, but before he could say anything, she continued. "You seemed . . . less than excited at the prospect just now, when your aunt spoke of it."

"Ah." He nodded in understanding. "There are few things in this world I love more than playing my instrument." The arch of his brow left little doubt what those few things were. "*But*—" He leaned in conspiratorially. "I sometimes feel . . . a bit like a trained monkey, on occasions like this." He leaned back and cocked his head to one side, examining her as one might a piece of art, or a horse. "'Twas perceptive of you to notice." A sly smile spread across his face. "Have you been watching me, Miss Stuart?"

She rolled her eyes and looked away before he could see the heat on her face—her cheeks must be crimson by now.

He chuckled, then continued his search, never glancing at her or even acknowledging her until suddenly, like a wildcat pouncing on unsuspecting prey, he pivoted to sit in the chair next to her. He was so close she could feel the heat of his body. He smelled of cedar, and oranges.

Her pulse was an unrelenting rhythm of breath blown over a hot coal, glowing hotter with each beat.

He leaned in. "Watching me or not, you've been avoiding me. Why?" His voice was smooth, self-assured, amused.

She opened her mouth to answer, but realized she had no idea what she would say.

Because you scare me.

Because I can't breathe properly when you're near.

Because you're an aggravating boor.

Denial seemed the best course. "You flatter yourself. I haven't been avoiding you. I've simply been enjoying an evening with friends." She aimed for a tone of lighthearted sophistication, but hit on shrill and shallow instead.

"Is that so?" He raised one impossibly perfect brow. "I've been trying to catch your eye all night, and I haven't exactly been subtle."

Arrogant man. As if he could demand her attention and expect her to obediently give it.

"I've no idea what you want, Mr. Sommerbell. Whatever it is, I'm not interested."

"Then why do you blush every time I catch your eye?" He took her gloved hand in his, lightly rubbing his thumb over her knuckles. "Jane." A smile played on his lips. Taunting. "You know as well as I do there's something between us."

His touch, so light it was barely a touch at all, was kindling. The hot coal glowing inside her ignited, bright, hot, angry and eager to incinerate anything in its path.

"What is *wrong* with you?" She snatched her hand away, then rose, towering over him. "There is *nothing* between us." His eyes widened. "I'm not here for your *amusement, Mr. Sommerbell*. The way you're acting, it's . . . it's *jackassery*." She spoke slowly, enunciating each word. "My life is not a game. And you"—she glared down at him—"are a boor."

Mama had submitted to such games. Look where it got her.

"Furthermore," she continued. "I have not given you leave to call me by my Christian name. Henceforth, you will call me *Miss* Stuart if you call me anything, which I hope you don't. Good evening."

She brushed past him, triumphant, but he sprang up and caught her, his ungloved fingers circling her forearm, his grip firm, but not tight. She could feel the heat of each fingertip pressing into the delicate flesh behind her elbow, the narrow gap of bare skin between her glove and her sleeve. He drew her closer until his lips were just a few inches from her ear. His warm breath tickled the fine hairs on her nape.

"Jackassery?" His voice was no longer smooth, but textured and rough. She felt it in the soles of her feet. "Listen to the music I play tonight. Know that I play only for you. Then tell me again there's nothing between us."

He brought his other hand to her mouth and softly, so softly, outlined her upper lip with his finger.

His touch sent a spark of awareness ricocheting through her, which finally, *disturbingly*, settled as an aching heat at the apex of her thighs. She could have easily broken away, except she found she'd lost control of her muscles. Even her breathing was no longer her own. It came in short, shallow gasps. She was well and truly stunned, caught in the trap he had so deftly set for her.

"Exquisite," he murmured. His feather light touch played over her lips again. *"Miss Stuart."* Then he dropped his hold of her and stepped back, a wicked smile playing on his lips as he reached in his pocket and pulled out a small piece of tortoiseshell. His plectrum.

"What do you know? It was in my pocket the whole time." Then he was gone.

Jane stood rooted in place, remembering how to breathe, trying to erase the feeling of his fingers on her arm, his hot breath in her ear, the spark of his touch on her lips.

You know as well as I do there's something between us.

She steadied herself. *He would not get the better of her.* And though every instinct told her to turn tail and run, she held her head high and walked purposefully to the sitting room.

"There you are, Jane." Cynthia was seated on the settee, her embroidery hoop in hand. "I was just about to come looking for you. Please, help yourself to some sherry." She gestured to the sideboard. "Percy's just about to play!"

He was seated at the far end of the room, hunched over a small wooden instrument, coercing it into tune. He looked up as Jane entered, his gaze piercing hers, eyebrows raised in a devilish arch, lips curling into a sly smile. She knew this look well by now. *Boor* did not go far enough.

Thankfully, the heat of his attention didn't linger on her, but returned to his instrument. He cocked his head sideways, eyes softening into the distance, listening intently to the tone of each string then adjusting until he was satisfied. She noticed the clean angle of his chin, the tendons in his neck, the quiet concentration on his face, the way his black hair seemed to soak up the candlelight . . .

She was staring again.

Annoyed, she strode toward the sideboard, poured a glass of sherry and found a seat next to her brother, purposefully turning her attention *away* from Mr. Sommerbell. She would not look at him again until she had to. She found herself studying her brother instead. Cam was absently holding a glass of brandy, lost in thought, seemingly oblivious to her discomfiture and Mr. Sommerbell's wayward glances. He looked tired. His studies often left little time for sleep, and his exhaustion turned him into a subdued version of the sunny, spirited brother she'd grown up with. She wished there was more she could do for him, for *both* of them, but as a man, Cam would always bear the burden of supporting her, and there was nothing of real substance she could do in return.

Then Mr. Sommerbell started to play and all other thoughts were swept away.

She'd never heard a guitar before, but it was obvious he was an exceptionally talented player. Melody and harmony flowed in an impossibly smooth succession of tones. Like water rippling over a million tiny pebbles. It started softly, building in intensity, until an angry storm of music emanated from the wooden body of the instrument, then quiet and hauntingly sweet again. The notes came faster than seemed possible, melody soaring above them all, sweet and sad and beautiful.

Mr. Sommerbell's gaze went inward, emotion playing clearly on his face. His fingers effortlessly played across the instrument's neck, and Jane couldn't help but remember how they'd felt on her arm. Her lips. *This must be what he looks like when he's making love—*

Oh sweet heaven, where did that thought come from?

Listen to the music I play tonight. Know that I play only for you. She closed her eyes to block out the disturbingly erotic picture of the man playing the guitar. With the loss of sight, the music gained in intensity. It became a monolith, commanding her full attention, pulling her deeper, bringing her back . . .

She was under the apple tree on that achingly beautiful afternoon with Ken, arms wrapped around him, lost in his eyes.

She was standing before Kendric's open grave, clinging to his father like a child, her body wracked with grief.

She was staring blankly at the small piece of paper that told her in a cheerfully looping script that her parents were dead, feeling for all the world like she was falling and falling and falling into a well with no bottom.

She was shaking with fury as she sat in her bedroom, packing the few belongings that were truly hers, unable to fathom how a cousin—someone with the same blood flowing in his veins—could be so cruel.

She was looking out the carriage window, enduring a pain in her chest that could only be her heart physically breaking as her home receded into the distance. The castle, the orchard, the village . . .

All of it, *all of it*, was in the music. The beauty of home, lost forever, her love, her grief, her anger, her loneliness.

How could he know?

A single tear squeezed through her eyelid and traced itself down her cheek.

When the music stopped, she sat with her eyes closed for a long moment, unable to face anyone or anything, *especially* not the man who'd so deftly pulled her back into feeling, into remembering all the things she most wanted to forget. When she finally, reluctantly, allowed her eyelids to raise, she was relieved to see that everyone's focus was still on Mr. Sommerbell, held in a moment of awe as the last of the reverberations receded from the strings.

His eyes, *of course*, were on her, but there was no arched brow, no smirk on his lips. He simply looked at her, searching for her reaction. He was vulnerable, somehow, in this moment, and she suspected this was the first time since meeting him that she was seeing behind the arrogant mask to the man he truly was.

Cynthia took a long breath. "Good heavens. That was stunning. Who's the composer?"

"I am." Mr. Sommerbell dragged his eyes from Jane to settle on his aunt. "I wrote it in my hotel the night after I got here, after I first came to your house."

The night after he'd met Jane.

Listen to the music I play tonight. Know that I play only for you.

"Your mother was not exaggerating your talent, dear boy. That took my breath away," Cynthia said. Jane still wasn't sure if she was breathing or not.

He played another piece, a lively, happy one, then put his guitar away and poured himself a glass of brandy. He and Cam sat side by side, not talking, just staring into the fire, sipping their drinks. Jane sat numbly for the rest of the evening, making small talk with Cynthia and Douglas. She was relieved when Cam finally yawned and suggested they start for home.

The younger Mr. Sommerbell bowed his farewell. "I hope to see you both again soon." He turned to her. "Did you enjoy the music, Miss Stuart?"

She saw another flash of vulnerability behind his careful nonchalance. This moment meant more to him than he would like her to know.

She couldn't help it. She haltingly gave him what he sought. "You have a gift, Mr. Sommerbell. I— Thank you for sharing."

FOUR

A SILENT, GREY FOG hung over the city as Percy climbed into the waiting coach. It seemed the mist had drifted into his mind, muting all sound and separating him from his surroundings by a hazy curtain of gossamer. One thing at least was in sharp relief—the relentless pounding of his head.

He'd been restless after leaving his aunt and uncle's house, with memories of the evening flashing through his mind. The heat of her sudden anger after his foolish and rather too blatant attempt at seduction. The pink satin of her lips on his fingertip. Her clean floral scent, like the wild roses that grew in the hedgerows at Grislow Park . . . and the image that was imprinted on the back of his eyelids, waiting for him every time he closed his eyes. Just as the final chords of her song had died away, he looked up, half dazed, to the vision of her, eyes closed, lips slightly parted, one crystalline tear tracing its way slowly down her cheek. He could compose a thousand songs to that one perfect diamond of a tear.

She was already his muse. He must have her for his lover.

Unable to sleep, he'd been awake till nearly dawn, playing guitar and drinking whiskey.

The coach lurched into motion, eliciting a similar lurching of his stomach.

Today was the first of three scheduled mill inspections, one to each of the Fulton Company mills now owned by his father. It seemed redundant, a spinning mill was a spinning mill, was it not? But when he'd pointed this out, the solicitors had only looked at him over their spectacles, sighed, and explained, oh so patiently, that these visits were not for his benefit, but for a show of authority, to demonstrate that the new ownership was keeping watch. *Ironic, really.* Percy had always detested authority of any kind, whether it be in the form of his governess, the vicar, a school master, Father . . .

But Mother was counting on him, so despite the thick fog in his brain, he'd done his best to dress the part of the authoritative mill owner, even donning the ridiculous hat and walking stick she'd forced on him. Despite all his efforts, the solicitors, two bony old men aptly named Mr. Brown and Mr. Grey, shot him looks of disapproval from the opposite seat. It was useless. He was a wandering musician at heart, not a man of business.

He watched out the window as the coach wound its way through the streets of Glasgow. He felt detached, as if he were observing the entire scene from a distance—the dirty city, the shiny black coach, himself inside it. Gradually, the wide streets of the business district narrowed and they passed through the middle-class neighborhood where his aunt and uncle lived. He'd not been farther east than this, but he knew most of Glasgow's mills lay in Calton, at the eastern edge of the city. He'd noticed the increased haze of coal smoke in that direction.

The cool fog began to take on a brown tinge and a fetid odor. There were no houses now, just two- and three-story stone buildings, grimy and in obvious disrepair with broken panes and missing roof tiles. Impossibly narrow alleyways branched off from the main road. Craning his neck to look down one, he caught a glimpse of tattered clothing hanging on a line between the buildings. An overflowing gutter lined the street. Cameron Stuart had described this scene to him last night. These were the wynds, the slums where the millworkers lived.

Men and women dressed in dingy clothes walked the streets, some with purpose, a few teetering along aimlessly, drunk. One man lay on the ground, asleep, a worn hat covering his face, a bottle still in his hand. A group of children huddled together, rags wrapped around their bare feet and hands to protect them from the cold. They glared at the sleek, expensive coach as it passed by.

His eye was caught by a girl no older than ten or twelve but with the grim, unflinching face of a woman four times that age. She was thin as a rail and clothed in rags, her cheeks streaked with dirt, her hair stringy and wild. She was sitting on a wooden crate, clutching a screaming infant. As the carriage rolled past, her piercing blue eyes caught his, holding him in an accusatory stare. A frisson of apprehension passed through him, and he jerked away from the window, leaning back against the seat and closing his eyes to escape the scowls of the men sitting across from him.

He reflected on his conversation with Cameron Stuart the evening before. As part of his medical training, Jane's brother had been assigned apprentice shifts in the public hospital, and he'd regaled Percy with stories of injuries and illness he'd seen the millworkers and their families fall victim to—afflictions of the lungs from breathing in cotton dust, severed fingers and hands, sickness brought on by exhaustion, dirty water, crowded living conditions, and lack of good food. According to

Cameron, the price paid for cotton cloth had plummeted just as the cost of bread increased, and the weavers of Glasgow—who just one generation ago were able to make a good living spinning thread and weaving cloth in their homes—were now forced either into the factories or, if they had the means, to emigrate to Canada or America. Tenant farmers, angry and desperately poor after being evicted from their ancestral homes, were streaming into Glasgow from the Highlands and Ireland. Discontent was brewing, Cameron had said, and violent revolt seemed inevitable. He'd advised Percy to take care, lest he become a target himself.

Percy hadn't paid close attention to the ledgers he'd been presented with in the last week, but he'd absorbed enough to know that the Fulton Company Mills operated at a profit, which seemed to be all the solicitors, and Father, cared about. Numbers on paper said nothing of the experience of the people working in the mills, however, and after his conversation with Cameron, he found that he did not, in fact, want to know the truth of it.

Devil it. He was supposed to be in Greece.

The coach came to a stop outside a four-story red brick building. It was in better repair than the houses of the wynds, with fresh white paint on the lintels and doors, but otherwise nondescript. The words *Fulton Company Mill Works* were painted in crisp white letters above the wide front door. Percy climbed down from the carriage, bowed with all the authority he could muster to the mill manager who came out to greet them, then followed the three men into the factory.

It was stiflingly hot. Little wisps of cotton fiber floated in the air, making him feel as if he were slowly suffocating. The spinning mule, a monster of a metal machine that stretched the entire length of the building, swung relentlessly back and forth, clanging a deafening, slow, droning beat that commanded Percy's headache to pound in rhythm.

Workers, some of them not more than ten or twelve years old, buzzed around him, attending to the needs of the machine. His sense of detachment became more pronounced, and he wondered for a moment if he was in a drink-fueled nightmare. Surely, this was not waking life. The desire to flee to fresh air and quiet was almost too much to bear. He couldn't breathe. He was lightheaded. Dizzy. Everything was distant, muffled.

The gritty, smoke-fouled miasma outside was a paradise compared with this.

Then he noticed the youngest children and reality snapped back into focus. They were waifs, three of them that he could see from where he stood. Pale, skinny, barefoot little things who couldn't be more than six or seven years old, scurrying underneath the mule as it swung back and forth. They took no notice of the group of men walking the factory floor. There were no smiles, no puerile banter, just blank faces staring intently at the underbelly of the mule, then disappearing beneath it. They were like the ghosts of children, darting in and out of the machine without seeing the world around them.

Suddenly, he remembered something else Cameron had told him the night before, after describing a particularly nasty injury he'd assisted with—a child's foot, crushed so badly by the mule that it had to be amputated. Percy had been shocked, then Cameron had explained that, due to the dangerous conditions, parliament had just passed a bill outlawing the hiring of young children to work in the cotton mills.

So why were they still here?

The manager was proudly espousing the number of yards of thread this particular spinning mule could produce in an hour. Percy waited for a wave of nausea to subside, then drawing on all his supposed authority, he took a breath and interrupted.

"What of those children?" He nodded toward the waifs. "What's their part in all this?"

The manager looked surprised at the question, and not a little annoyed to be cut off in the middle of his speech.

"They're scavengers, sir. They sweep up the bits of cotton that fall under the mule."

Mr. Grey jumped in, speaking slowly, as if Percy were a child himself. "Another example of the efficiency of the modern spinning wheel. Every bit of raw material is utilized and turned into profit."

"Was there not just an act passed by parliament, forbidding young children from this work?"

The men were stunned for a moment, looking at one another as if to be certain they'd heard the question correctly, then silently agreeing that, yes, they'd heard right and, yes, this young man was indeed as ignorant as all that.

"The wee ones are best suited to the task. Without them, cotton would go to waste. Profits would decrease." The manager was clearly galled at having to explain the obvious.

"But it's the law of the land. Surely—"

"What parliament does not understand," Mr. Brown said, clearly losing patience, "is that being put to work is what's best for these whelps. It keeps them off the streets. Instead of joining the criminal class, they contribute."

"It's really nothing to worry about, sir," Mr. Grey added smoothly. He really did think Percy was a child. "The act is unenforceable. No fines have been leveled against any of the mills, nor will they be."

Another surge of nausea, worse than the last. No wonder the workers of these mills were on the verge of violence. How could they not be?

He would surely retch if he kept up this line of questioning, and since casting up one's accounts was not exactly in line with a show of authority, Percy stood back and listened as the manager droned on, proudly showing off every nook and cranny of the factory as if it were the very pinnacle of human ingenuity. The man seemed to give no further thought to the small apparitions darting in and out from under the mule or the vacant-eyed older children and adults working around them—as if they were not flesh and bone, but simply an extension of the machine that spun cotton fibers into thread.

Either this man was crazy, or Percy was stark raving mad. It was not possible that both were sane.

⸻ ⚬ ⸻

The ride back to the hotel was wretched, his churning stomach and pounding head made nearly intolerable by the jouncing of the coach over the cobblestones. Thankfully, the solicitors had given up trying to talk. They just watched him with silent, disapproving frowns, until at last they reached St. Andrews Square and his hotel. He nodded a quick farewell, then climbed down, noticing that the fog had lifted, revealing a pristinely clear day.

Though part of him wanted nothing more than to retreat to his room and crawl into bed, a larger part was repelled by the prospect. After the stifling heat of the mill and the roiling of the enclosed carriage, his body craved fresh air and open space, so he started off on foot, aiming himself toward the open parkland of Calton Green. He loosened his too-tight cravat as he walked—his appearance made no difference now—and drew in several deep breaths in an attempt to will the nausea away. It was for naught. He'd barely made it to the edge of the Green when his stomach heaved. He scrambled to the side of the path, then cast up his accounts, relieving himself of the little bit of buttered toast and coffee he'd managed to choke down before leaving the hotel hours earlier.

When he was quite sure he'd vomited up everything that could be vomited, he fumbled in his pocket, searching for the flask he'd had the foresight to bring with him that morning. He took a swig, then swished the whisky in his mouth, pursing his lips to spit—

"Mr. Sommerbell?"

He froze. It was her. The one woman in the world he most wanted to impress had stumbled across him retching in a public park, with a mouthful of whisky he had no intention of swallowing, and not even a handkerchief to clean the filth from his face.

Hell and the devil.

Without turning around, he returned the flask to his pocket, spat the whisky into the bushes as quietly and unobtrusively as one could spit whiskey, retrieved the cane that had escaped his grasp, then straightened up and turned around, attempting a look of perfect composure despite the very obvious fact that he'd just lost his breakfast to the shrubbery.

From the look of concerned derision on her face, it was clear she wasn't fooled in the least.

"Miss Stuart."

"It *is* you. Are you quite well, Mr. Sommerbell?"

"Of course." He shot her a wry smile. "Do you, by chance, have a handkerchief I might borrow?"

She produced a small piece of linen from the pocket of her cloak and gingerly handed it to him. Nodding his gratitude, he wiped his brow and mouth, inhaling the clean, wild rose scent. It was better than any medicine. His head felt clearer than it had all day.

"My thanks." He tucked the cloth into his pocket. "I'll have it laundered and returned to you." *He would do no such thing. He would keep that handkerchief as long as it smelled of her.*

Probably she assumed he was ill from the aftereffects of drink, which was at least partly true, but even with the look of mistrust she was facing him with, she still stole his breath. She'd allowed the hood of her cloak to slip off, leaving her head bare. The sunlight lit up her hair, turning it into a wreath of shining red gold and adding sparkle to the deep blue pools of her eyes. Her creamy skin glowed in the morning air, color bloomed on her cheeks. She wore a plain cotton dress and a rough woolen cloak, but she bore herself with an effortless grace and poise that made his pulse race.

If he continued the game of the previous evening, she would flee like a frightened bird. He must start slowly. No sudden movements. So, he donned his most polite, nonthreatening smile.

"Walk with me? I've had a most unsettling morning. I'd appreciate the company."

She gazed at him for what seemed an eternity, searching for something. Then finally, "Your behavior last night was reprehensible. If you try anything like that again, I'll leave in an instant, whether you're ill or not."

He grinned. "I'd expect nothing less."

He didn't want to drive her away, so he didn't offer his arm. He resisted the urge even to turn his head to look at her as they set off side by side through the park, steps in sync, close, but never touching. She was obviously still shaken by the events of the previous evening, and she must be made to feel at ease before any further progress could be made.

He found himself telling her about his trip to the mill. Everything he'd experienced, everything he'd seen and felt. Perhaps she would feel a similar horror toward the place. Perhaps it would cast him in a more sympathetic light, and give her an explanation for his illness other than simple drunkenness. She listened quietly, or at least he supposed she was listening. She said nothing when he reached the end of the story, and they walked in silence for a few moments. He wanted desperately to turn to look at her, to divine what she was thinking, but he didn't dare.

Finally, she spoke, "I understand now why you were ill. I apologize, I assumed it was from overindulgence."

"Don't apologize. It was an understandable assumption." He stopped and turned toward her, not touching, not even attempting, not even *thinking* of touching. "I'm the one who should apologize. For my behavior last night. I wasn't . . . It wasn't kind, or right of me."

He drew a breath. "I'd be greatly honored to be given the chance at a fresh start."

She looked at him intently for a moment, gave him a small nod—*accepting his apology?*—then resumed walking, forcing him to catch up with her swift strides.

"My brother's told me of the mills. He sees them, the workers, in the infirmary. Some are from Glasgow, but most are country folk from the North, or from Ireland." The words tumbled softly from her perfect lips, and it took all his concentration to focus on the meaning of them rather than the music of her rich, breathy alto. "There's more money to be made from grazing sheep than renting to farmers, so the lairds evict them and they have no choice but to come looking for work. *Improvement*, they call it." Her stormy eyes stared straight ahead. "'Tis cruelty, plain and simple." She turned her head to look at him. "They're good people, Mr. Sommerbell. Not any different from you and me."

"Your brother told me some of his stories last night. I'm glad he did. But *being there*, 'twas worse than I could have imagined. Those children, Miss Stuart, they're so young, and small. They work twelve hours a day, six days a week." They were walking through a secluded patch of woods now, the first bits of spring green just poking through the dead browns of winter. The air was fresh with the scent of damp earth. "At that age, I was tramping through the woods with my sister. Making mischief. Learning my first chords on the pianoforte."

"I was the same," she murmured. "Always outdoors." She paused, then turned to look at him. "What do you intend to *do*, Mr. Sommerbell?"

"Do?"

He intended to take this woman to bed, then get the hell out of this godforsaken city. That's what he intended to do.

"About the mills. Your father owns them, does he not? You must have some influence."

Of course. The mills.

He took off his hat and ran a hand through his hair, liberating it from the careful order he'd combed into it earlier in the day. "I'm not sure I *can* do anything. My father's the owner, not me. He's like those solicitors. He cares only for the profits."

She was quiet for a moment, and when she spoke, her voice was a susurrus, almost indecipherable from the sounds of the forest around them. "You're lucky to have a father who cares enough to provide for his family, Mr. Sommerbell, even if the means are incomprehensible to you and me." Then louder, as if she'd not spoken the first part, she said, "It's hardly my business, but it seems you could do *something*. You are his only son, are you not?"

"Yes, but he doesn't make a habit of listening to me." Any suggestions Percy might make regarding Father's business would most certainly fall on unlistening ears.

But perhaps he could at least pretend to try.

An idea began to take shape. "According to your brother, there are mill owners in Glasgow who take some responsibility for the welfare of their workers. Funding schools. Better hours of work. Things like that. I suppose I could talk with him more. Learn what these men are doing and how, and present them as options to my father."

Visiting her brother would be the perfect excuse to see her again.

They'd now come close to the River Clyde, a more popular section of the Green. The early spring sunshine seemed to put the residents of the city in a buoyant mood. Couples strolled and laughed. Children played. Housewives chatted happily as they laid laundry in the sun to dry, the bright white linens flapping gaily as they shook them out in the chill breeze coming off of the river.

He gestured to the scene. "On a day like this, one could almost imagine Glasgow to be a pleasant city. Pity it's so—"

"Horrible?"

He whipped his head to look at her. She'd interrupted him. Even more incredible, a coy smirk played on her lips.

Was this the first time he'd seen her smile?

"I was going to say dirty, or perhaps befouled. I'd accept horrible."

"It's abysmal." Her eyes locked with his. Challenging.

"Loathsome."

"Noxious."

"*Nauseating.*" He raised a brow, daring her to best his coup de grâce, but instead, her smile widened, and she laughed—a rich throaty legato that wound itself around him, through him, smoothing all the rough places inside.

He laughed with her, and for a single, perfect moment, they stood in the sunshine, laughing together like children, all else forgotten. Then it was over. Her face clouded. She looked away.

He would do anything to see that smile again. To hear that laugh.

"It would be good, Mr. Sommerbell, if you talked more with my brother. He knows many men in Glasgow. I'm sure one of them could help you."

They'd come to a bench, and he sat, leaning back, basking in the warmth of the sun and the memory of her laughter. "Sit with me?"

For several long moments, she stood, weighing her options. Sit, remain standing, retreat. Then, to his great satisfaction, she let out a resigned sigh and sat—as far from him as was possible—on the small bench. Her eyes settled on a crabapple tree just across the path. It was covered with little white buds that would soon burst into bloom.

Now. Now he could delve just a bit deeper.

"Tell me, Miss Stuart, how is it that you came to have such an interest in fruit trees?"

FIVE

WHAT ON EARTH WAS she doing? All she wanted in the world was to avoid this man, and—setting aside the unsettling episode in the dining room the night before—she'd been largely successful. But something was different this morning. He'd not pressed her. Indeed, he'd been the perfect gentleman, the opposite of the wildcat she'd encountered the night before, and somehow, he was bending her to his will. Evaporating her resolve. She'd agreed to walk with him. She'd laughed with him. And now here she was, sitting with him, *alone*, on a bench in Calton Green.

Of course it was an act. He wanted more from her than polite friendship. He'd said as much the night before. But she was like a moth drawn to the light. No, she was less than a moth, for unlike that unthinking creature, she knew the dangers of flying too close to a flame.

For days, the city had been covered by an oppressive blanket of clouds. When the morning fog lifted, revealing a pristine blue sky, Jane had been unable to resist the promise of sunshine on her skin. She'd abandoned her pile of mending, wrapped herself in her cloak and aimed her steps for the Green, the only place in Glasgow—besides the prohibited botanical gardens—where she could be entirely surrounded by grass and trees. She'd let the hood of her cloak slip off, savoring the chill breeze on her face. It cleansed her, and she was almost, *almost* washed clean of the unwelcome feelings of the evening before.

When she'd realized who the man hunched by the side of the path was, her first impulse was to walk right by, to preserve the beauty of the day and not sully it with an awkward encounter. But an inconvenient sense of compassion had come over her. He was the Sommerbells' nephew after all. What sort of friend would she be to Cynthia if she just left him there, retching in the bushes?

Listening to the honest emotion in his voice as he described what he'd witnessed in the mill, she found herself wondering if she'd been too harsh in her assessment of him. Certainly, she no longer feared him, and while she did not *like* the man—she could never forgive his predatory behavior of the previous evening—she felt oddly at ease in his company. She'd surprised even herself when she'd interrupted him in such a silly way as he described the city. For that brief moment, she'd been her old self, bantering with Ainsley, or Cam, or Kendric. Dissolving into laughter. It had felt good, yet equally disturbing that such a rare moment of pleasure had come, unbidden, in the company of Mr. Sommerbell.

And, of course, there was the music he'd played.

No, she wouldn't think of that. She couldn't allow the unwelcome feelings he'd unearthed to climb back into her consciousness.

"Tell me, Miss Stuart, how is it that you came to have such an interest in fruit trees?"

She should have been terrified by the question, but strangely, she wasn't. Perhaps this was an opportunity to practice telling the parts of her story she *could* tell.

"There's an orchard. Near the village where I grew up." She spoke slowly, choosing her words carefully. "It had been abandoned. The trees were ancient. Most did not bear fruit of any quality." She paused, sifting through the story to determine which parts she would tell. "One winter, I found a book on the culture of fruit trees in my father's library, and I came upon the idea of rehabilitating the old trees. I asked the landowner if I could attempt it, in the spring, and he agreed."

No need to mention the library was in a castle, or that Father *was* the landowner.

"Were you successful?"

"Not at first. I'd no idea what I was doing. But I learned. Eventually, I improved the production of the orchard tenfold." She couldn't help a small prideful smile.

"How old were you?"

"Ten when I started."

His eyes widened. She could see him trying to picture her as a girl, working among the apple trees. "I *did* have help, more in those early years before I was big enough to properly work the larger shears and saws. The groundskeeper, and Ken—" She broke off. *That was not a name she would ever bring up in the company of Percy Sommerbell.* "And his *son* helped me, but I was allowed to direct the work."

"But why? What drew you to the idea?"

She thought for a moment. "At first, I suppose I simply wanted to prove I could do it. But, in time, I became fascinated with the trees, learning what they needed. I liked providing fruit for the village . . . and my family." *And the servants. And the tenants.* "'Twas a far sight better than needlepoint, or whatever ladylike things my mother would have preferred me to do." And because the story wouldn't be complete without it, she added, "Eventually, I became interested in breeding. Developing new varieties."

"Breeding. As one would breed horses or sheep?" His brows rose.

"Aye, though the mechanism is different, obviously."

"Different how?"

"It's complicated. It'll bore you."

"Try me." His head tilted to the side. He smirked. "Perhaps I'm more clever than you think."

Pointedly, she looked away. This man was insufferable.

"Well?" he asked.

She sighed. Where to begin? "Fruit trees can be propagated, or reproduced, in two ways. The most common is the method your uncle and I discussed last evening, where one grafts the wood of one tree onto the roots of another. With grafting, you can be sure you'll harvest the variety of fruit you want. 'Twill be exactly as its parent was. The other process is what I experimented with in my breeding trials. This is called sexual reproduction—"

Sexual.

Mr. Sommerbell's eyes widened. Heat reverberated between them. This was exactly why Mama had discouraged her interest in breeding. It was too lascivious she'd said, not a fit pursuit for a young girl. Jane had only laughed and thanked her stars that Father took her side in the matter. How could studying the reproduction of trees lead to ruin? But as she breathed in Mr. Sommerbell's heady scent, and felt a sudden awareness of the space between her thighs, she realized that perhaps Mama had a point after all.

Their eyes met, and it was as if they'd come up to the edge of a high cliff and made a tacit agreement not to jump. He cocked an eyebrow, a carefully subdued expression on his face. "How does this *other* kind of reproduction work?"

She cleared her throat and looked away, focusing on a pair of robins flitting in a nearby alder, collecting leaves and twigs to make their nest. *Let us not bear witness to them mating.*

"In the spring, when the trees are in bloom. Each blossom has a male organ, the stamen, and a female organ, the pistil." Her cheeks were on fire. "The stamen produces pollen, a kind of sticky yellow dust that's the ... the male essence of the tree. The pistil is where the eggs of the tree are found. They eventually become the seeds."

She sneaked a glance at him. He was staring at her intently, brown eyes wide and sparkling.

This was only science. Logical. Reasoned. Rational.

"'Tis the bees that do the real work. When she visits a flower, a bee intends to collect pollen and nectar to make honey, and to feed her hive .. . But in the process, some of the pollen sticks to her body. When she lights on the next flower, perhaps on another tree, some of the pollen from the first blossom is left behind. On the pistil. The blossom is fertilized. A fruit grows, and a seed, presumably with characteristics of both parent trees ... But it's not predictable, not any more than you can predict what the child of a particular man and woman will look or act like."

"If the bee does the work, how can you cross two particular trees? Surely, you can't put a harness on him and direct him where to go?"

"The bees who do the work are all *female*." She corrected him. "The males don't do anything really, except eat and mate with the queen." Her eyes were still carefully trained away from him, but an irritating chuckle floated to her from the other side of the bench. "The male's reproductive organs are ripped from his body when he mates, along with the entirety of his abdomen. He does it only once." The chuckling ceased. "To answer your question, no. You can't harness the bees. Breeders simply wait for them to do their work and hope a new, desirable variety will emerge. It can take a very long time. My idea was to do the bees' work myself. I collected pollen from one tree and painted it onto the pistils of another. Then I planted the seeds."

"*Your* idea? You mean no one has ever done it that way before?"

"Not to my knowledge. It's always been left to the bees."

"So? What happened?"

"I don't know. None of the trees were old enough to bear fruit when we left Darnalay."

The familiar lump formed in her throat as she thought of the little stand of saplings she'd left behind. She'd poured so much time and care into those trees. The method was nothing she'd read about in a book, just an idea she'd had after watching bees skipping from one tree to the next, distributing pollen. She'd used Mama's old rouge brush to paint the pollen from the ancient and very productive Wine Apple onto the pistils of a Golden Russet tree Father had bought near Glasgow. Her idea was to combine the traits of a hearty apple like the Wine, fit to grow in the Highland climate, with the sweet juice and storing properties of the Golden Russet. She'd marked the branch she'd pollinated, collected the apples in the fall, and the following spring, she'd planted fourteen seeds. Twelve had germinated.

It was a silly idea, but she'd tried it anyway, just to see what might happen.

"*If* they're still there, they'll bear fruit this autumn." *And she wouldn't be there to harvest it.* The lump in her throat grew. Odd that the pain of losing those little trees brought up this emotion, when she had become numb to the loss of so much more.

"That's marvelous. *Marvelous.* Creating new apple trees by acting the part of a bee . . . It's truly never been done?" The wonderment in his voice only made things worse.

"It doesna matter. The orchard's no longer mine to tend."

A heavy silence settled between them. She didn't know what to say. She wouldn't be able to say it even if she did.

"Darnalay. That's where you're from?"

Confound it. She'd not meant to give that away. Why was she sitting here anyway, talking to his man? This was precisely the situation she most wanted to avoid.

A cross of anger, fear and guilt germinated, pushing up a familiar, poisonous green shoot.

"Do you miss it?" His voice was soft. He was trying not to frighten her, trying to trick her into telling him her secrets.

The shoot grew taller, sprouted ugly, broad leaves. Where was that serviceable numbness she'd settled into before she met this man?

"It's all right. You don't need to tell me," he murmured. She felt his hand on her shoulder. "You're safe with me, Miss Stuart."

It was as far from the truth as was possible, yet somehow the certainty in his voice pushed the pain away, just a little, and she wondered what it would be like to lean into him, to press her cheek against the finely spun wool of his coat, to feel his arms around her—

What was she thinking? The man was a rogue. Just because he'd behaved himself for one morning was no reason to change her opinion of him.

She drew in a steadying breath. "Thank you, Mr. Sommerbell. I should be getting home now." She rose. "I trust you're well enough to get yourself wherever you're going?"

"Of course." He stood. "I shall call on your brother soon to discuss the mills."

"He's away most days. You're not likely to catch him."

"We could arrange something on a day that's convenient then. An excursion? My aunt already suggested it. Something to divert me from the mills, and your brother from his studies." His eyes, once again those of a wildcat stalking its prey, met hers. "You might join us?"

She didn't answer. She couldn't. She simply turned and strode toward home.

———•◦•———

Percy sat by himself after she left, watching the cheerful citizens of Glasgow and pondering the pieces of the puzzle he'd just acquired. Frustrating. No matter how he turned them, there were still too many missing to make a sensical picture of her past.

Jane and her brother were alone in the city, yet she spoke of her parents, of a place called Darnalay where she'd tended an orchard and grown fruit for a village. Just the mention of it had touched a nerve so raw she'd been speechless from the pain. *Then why had she and Cameron left, and come to a city she so obviously despised?* It couldn't have been for want of money. Her brother had enough coin to rent a house and attend university. Her father was well-off enough to possess a library. She was educated, spoke proper English, albeit with a soft, musical brogue she seemed to be trying to hide. All the signs pointed to a landowning family, perhaps even gentry. Or a vicar? But if not money, then what drove them here? The death of their parents? Then why the secrecy? Had they been disowned? Run away from something . . . or someone? That seemed possible, but what? Whom? And why, if her mother had desired her to act as a lady, had she been allowed to pursue a hobby that resulted in her uttering the word *sexual* without a second thought?

His headache was returning. The sun was too bright, the puzzle too difficult. He sat back on the bench and closed his eyes, allowing his thoughts to blur to a more comfortable truth. He didn't care where she came from, or why. He wanted her. He wanted to be her comfort, to hold her. Wanted to be welcomed into the depths of her eyes, the curves of her body. He wanted to hear her laugh again, and again, and again.

Percy enjoyed the sexual act, very much so, but he knew from experience that the longing, the anticipation of a slow seduction, was infinitely more enjoyable than a quick tumble with an over-eager partner—and Jane Stuart would be a lover to be savored, her secrets unfurling slowly, like the petals of a flower. Just as soon as he thought he'd learned her, she surprised him with her devious humor, her beautiful science, her deep, secret pain.

What he felt was more precious than simple arousal. It was inspiration, the purest and most powerful he'd ever felt.

Already he had two new compositions floating in the back of his mind. The first was a vivace—lighthearted and joyful. It was the moment she'd interrupted him. Their inane back and forth. Her laughter. She was a viola, rich and smooth. Playful. He was a pianoforte, bubbling up around her, lifting her up. The other was slower. A sultry, warm adagietto. It was the charge in the air just after she'd said the word *sexual*. Her viola played an airy, shimmering tremolo. His pianoforte, the melody of seduction . . .

He realized suddenly that his remaining time in Glasgow—it was only a week until he was scheduled to return to Northumberland—was too short. Even if things progressed smoothly, even if he could arrange an outing, steal more time alone, gain her confidence, it would still take a week's time just to win a kiss. Extending his stay in this *nauseating* city—he smiled at the memory—was out of the question. He must put distance between himself and those nightmarish mills as quickly as possible, and yet . . . she was too extraordinary, too precious to rush and risk losing altogether.

He could ask her to become his mistress.

The thought came unbidden, from whence he did not know. He'd never had a mistress, never even contemplated such a thing. It had always seemed too confining an arrangement. But if she were truly running from something, perhaps she'd welcome his protection. He could get her out of the city, set her up in a house in London, or in the country if she preferred, even take her with him to Greece. She could be a refuge from Father's disapproval, Mother's entreaties. He could go to her—*be with her*—whenever he wished. His pulse quickened at the thought of her waiting for him, welcoming him with her body. His cock stirred, signaling approval all its own.

He sat for a time, staring at the river, dreaming of what could be. Then he rose and started back toward his hotel.

SIX

LIBERTY OR DEATH IS our Motto, and we have sworn to return Home in Triumph, or return no more …

—From 'The Proclamation of provisional government'
Glasgow, 1 April 1820.

THREE DAYS LATER, JANE found herself once again in the company of Mr. Sommerbell, speeding through the countryside in a hired landau, top down to let in the Scottish sunshine. She'd no idea where he'd found a carriage this lavish in Glasgow. She'd never seen its like in the city, nor anywhere else for that matter. It had only two seats—a *landaulette*, Mr. Sommerbell had proclaimed it, with a smirk, and an exaggerated French accent. Thankfully, Cam occupied the seat beside her. Mr. Sommerbell was perched high up in the driver's box, his guitar beside him.

The soft, cream-colored leather was like sitting on a cloud, and the carriage was sprung so well she almost didn't notice when they moved off the cobblestones and onto the dirt road of the countryside. It was painted, wheels and all, a garish hue of bright yellow. *Canary? Daisy?* It was the color one would expect on a post-chaise hurtling down a country highway, not on a private carriage in the city. It seemed designed to attract attention, and if that was indeed the intent, it had worked. Everyone they'd passed had gawped. At one point, a group of children even ran after them, trailing along for nearly a mile, laughing. Mr. Sommerbell and Cameron simply laughed back, but Jane wanted to melt into the plush cushions. She felt ridiculous, exposed, and entirely uncomfortable.

It didn't help that nearly all the residents of Glasgow were out this morning, abuzz with the news of the day. They'd woken to a poster plastered to walls and lampposts, a proclamation, anonymously written, calling for a general strike and demanding the right to Scottish self-rule. Cameron had been out early to read the document for himself. He'd come home wide-eyed and excited, reporting that a strike did indeed appear to be imminent. Rumors were flying. He'd heard that radical militias were preparing to march on the city and burn it to the ground. He'd heard the proclamation was, in fact, the work of the Chief Constable, an attempt to draw the radicals out of hiding for arrest. He'd even heard that the French, in league with Scottish insurgents, were amassing an army set on invasion. It was impossible to know the truth.

Jane's instinct was to lock the doors, draw the drapes, and stay inside until the danger had passed. But when she'd suggested that perhaps this wasn't the best day for a country excursion after all, and quietly reminded her brother of the fifteen dead at Peterloo, he'd brushed her concerns aside. The strike, if it happened at all, would not take place until Monday, he said, and even if violence *did* occur, they'd be safe in the countryside. Cameron had made it clear that *he* would go with Mr. Sommerbell, with or without her, and so she'd reluctantly agreed to come, if nothing else to ensure her impetuous little brother stayed out of trouble.

Mr. Sommerbell seemed as oblivious to the danger as Cameron. His formal attire of their previous meeting was replaced by worn buckskin breeches, a sloppily tied cravat, and a somewhat rumpled, though fashionably cut, green coat. He'd taken off his hat, and the wind whipped his black hair in every direction. He seemed to revel in the day—completely comfortable in his own skin, brimming over with exuberance.

Curse it. She was staring again.

The sunshine had returned. The entire countryside was coming to life, and they were driving to a pleasure garden called Willow Creek, which Cynthia had described as a country oasis, perfect for a picnic. Jane *should* have been pleased. It had been ages since she'd gotten out of the city, but instead she found herself wrapped in thick layers of annoyance and dread. Dread of the danger in Glasgow. Annoyance with her brother, and with Mr. Sommerbell, but mostly with herself for allowing that infuriating man to co-opt her thoughts. For agreeing to come on this foolish errand in the first place . . . and underneath it all was the black dread that had been building inside since the moment she'd met Mr. Sommerbell, a sense of foreboding, laced with guilt. This unbidden preoccupation with Cynthia's nephew was a betrayal. A betrayal of the one thing, the one *person*, she'd loved the most.

Cameron sat next to her, eyes half-closed, face upturned, strongly resembling a lizard sunning himself. He was, of course, completely oblivious to her distress. A day off was a rare occurrence for him, and though he *was* a fool, he was a hard-working fool. He deserved to enjoy himself. She would try to project a happy mood for his sake.

The road followed a small river. Cold clear water flowed over flat stones and around boulders, undulating, occasionally agitated enough to break free in a spray of white foam. They rounded a bend, and the stream diverged, snaking its way around a large enclosure bordered by a stone fence, then disappearing behind a cottage. The enclosure contained row after row of what appeared to be very small trees, lined up like infantrymen and marked off with wooden stakes. Sheep grazed in one corner, happily foraging the first flush of spring grass, and the cottage was brightly whitewashed and well kept.

Whenever he could, Father would return home from a trip to London with a new apple or pear tree purchased from Whitehall, a nursery near Glasgow. This might be the place.

Mr. Sommerbell turned the carriage into the drive. *They were stopping here?*

He drew the horses to a halt, and in one quick movement, he leapt down from the driver's perch, opened her door, and swept into a dramatic bow. "Welcome to Whitehall Nursery, milady."

Of course he had no idea of the connection.

Why were they stopping here?

She looked to Cameron. A wide grin spread across his face. He'd been in on this. "We thought to surprise you since it was on the way. Sommerbell's uncle says they have all the latest and greatest fruit trees."

Her brother apparently had not made the connection either.

Both men seemed exceptionally pleased with themselves. They looked at her expectantly, sure she'd be overcome with joy. *But really, what good is a tree nursery if you don't have ground to plant trees on?* She looked out over the spindly saplings. Just sticks really, with no leaves or blossoms this early in the year. Surprise quickly changed to agitation, sharp and hungry. *What was she supposed to do here?*

She turned to her brother, ready to dig into him with the talons of her anger, then stopped. The look on his face, so mirthful, so eager, so much like the boy he'd been before . . . No, she could not poison his mood with her own. She drew a steadying breath, forced her lips into what she hoped looked like a smile of delight, then accepted Mr. Sommerbell's outstretched hand. She did not meet his eyes as she stepped down from the carriage.

A man who must be the proprietor emerged from the cottage and strode toward them. *What would they say to him?* They had no intention of buying anything. Surely, he would not want to waste his time on three loiterers. She looked to her two escorts, both smiling like buffoons. This had been their idea. They could very well do the talking.

The man introduced himself as Mr. Olsen, and at first, he *did* seem a bit confused. It wasn't every day a group of young people descended on his orchard in an absurdly bright yellow carriage, with no intention of buying anything. But as soon as Mr. Sommerbell mentioned the name of his botanist uncle, the man warmed and offered a tour.

With his usual bonhomie, Cam struck up a conversation with Mr. Olsen about trees and politics and who knows what else. Jane trailed behind, half-heartedly looking at the smooth wooden tags affixed to each tree. There *were* a few she'd not heard of . . . Of course, Mr. Sommerbell chose to hang back with her rather than converse with the others. The man seemed incapable of leaving her be.

He allowed her a few minutes of silence before attempting conversation. "How do you find the nursery, Miss Stuart?" He peered at her with that self-satisfied smile, sure her answer would be in the affirmative.

The only reason to pretend satisfaction was her brother, and her brother was not listening. "How do I find it? I find it pointless, Mr. Sommerbell." She strode ahead of him.

He caught up with her. Too quickly. "Ah, but Miss Stuart, how could you *not* be pleased? The day is fine. We've escaped the city. You're surrounded by what you love best." He touched her arm. "What must a man do to earn your smile?"

She jerked away. "Just stop."

Again, she outpaced him, and again, he caught up. This time, he turned and walked backward in front of her, nettling her with his cocky grin. *If only there were a rock in his path. If only he would stumble.* "You, Miss Stuart, need a diversion. Something to distract you from yourself."

Suddenly, he reversed course, darting toward her and snatching her bonnet off her head.

"Mr. Sommerbell!" She lunged forward, trying to get it back, but the ribbons slipped between her fingers. Why hadn't she tied the blasted thing on?

He turned and threw a mischievous grin over his shoulder, daring her to follow as he took off toward the far corner of the enclosure.

Cam and Mr. Olson were now well ahead, absorbed in their conversation and taking no notice. Her brother had completely abandoned her. Her eyes darted back to Mr. Sommerbell. He was taunting her now, jogging backward and waving the bonnet in her direction. With a sigh of pure annoyance, she followed.

He reached the fence well ahead of her and vaulted over, as graceful as a cat, then—bonnet tucked securely behind his back—he turned and offered her his other hand. She ignored him, scrambling over the low stone wall of her own accord.

"This is ridiculous." She straightened up and continued her pursuit. "Just give it— *Oh!*" Without a word, he tossed the bonnet back to her. It soared gracefully through the air, and she caught it, lunging precariously to avoid slipping in a patch of mud.

"Wait here." He grinned at her, and she stood, hands on hips, watching as he sat himself in the grass by the streambank and calmly removed his boots and stockings.

"What are you doing?" she asked.

He looked up, as innocent as a wee boy. "I shall obtain a token for my lady, one that will lighten her mood. Perhaps, if I'm lucky, it might even put a smile on her face."

He rose, barefoot now, and made an exaggerated bow, then turned and waded into the burn, wobbling a bit as he traversed the sharp stones of the streambed. She followed his trajectory and realized where he was going. Just beyond the far bank, under the trailing boughs of an old willow, there was a stand of kingcups, one of the earliest spring wildflowers. The small yellow blossoms bobbed in the breeze, bright and cheerful. She couldn't help but notice just how well their color matched the garish hue of their carriage. *Kingcup yellow.*

As she watched him make his way across the stream, an idea formed in her head. Something she'd noticed out of the corner of her eye as she struggled over the stone fence . . . Perhaps it was an instinct from a childhood spent with three boys as playmates. Perhaps it was simply her desire to once and for all wipe that arrogant smile off his face. Whatever it was, she didn't feel either able or willing to resist the temptation.

She walked quickly back to the fence, keeping an eye on Mr. Sommerbell's retreating form, making sure she was unobserved. *Exactly as she'd thought*, a slithering mass of slowworms writhed together on a shelf notched in the weathered stone of the fence. There were at least a dozen of them. Likely, they'd just emerged from their nest, lured from their hibernation by the spring sunshine. She watched for a moment, transfixed by the scales shining bronze in the sunlight, the forked tongues darting in and out. They were beautiful specimens, some nearly two feet long.

By the time Mr. Sommerbell returned, Jane was sitting on the side of the streambank, knees drawn up to her chin, innocently watching the clear water flow over flat stones. He presented the small bouquet he'd collected with a flourish, and she accepted, hoping the smile she gave him was not overly cheerful. He met her eyes and smiled back. *He thought he'd won.*

She looked back toward the landau. "Cameron and Mr. Olsen are almost back to the carriage."

"Indeed. On to the next adventure." He sat to pull on his stockings. She watched. He tugged one boot on. She watched. He tugged the other boot on . . . and went white as a sheet, emitting a shrill, savage shriek—a sound decidedly more animal than human, and as far from smooth velvet as a sound could be. He kicked his foot wildly, and the boot flew in a wide arc, landing with an audible *squish* in a particularly wet patch of mud.

Victory.

"*What the devil?*" He ran to where the boot had landed, turned it over, and jumped back, eyes wide in horror as a large slowworm slithered into the grass.

She couldn't help it. She laughed, harder than she had in months, or years even. Her body shook with mirth, her stomach ached, tears welled in her eyes. It felt so *good* to break his perfect facade. Although a part of her knew she wasn't being exactly fair . . . *No, this was fair. He deserved it.*

Mr. Sommerbell's pallor quickly turned to a red flush. He stormed back to her, one stocking foot covered in mud, the other booted. All attempts at charm were forgotten in the force of his rage. "*You.* You. Put that . . . *thing.* In my boot. What the devil were you thinking, woman? *A damnable snake?* You could have bloody well killed me!"

It appeared Mr. Sommerbell had a fear of snakes. A somewhat unreasonable one. "It wasn't venomous, and it wasn't a snake. 'Twas a slowworm, a *legless lizard.*" She shrugged. "Harmless. Unless you happen to be a grub. I'd have thought you'd crossed paths with them in your child-hood, Mr. Sommerbell. Or don't you have slowworms in England?"

"I make a point of avoiding anything resembling a snake. And that . . . that *thing* was bloody close enough." He was sullen now, his anger quickly receding to embarrassment. "My sister tormented me with the devils when I was a boy. I *hate* the blasted things," he muttered.

"Well, I truly am sorry, then, Mr. Sommerbell. I'd thought to have a bit of fun. I didn't mean to frighten you."

"I wasn't frightened. I just hate snakes is all."

"Yes, of course." Now she was the one with the self-satisfied smile. "Shall we rejoin my brother?"

She set off toward the landau where Cam and Mr. Olson now stood, still engrossed in conversation. Whatever did her brother find to talk about with strangers? Jane would never know, but she was grateful he had a knack for it so that she did not have to. Mr. Sommerbell trailed behind, one boot clean and one encased in mud, squishing slightly as he walked.

Seven

Percy's foot was wet. And muddy. His pride was in worse shape yet. Of course she couldn't have known of his nonsensical fear of snakes. But still, what kind of woman did such a thing?

Jane Stuart, apparently.

But as he trailed behind her, he noticed something—a confidence, a swagger that hadn't been there before. And the way she'd laughed . . . the way she'd thrown off the trappings of her sullen mood and transformed herself into a trickster, a veritable puck, scheming, gleeful, unapologetic. Now that the moment of terror had passed, it hardly mattered that her mirth had been at his expense.

She glanced back over her shoulder, and in his mind, the victorious smirk on her face was a seductive, teasing grin . . . *She turned and led him back to the streambank, disappeared behind a curtain of willow boughs. He followed. She was lying in a pool of sunshine, her expression heavy with wanton desire, her skirts drawn up to her waist, legs spread wide in invitation . . .*

He shook his head to banish the erotic image. This was neither the time nor the place for such thoughts . . . but *damnation*. She would be a glorious lover.

They were nearing the carriage. "Jane!" Cameron was excited. "Mr. Olsen says the Earl of Banton stopped here sometimes, on his way from London. This is where he got your trees." He looked to his sister expectantly, as if his words had some hidden meaning.

Her stride stiffened as she approached her brother and the nurseryman. She said something that Percy couldn't hear.

Mr. Olsen's face brightened. "I sold him a Ben Davis apple from America the last time he came. Tell me, miss, have you gotten any fruit from it yet?"

"I couldn't say." He'd caught up to her now, but she spoke so softly Percy could still barely hear. "I haven't been to the orchard for quite some time."

"Ah. I'll have to ask the Earl himself when he happens by again then. It's a rare one. Cost me a pretty penny, it did."

Cameron and Jane exchanged a glance.

"He died. The Earl. A year ago. I dinna think his successor is interested in trees." Cameron looked into the distance as he spoke, avoiding Mr. Olsen's gaze.

The silence stretched. Uncomfortable. Jane stood, rooted in place. Even Cameron seemed to have lost his knack for words. *Who was the Earl of Banton?* The owner of the orchard from the sound of it. A friend of their father's? Percy would ask Cameron when the chance arose, but in the meantime, he'd seize the opportunity to play the gallant hero and save the lady from her discomfort.

He cleared his throat to break the tension. "I believe it's time for us to depart. The pleasure gardens await. Thank you, Mr. Olsen, for your hospitality."

———◦———

Percy and Beau had frequented the gardens of Vauxhall in London during the summer of debauchery that separated their graduation from Oxford and their departure to the Continent. They would drink to excess while taking in the spectacle of the lights, then stroll through the dark of the enclosed walks in search of willing partners for amorous play. Beau preferred men, Percy women, but they were accepting of either. If they were successful in their search, they'd bring their new lovers back to the apartments they shared for a drink-fueled night of pleasure . . . But the gardens of Willow Creek were nothing like that, and gazing out over them, Percy found for the first time his memories of those nights seemed just a bit too hedonistic, too self-indulgent. Artificial.

These gardens were just a patch of well-tended country, really. Idyllic, but plain. *Uncontrived, uncomplicated beauty.* A rolling meadow was bordered by a small river that wound its way through birches and willows still barren of leaves. At one end, the stream widened into a pond in which he could make out lily pads just starting to emerge. He let his eyes wander over the scene, searching . . . Several rowboats were drawn up on the bank. *Perhaps he could convince her to ride with him.* On the far side of the pond was a folly built to look like the ruins of a medieval castle, complete with a stone tower. *That held promise.*

He tied up the horses, then they set out over the meadow toward the river. Cameron spread their blanket on a sunny patch of grass near the bank, not far from where it flowed into the pond. Percy had instructed the hotel staff to spare no expense when filling the picnic hamper, and was satisfied to find they'd followed his orders. There were pork pies, boiled eggs, several cheeses, pickles, a loaf of crusty bread, fresh oranges, pears, cake, biscuits, a fruit pie, two bottles of claret, and, courtesy of Uncle Douglas, a bottle of French brandy.

"Heavens, are we expecting the entire Scots Guard?" Jane hesitated for a moment then reached for a pear. She gripped it lightly, acquainting herself with the feel of its skin, the weight of it in her hand. She brought it to her nose, closing her eyes as she inhaled deeply.

Damn. He wanted this woman.

Thankfully, Cameron was too focused on the feast laid out before them to notice Percy's ogling. He finished off a pickle, then took up a plate, piling it high with two pork pies, boiled eggs, cheese and more pickles.

Percy uncorked the claret, offering the siblings each a glass. Cameron eagerly accepted. "Fill it up. 'Tis a rare day, and I intend to enjoy every drop."

Jane watched with lowered eyes as Percy filled her cup. Her eyelashes were thick and lush, the same dark auburn as her hair. He finished, and by pure happenstance, they both glanced up at the same moment. Their eyes met, and—*hallelujah*—she did not look away. A slight blush spread across her cheeks, and incredibly, she smiled. It was only a small smile, gone in an instant, but *still*. A shiver went up his spine.

Luncheon was a companionable affair. Cameron ate heartily while keeping the conversation flowing with questions about Percy's musical pursuits and his growing-up years. Percy told them of his boyhood at Grislow Park, tormented by his sister and coddled by his mother. He told them of his travels with Beau to the Continent. Of meeting Mauro in Prague at a late-night musicale, and eventually following him to Italy to study guitar while Beau painted the landscape. Jane's brother had a knack for comfortable discourse, but Percy had begun to notice that he always steered the conversation away from himself, asking questions, showing interest in the answers that led to more questions. They'd talked for at least an hour at his Uncle and Aunt's dinner party, and by now, Cameron knew almost the entirety of Percy's life story, but he'd not learned one thing about Cameron other than some details of his current life in Glasgow, and the one quick, mysterious comment about the Earl of Banton. He must hold the same secrets as his sister, Percy realized. He just held them differently.

Jane sat quietly, listening. She ate the pear, taking small bites, savoring each one. Percy had to avert his eyes to discourage the erection that stirred to life at the sight of her soft lips, wet with juice. *This was getting ridiculous.* After the pear, she took some cheese, a boiled egg, bread with butter and more fruit. He was glad when she accepted another glass of claret. He didn't want her foxed, but he *did* want her comfortable, and this was one way to accomplish that.

Cameron didn't bring up the subject of the mills, and though thoughts of Jane Stuart's lips were paramount, Percy still wanted to discuss the topic, ideally *before* he propositioned the man's sister.

He'd finished inspecting the entirety of Father's holdings over the last few days. Each mill he visited was worse than the last, and he'd come to the conclusion that he must start formulating a plan for reform, not just as a show for Jane, but for his own piece of mind as well.

It wasn't just the children, though that was bad enough. It was the vacant stares on the faces of the adults—as if they'd given up being human. It was the man, no older than Percy, doubled over, coughing and wheezing, then quickly hiding away the bloody handkerchief he'd held up to his mouth. It was the woman, belly huge with child but thin as a rail everywhere else, who'd collapsed from exhaustion in front of him and been carried away.

It was impossible not to sympathize with their plight. Percy himself would surely join in a strike if he were one of them. He'd play the fife while they marched in the streets. But he was also his father's son. He collected an allowance, a generous one. He'd have an immense inheritance when Father died . . . and the truth of it was that all that wealth, all that luxury Percy had grown accustomed to, had all been gained on the backs of those very same workers.

For now, he could escape this reality, leave Glasgow, flee to Greece and bury himself in sensual pleasure until all else was forgotten . . . and that was exactly what he intended to do, hopefully with Jane Stuart at his side. It wasn't as if Father would listen if he tried to argue for change anyhow. But what would happen if—*when*—Father died? Uncle Douglas had been wrong about marriage, but he'd been right to urge Percy to think of the possibility. All the factories, and all the misery and cruelty inside them would belong to him and him alone. His responsibility.

Responsibility. He detested the word, but still . . . *what would he do?* He could choose to leave the solicitors in charge and continue to enjoy an income generated by the abuse of human beings, or he could sell the mills, allowing someone else to continue that abuse. Both choices seemed cowardly. They left the barbarity in place, the children under the mules. Percy was many things—an artist, a rakehell, a free spirit—but he was *not* a coward.

He finished packing away the food, then poured himself and Cameron each a glass of brandy.

"Did your sister tell you of my experience at my father's factory?"

Cameron nodded. "Aye. You want to learn about the models for reform. I told you all I know the other night." He took a sip, exhaling through his teeth. "But there's a lad, Richie Owen, works apprentice shifts at the infirmary with me. His father owns New Lanark."

New Lanark. The name sounded vaguely familiar, but Percy couldn't think of where he'd heard it.

"New Lanark? Is that a mill?"

"Mills. Plural. And a village," Cameron replied. "Just up the Clyde. People come from all over to see it. Richie's father's done away with child workers. Built schools for them instead." Cameron paused. "He's done other things, too. Good things. But I dinna know the details."

"And these mills are successful, without child labor?"

"That's the way Richie tells it. I dinna get the sense he and his father see entirely eye to eye . . . but he speaks well of the factories."

"I'd be grateful for an introduction."

"Dinna mention it. You'll get along. Richie's a good lad."

Cameron seemed content to end the conversation there, but Percy couldn't hold back. "Tell me more about the injuries you've seen. Is it only children who are hurt, or are there dangers to adults as well?"

Cameron opened his mouth to answer, but Jane rose, interrupting him. "I'm going to take a turn around the pond before we leave."

"Suit yourself." Cameron shot his sister a lopsided grin that held a hint of inebriation. To Jane's two glasses of claret and Percy's three, Cameron had imbibed four, and was just now pouring himself a second brandy.

She nodded and set off. Her head was bare—the straw bonnet lay beside Cameron on the blanket—and Percy had a perfect view of the creamy skin of her nape as she strode away. His eyes wandered lower over her luscious curves, noticing how she swayed when she walked . . .

". . . mostly children who are wounded badly enough to put them in the hospital."

Cameron was answering his question, and Percy had, once again, been leering at the fellow's sister. Luckily, in his slight haze of inebriation, Cameron didn't seem to notice, but Percy was sure his luck would run out at some point.

" . . . Adults have lesser injuries, though lung attacks arnna uncommon. Of course the exhaustion makes them more susceptible to disease, an' the lack o' good food. I dinna blame them for wantin' to strike. 'Specially with what so many of them have been through, in the name of *improvement*." Cameron spat the word out as if it were the bitterest of pills. "I'd do the same, 'twer me . . . though, with Janie dependin' on me . . . She relies on me, ye ken." Apparently, drink brought out the brogue in this lad.

This was as good a time as any to pose the question that'd been on Percy's mind since they'd left the tree nursery. Now that Jane's brother was slightly in his cups, he might even get an honest answer.

"Who's the Earl of Banton?"

Cameron's expression darkened. "I shouldna mentioned him. Janie wasna happy I did."

"Was he the laird in Darnalay? Where you came from?"

Cameron heaved a sigh. "Aye."

"I wondered if he was the landowner who allowed Jane to work his orchard. A friend of your father's?" Mayhap he was being too forward, but he couldn't help the curiosity.

"Sommerbell, I—" Cameron started, then stopped. Thinking for a few moments before opening his mouth again. "I dinna like keepin' secrets. *I'd* tell you straight out, but 'tis her secret too." He pointed his chin toward where Jane was walking by the streambank. "And she wouldna want me sayin'." There was a long silence, then Cameron's eyes narrowed. "I'm nae used to lookin' after my sister . . . but ye ken I'd kill you if you try to take advantage o' her."

He should have known this was coming. "Your sister is lovely. Truly. But I leave Glasgow in less than a week." *Both true statements.*

Cameron nodded, satisfied as only a man in his cups could be. He removed his coat, balled it up and put it under his head for a pillow. "Time for a wee nap. Watch Janie, will you? I'll rest easier knowin' there's a set o' eyes on her."

"Of course." Percy would do much more than watch her, but Cameron needn't know about that.

EIGHT

THE FOLLY WAS BUILT to resemble a ruined medieval castle. Stone archways and half walls enclosed a space that would have been the great hall in an authentic structure, but it was much too small to be believable—less than half the size of the great room at Darnalay. To one side stood an intact stone tower decorated with Gothic crosses. Large arched windows bisected by iron mullions were spaced evenly all the way around to the summit. The top was enclosed by a sturdy looking parapet, suggesting it might be possible to climb up and look out over the countryside.

The place was deserted. No wind stirred. The slanting afternoon sun cast an aura of enchantment, and Jane could imagine she was wandering into the land of the faeries, like a girl from the stories Freya Riley—one of the castle maids and Mama's closest friend—had told her as a child.

She could still see the figures of her brother and Mr. Sommerbell sprawled on the blanket in the distance. She'd been glad to leave their conversation behind. Certainly she sympathized with the plight of the millworkers. If things had happened differently, she and Cameron might have been among their ranks. But she found she was in no mood to dwell on what was wrong with the world. Instead, for the first time in a very long while, she wanted to think of the past—of the girl she'd once been. There was something about the episode with the slowworm . . . as if she'd been asleep, then suddenly jolted awake and climbed out of a dream to remember who she was. A girl who could laugh, who took pride in besting the boys and surprising everyone with what she could accomplish.

As she approached the folly, she felt herself slipping back even farther in time. In her child's mind, there'd been no hard line between science and magic. She'd seen them as equals, and been just as eager to look for faeries inside a blossom as she was to identify its stamen, carpels, and sepals.

She was exploring a magical wood. There, just in front of her, were the ruins of an enchanted castle. A fortress where no one had set foot for hundreds of years . . . But perhaps someone was here, perhaps a princess dwelt at the top of the tower, forever a prisoner until her prince came to free her . . .

She shook herself. *Silly.* She was no longer a child, and this was just a folly. A fake. Built to lure patrons to the gardens. She *would* climb that tower, though. Perhaps she'd be able to see all the way back to the city.

A wooden staircase spiraled up the inside, just as she'd supposed it might. The windows were much larger than they would have been in a real medieval tower. Shafts of afternoon sunlight slanted through, given shimmering, ethereal form by the specks of dust floating in the still air. The entire space was bathed in a warm golden glow and once again, she had to work to push young Janie's flights of imagination away.

She'd made it halfway up when footsteps sounded below.

"Miss Stuart?"

Of course. It was him.

She said nothing, but she heard him begin to climb, the dull thud of his footfalls breaking the golden silence. He rounded a corner, and she could just make him out—a silhouette hidden in shadow. The disheveled black hair. The angled planes of his face. The arch of his brow . . . If there *were* a princess imprisoned in this tower, this was not the chaste prince come to rescue her and carry her away on a white horse. No, this man had arrived on a black stallion. He was the wickedly gorgeous villain who had come, not to rescue, but to ravish.

She was standing in a shaft of sunlight. He stopped short at the sight of her, staring unabashedly.

"Jane." His voice lowered to that same dark, sultry tone she remembered from their encounter in the dining room. She opened her mouth to respond, to admonish him for using her name, but he held up a hand, commanding her silence. "Don't. Move."

She *didn't* move, not so much because of his directive, but because she was caught. The shimmering beam of light held her. In time. In space. In this moment, he was no longer a predator, but a devotee, and she was no longer the exiled bastard of a nobleman's mistress, but a Lady, bathed in golden light. Powerful. She stood three stairs taller than him. His eyes worshiped her.

He closed the distance between them. One stair. Two stairs. Then he was on the tread just below her. His breath was ragged in the silence. His scent enveloped her, weaving together with the sunlight, strengthening the enchantment that held her in place. His eyes sought hers, and she did not look away. She allowed him to delve as deeply as he wished, to see every bit of her—because, in this moment, she had nothing to hide. She was no longer the scared, empty girl she'd let herself become, but the strong, luminous woman she'd once dreamed she could be.

Without breaking eye contact, he held out his hand, as if asking for a dance. She gave it, watching as he slowly, finger by finger, slipped off her glove. Her body began to hum, then vibrate as he brought her bare hand to his lips, brushing her knuckles with the lightest of kisses.

Later, on one of the many nights she would lie awake, remembering, she would decide that this was the moment she should have made her escape. Should have left him and run—back to her brother, back to the comfortable torpor of her life in Glasgow. If she *had*, perhaps she still would have been able to forget him, to relax back into numbness and avoid all that was to come . . . But alas, she did *not* jerk her hand away, nor did she run. She simply stood there and watched as he paid homage with his lips.

She closed her eyes and felt him turn her hand. Felt his lips soft against the inside of her wrist. The buzzing sensation grew, then something small exploded inside her. She was dizzy, losing her balance. She gasped, lost his hand, reached for him again—for anything solid to avoid falling down all those stairs below. Her fingers landed in the smooth silk of his hair. He groaned at her touch, and her eyes flew open to the sight of him gazing up at her with a blazing heat that hit her like a lightning strike.

She blinked, and a vision of Ken flashed through her mind. Her beloved. Her prince on a white horse. The man she would remain faithful to until her dying breath.

What was she doing?

Like a drowning victim coming up for air, she broke away, and because she didn't know what else to do, she bolted up the stairs, running blindly from what she'd just done.

For a few long, ragged breaths, Percy stood rooted in place. Mayhap it was the way the sun played through the windows, or the claret, or that bloody snake she'd put in his boot. Whatever it was, Jane had opened herself to him. *Finally.*

He'd forever remember rounding the staircase and beholding her above him, bathed in sunbeams, hair lit up in a crown of red-gold light. A queen. The way she'd looked at him, proud and certain. The way she'd yielded her hand. The white-hot fire that had burned between them for the briefest of moments before she'd remembered herself and run away . . . He needed her. *More* of her. As much as he needed air to fuel his next breath.

It would be now or never to press his suit.

He bounded up the stairs, taking two at a time, emerging into the open air to find her standing with her back to him, gazing out over the parapet. One couldn't see the buildings of the town from this distance, but to the south, the clear blue of the sky was polluted with a dirty brown haze. The mills.

She must have heard the tread of his boots on the hollow wooden deck, but she didn't turn as he approached. He came to a stop beside her, joining her in looking out over the green hills. The picnic blanket was visible from here, her brother reclining on it, no bigger than an ant. Percy realized he was still holding her glove. He held it into her line of vision, a peace offering. She took it, and in the brief moment of exchange, he caught a glimpse of her face. The sultry golden angel he'd just kissed was gone, in her place the scared, sad-eyed beauty he'd come to know.

"Jane— Miss Stuart. Please. I didn't mean—"

She pulled her glove on. "Go. Away. Mr. Sommerbell." Each syllable was carefully enunciated. Controlled.

His hand was resting on the parapet, just inches from hers. He slid it toward her, slowly, until he felt the smooth touch of her gloved hand connecting them. She didn't move away. He counted the breaths. One. Two. Perhaps she would allow—

She jerked her hand away. "I said, go. Away."

"But. What just happened . . ." He exhaled. "I desperately want to get to know you. *Please*."

"What just happened 'twas a *mistake*." Her voice wavered, losing its controlled edge. "I dinna know why I . . . I shouldn't have allowed it."

"It was only a kiss on the hand," he reminded her. "'Twas innocent."

"*Innocent*?" She turned her head to look him in the eye. "There can be nothing between us, Mr. Sommerbell. You must understand that." She looked away and closed her eyes. "I should never have allowed it." She seemed to be speaking more to herself than to him.

There was so much anguish lurking beneath the surface of her words. He wanted to take her in his arms, kiss her until she could no longer feel the pain of whatever it was that haunted her, but he knew if he moved so much as an inch, she would be lost to him, perhaps forever. So, instead, he gave her something infinitely more precious, and infinitely less comfortable—honesty.

He took a breath, exhaling slowly. "Jane— Miss Stuart. You were right. When you said it was a game . . . that I was toying with you. I *was*. And . . . I'm sorry. The fact is, I *like* you. A great deal, and I . . . I suppose that's how I thought to show it." He paused, then added another bit of truth. "I'm an ass."

She didn't respond, but she also didn't move farther away. He took another deep breath, steadying himself for the words that came next.

"Come with me. To Northumberland."

She stiffened, but still didn't move.

"I have an allowance. You could have a house. Land for an orchard."

He held his breath through the long silence that followed.

"You're asking me to be your mistress." Her words were stiff and controlled again. It was impossible to guess what she was thinking.

"We needn't call it that. It could simply be an . . . an *understanding*. You would want for nothing. We could travel. Anything you wish."

"And what would be the benefit to *you* of this *understanding*?" She turned to him, her gaze accusing.

"I'd ask for nothing that's not willingly given." And it was true. He had never, would never, force himself on a woman. "You would be a muse for my music. A friend. And, eventually, when you're ready, I hope we could be lovers."

There. He'd said it.

"And if I don't *want* to be your lover? If I accept the house, the orchard, all of it, but refuse your bed? What happens then?" Jane's voice rose, her eyes flashed with anger. "I'll *tell* you what happens, Mr. Sommerbell. You'll tire of me. You'll throw me out. I'll be even worse off than I am now." She paused and turned away again. Dismissing him. "'Tis bad enough living with my brother. I'll never be your lover, Mr. Sommerbell, and I have no interest in being your dependent."

He'd hoped it wouldn't come to this, but she'd left him no choice. "I could have a contract drawn up. When—*if* we part ways, you'd be entitled to a sum of . . . say, a thousand pounds?"

She drew in a breath. That was enough for her to live comfortably for the rest of her life. It was also more than what his allowance could bear, but he'd think of that another day.

"You're your father's heir, are you not? You'll want to marry someday. Have children of your own. Where would I be then?"

How little she knew of him.

"I'll never marry. I don't believe in it."

"Don't believe . . . in what? Marriage?"

"Yes. Marriage. Wedlock. Prison. Being shackled together *for life*. What I'm offering is a thousand times better. When we tire of each other, we go our separate ways. You with your thousand. Me, with my freedom."

She shook her head. "I know how these *arrangements* work. They're not better than marriage." The bitterness in her tone was startling. *Had she been someone's mistress?* It seemed unlikely given her reaction to a simple kiss on the hand, but . . .

"Were you the Earl of Banton's mistress?" The question was out of his mouth before he had time to think better of it. "It wouldn't change my mind."

She turned on him, eyes wide and angry, then suddenly seemed to think better of her attack. She closed her eyes and drew in a deep breath, releasing it in a long sigh, then turned away again, looking out into space. "The Earl was my *father*, Mr. Sommerbell. My father and Cameron's."

He sucked in his breath. "Then why . . ." He wasn't sure how to finish the question.

Why are you alone?

Why are you in Glasgow, in a rented house, and with only one servant?

Why does Cameron bear the burden of supporting the both of you?

But there was no need to finish the question. She knew exactly what he was thinking. "Because my mother was not his countess. That title belonged to another woman."

The puzzle pieces clicked into place. The secrecy and discomfort, her education and fine manners, their modest means. Jane and her brother *were* high born, but born on the wrong side of the blanket.

"She was his mistress."

"His housekeeper, officially. But for twenty years, they shared a bedroom. I suppose you could say they had an *understanding*. One that doesna include Cameron and me."

But he'd brought her trees, given her access to his library . . . "But your father acknowledged you. Surely—"

"Aye. At least I thought he did. I thought he *loved* us. But what kind of father provides nothing for his children? *Mama* was accounted for. She'd have been a wealthy woman had he died first, but she died alongside him, and there was nothing for us in his will. We werna even mentioned."

Another long pause.

"I don't know what to say . . . Truly. I'm sorry."

"What's done is done." She stared, unseeingly, into the distance, lost in thought. The sun disappeared behind a cloud for a moment, then the world brightened again. Their father had been everything Percy's father wasn't. Present. Giving. Loving. Yet he would be left with a fortune, while Jane and Cameron had nothing.

"Tell me about them?" The words floated out of his mouth, then drifted away into the still air. He'd just decided that she would not, in fact, speak, when she did.

"Mama grew up in London, in a great house. The daughter of a footman and a chambermaid. She had an education, and a . . . a taste for the finer things. She was pretty. She became a . . . a *courtesan*."

"That's how she met your father."

"Aye. According to him, she was the most beautiful woman in all of London. He loved her. I know he loved her . . ." Jane stared straight ahead, as if she could see her parents standing before her. "When she found she was with child, he moved her to Darnalay, to the castle. Then, I was born. Then Cameron."

"Darnalay. The way you say it, it sounds like Heaven."

She sighed. "'Tis just a castle, and a village, and the glens where the tenants have their farms. Lady Elinore—Father's wife—she never went there. She preferred to be in London. My parents could be together in Darnalay. Have a family. And they did. *We* did, or I thought we did, until—" Her voice broke. She looked away from the apparition in front of her, blinking as if to ward off tears.

Once again, he moved his hand to rest beside hers, offering the comfort of his touch. "Until they died." He finished for her.

This time, she didn't move her hand away.

"How did they die?"

"Father had business in Edinburgh. Mama went along to do some shopping. They were coming home. Their carriage lost a wheel. It skidded down a brae, and they were both killed. Instantly."

The pain in her voice was too much. He took her gloved hand in his, lacing their fingers. "Jane. I'm so sorry."

"Death happens. All too often." She didn't release his hand.

"Who inherited the title? Did he have other children? With his—"

"Wife?" she interrupted. "No. Lady Elinore died childless just before my parents did. But it wasna for lack of trying. Father would—" She stopped herself. "It doesna matter."

"It matters to *you*. Tell me. I won't think less of you."

She sighed. "He married her just after Cameron was born. He *had* to, apparently, something about his inheritance and our grandfather's will. But every spring, he'd go to London, to take his seat in the House of Lords, and I suspect he also went to . . . to try to get an heir on Lady Elinore. Mama'd lock herself away for days after he'd left . . . crying . . ."

There was a pause. They stood, hand in hand, looking out over the countryside.

"Who inherited the title?" He repeated the question. He had to know.

"Our cousin. The son of Father's younger brother."

"And he wouldn't allow you to stay?"

"We wrote him, asking. But then a letter came. It said he planned to take up residence and demanded we leave immediately. So, we took all the money we could find, Mama's jewelry, and we left."

"Your cousin would be so cruel?"

"Aye." Her voice grew distant. "I dinna know him. I've never even met him."

"Never *met* him? Surely he'd been to the castle if he was the heir?"

"I'm not sure, but—" She shook her head. "I dinna think my father and my uncle were on good terms. Father never spoke of him."

Without warning, she pulled her hand away and turned to him, her blue eyes a tempest of emotion. She'd lost so much—her parents, her home, everyone she'd ever known, save her brother . . .

"Now you know, Mr. Sommerbell, why I can never agree to be your mistress." All traces of brogue were suddenly gone. She'd regained control. "I will *not* put myself in my mother's place, nor will I put my own children in the place of my brother and I."

And there it was. The reason for her grief, her distrust of him. It all made perfect sense.

Yet he couldn't just let her go.

He let out a breath. *What could he possibly say to make her change her mind?* "Thank you. For telling me. Trusting me. But you are *not* your mother. I'm not your father. We certainly needn't have any children together." He took both her hands. Pleading. "I can give you a home. It won't replace what you had, nothing can, but it would be better than . . . *this*." He gestured around him, indicating the smoky skies, her brother sleeping below them. "You could have an orchard, a house of your own. And Jane, I *swear* to you, you need not share my bed. If you come with me, it's without expectation. If we become lovers, it will be because you choose it."

And he was surprised to realize he actually meant it. She'd been through so much, lost so much. It was within his power to give her a home, a new life . . . and though he might die if he never had the satisfaction of her body, the feel of her skin on his, the joy of driving into her and fusing himself with her . . . even if that never came to be, he could not, *would* not be the one to take her home away from her. Not after what she'd been through.

She gave him one last wide-eyed, agonizing look then dropped his hands and darted across the wooden floor, down the staircase and out of view. A minute later, she emerged from the bottom of the tower and strode quickly toward her brother. Percy stood there for a time, watching her retreating form. Then he drew in a deep breath and followed.

NINE

JANE NEARLY RAN BACK to the glade where her brother lay, eyes closed and softly snoring. His head rested on his wadded-up coat. It would be terribly wrinkled, probably grass-stained. Obviously, the man relied on someone else—*her*—to keep his clothes in order.

Her mind was spinning with the events of the last hour. The tower. The kiss to her hand. The excruciating guilt that followed, then the sudden shock. *He'd asked her to be his mistress.* And, somehow, in an effort to hide the true reason for her refusal, she'd told him much, much more than she'd ever intended for him to know.

Even as one side of her mind cataloged all of the reasons she could never accept his proposal, the other side couldn't help imagining . . . A home. An orchard. A way out of the city— *no.* That would never happen. *Could* never happen. For all she knew, his promises were nothing but lies intended to lure her to Northumberland where she knew no one, and abuse her, then leave her destitute.

But he was Cynthia's nephew. Surely that was some insurance against the worst case?

Even if it *was* true, that becoming his lover wasn't a condition of the proposed *understanding*, she'd no doubt he would pursue her relentlessly once he had her to himself. And, in truth, after what had just transpired in the tower, she wasn't at all certain she'd be able to resist him.

Bother Cam and his rest. Already she spied Mr. Sommerbell on the far side of the pond, walking briskly toward them.

She toed her brother lightly. "Cam, wake up. 'Tis time to go." She knelt down and began packing up the empty glasses. She would have everything ready to go by the time Mr. Sommerbell returned. They would leave, and there would be no need to talk to him again until he'd deposited her safely back on her doorstep, at which point she would give him one word—*goodbye*—and be rid of him. Forever.

Cam opened his eyes slowly, observed her movements for a few seconds, then shot her his laziest of grins. "'Tisn't late. Have another glass of wine." He closed his eyes again.

Infuriating brother. All of his days spent toiling at his studies, and he chose *now* to turn lazy.

"There are clouds gathering. We dinna want to be caught in a storm in that open carriage." It was true. Milky white clouds had obscured the sun. It did not, in fact, look like rain, but that was beside the point.

Cam opened his eyes, glanced up at the sky, then closed them again. "Those arnna rain clouds and you know it. Anyway, the carriage has a cover." He sighed dramatically. "I dinna think I could move if I tried. Mayhap it's some kind of sleeping illness. Those *do* happen, you know."

Mr. Sommerbell had cleared the lake. "Cam. *We must leave.*"

Finally catching on to the urgency in her voice, her brother blinked his eyes open and sat up on his elbows. He took in her troubled countenance, then the man striding along the streambank toward them. Con-

cern clouded his face. "Did Sommerbell overstep his bounds? If he did,
I'll—"

"No." *Yes.* "But Cam. I told him everything. About Darnalay . . . and
why we left. I dinna know what came over me."

"He asked about Father?"

She nodded.

"He asked me, too. I told him I couldna say out of respect to you." He
paused. "I'm sorry. I shouldna said ought at the nursery. I just . . . I got
excited."

She sighed. "Isna your fault. 'Twas *me* who told him."

"Did you tell him about Ken, too?"

"No."

A sudden stab of grief slashed through her, almost knocking her
down. It had been so long since she'd heard Ken's name spoken out loud.
And after what she'd just done, that moment in the tower . . . A hard
lump formed in the back of her throat. Her lower lip began to quiver.

Mr. Sommerbell was just a stone's throw away. Jane looked to her
brother, panicked. She must not let that man find her crying.

Wordlessly, Cam poured a small amount of amber liquid into a glass
and thrust it into her hands. *Brandy? Whiskey?* "Drink this. It'll help.
And stop worrying. I'd wager Sommerbell doesna care a whit who our
parents were."

He was right of course, but there was so much Cam didn't know
about the conversation on the top of that tower. And she could never
tell him.

He was also right about the brandy. It must be brandy, as it had a
different flavor from the whisky Father had sometimes allowed her to
sip. She welcomed the warmth as it burned down her throat and settled

in her stomach. The sensation helped quiet the grief. It was no longer a sharp pain, but a more familiar, and manageable, ache.

She turned her back on both men, clutching the glass with white knuckles and pretending to study the fields in the distance.

"Sommerbell!" She could hear the lazy smile in Cam's voice. "My sister tells me it's time to depart, yet I fear I canna yet move from this spot."

The whisper of movement, the hint of his scent. He'd arrived at the blanket. "Shall I play something to cap off the afternoon?"

Cameron grunted his assent.

"What are you in the mood for?" Mr. Sommerbell asked.

"Something lively. There's too much melancholy in this world as it is."

Apparently, they'd made a silent agreement to ignore Jane and her request to leave. *Confounded men.* All she wanted was to go home so she could cry in peace.

The sound of tuning came next. "This is a saltarello, an Italian country dance. 'Tis lively enough."

The Italian word rolled effortlessly off of Mr. Sommerbell's tongue and floated to her like a warm breeze. She gripped the glass tighter. *What was wrong with her?*

Then he began to play. A whirling melody running effortlessly through a low, driving rhythm. The music swept her thoughts into a cyclone of jumbled images and emotions, which she seemed to be viewing only from a distance. She gazed at the messy contents of her mind as if they were so much scenery, and was glad for the reprieve.

Then the song was over. He played a few others, each slower than the last. By the end, she was relaxed into herself, leaning heavily on her drawn up knees, her chin resting on her clasped hands, her eyelids drooping, her body languid, and her mind, amazingly, at ease. She wanted to believe it was the effects of the brandy, which now lay empty beside her, but she knew it was the music that had calmed her. *His* music.

She heard him put away the guitar, but still she didn't stir. Her relaxed state would be shattered the moment she did, and all the confusing and disturbing thoughts would tumble back to the fore.

Cam's gentle voice came to her finally. "Janie, off the blanket with you. It's time to go."

With a sigh, she rose and started toward the carriage, allowing the two men to follow with the blanket and the picnic basket. She just needed to make it home, then she would have peace and be able to sort out her thoughts.

She was upset, that much was clear. She wouldn't even face his direction, so he'd poured himself into his music. If he couldn't comfort her with his body, he could, at least, give her that. After the saltarello, he'd chosen pieces with slower tempos—adagio, lento—soothing melodies that would wrap themselves around her, just as he longed to do. And his efforts had been rewarded. Her body, at least, had visibly softened. Her mind, though? He would give anything to know what was going on in her mind.

The music's spell had been broken the moment she rose from the blanket. Agitated once more, Jane strode quickly toward the carriage, not even glancing back to be sure he and Cameron were following. Thank goodness her brother was so amiable. Without him, the whole situation would have been intolerably tense. They strolled together in her wake, Percy with his guitar strapped to his back and the folded woolen blanket in his arms, Cameron toting the picnic basket.

"She told you about Father," Cameron said, more as a confirmation than a question. "I'm glad. I hope you were kind about it?"

Percy shrugged. "It's no matter to me who your parents were. I'm sorry, though, that you were left in such a poor situation. It seems your father could have had more forethought."

Cameron shot him a wry look. "No one expects to die unexpectedly. I choose to believe he *meant* to add us to his will, but he put it off. For too long, as it turned out."

"I'd be angry in your place."

Jane's brother shrugged. "Canna be changed. We're not bad off really. We've enough to pay for my training and a place to live."

One more example of the ridiculous nature of marriage. By all natural rights, Cameron should have been his father's heir, yet the lack of a thirty-minute church ceremony prevented it. How odd that humans had created these rules, so detached from the reality of life.

They arrived to find Jane already sitting in the landau. She still wouldn't meet his eyes, choosing instead to stare determinedly at the empty space in front of her. The clouds were thickening, their perfect day threatening rain.

She remained silent as Percy and Cameron wrestled the top up. At least the passengers would stay out of the rain. The driver's box, Percy noted dryly, had no such protection. He stashed his guitar and the picnic basket on the floorboards, untethered the horses, then climbed up, prepared to see just how fast the hired outfit could go.

By the time they passed the nursery, the day had turned downright depressing, a steady mist thickening into drizzle. Had the weather been clear, there would have been plenty of light at this hour, but the increasing gloom banished the very notion of brightness. Percy's thoughts wandered about in a melancholy minor key, grey as the weather. *Jane.*

The oppression of the factories . . . It was all rather hopeless, but as was often the case with bleak thoughts, allowing his mind to make music of them gave him a certain sense of peace.

The carriage rumbled over a bridge that spanned a canal, and something on the bank, near the towpath, caught his eye. A figure. *A man?*

It was impossible to see anything clearly in the fog, but if it was a man, he appeared to be laid out, asleep in the grass.

This was no weather for a nap by the canal . . . Percy felt a sudden chill, but there was no reason to stop. It was probably only a log, or a large rock.

No. It didn't look like a log, or a rock. It looked like a man, and he couldn't in good conscience drive on without at least checking to be sure all was well.

He brought the horses to a quick stop. Cameron poked his head out as Percy climbed down. He motioned for Jane's brother to follow, and together they descended the bank toward the prone figure, grasping at the rough stones of the bridge to balance themselves on the steep decline.

It was, indeed, a man. He lay in the long grass on the canal side of the towpath. He was older than Percy—*thirty, maybe?*—dressed in a worn greatcoat and breeches, boots scuffed and dirty. A battered hat lay nearby. The man's eyes were closed. The shadow of a beard darkened his face, and his cropped brown hair, wet from the rain, stuck out at wild angles.

"He's bleeding . . ." Cameron was to him first. "Sir, *can you hear me*?"

Percy could see the blood now, a large stain of red brown on the man's coat. Cameron gently touched his neck, feeling for a pulse, and Percy heaved a sigh of relief to hear the man's pained groan. At least they hadn't stumbled upon a dead body, though a mortally wounded man wasn't much better.

Cameron was focused completely on the patient, giving orders without even looking to be sure Percy was there to follow them. "Fetch the blanket. And the brandy." Gone was the half drunk, jovial young man he'd picnicked with. In his place, a terse physician expecting to be obeyed.

Happy to follow orders, Percy climbed back up to the road, meeting Jane as she disembarked from the coach, looking alarmed.

"What's happening?" she demanded. "Where's Cameron?"

"There's a man. Wounded." He indicated the direction. "Your brother's with him— He needs the blanket. And a bottle of spirits."

Wordlessly, Jane disappeared into the carriage, then re-emerged with the needed items.

"Your brother has it well in hand. There's no need for you to—" He attempted to take the blanket and the bottle from her hands, but she brushed past him.

"He may need my help," she called over her shoulder. "And yours. Come."

Apparently, neither of the Stuart siblings hesitated to take charge in a crisis. Percy's stomach was roiling, his pulse pounding. He had significant doubts about his own capabilities, but he would do his best to follow their lead.

They arrived by the canal to find that Cameron had removed the man's coat and torn open his shirt, exposing an ugly wound on his shoulder. The shirt was soaked with blood. The man's eyes were open, and he was staring at Jane's brother, mouthing words so faint that Percy doubted even Cameron could make out what they were.

Small black dots invaded the periphery of Percy's vision. He blinked hard, willing them away.

Cameron seemed to sense his sister approaching. "Bullet wound. Says his name's Will. Brandy."

Jane handed him the bottle.

"Sommerbell." Cameron motioned for Percy to come closer. "Hold him. Here." He showed him where to grip the man on his opposite shoulder. It was a relief to crouch down, closer to the ground. The black dots faded. "Stand clear, Janie. Tear this for a bandage." He ripped off a wide swath of the man's shirt, handing it to his sister. Without hesitation, Jane accepted the bloodstained linen and began tearing it into strips.

Cameron bent down and spoke in a slow, clear voice. "Will, brace yourself. This is necessary, but it will hurt." The man grimaced in acknowledgement. Cameron looked to Percy. "Ready?" Percy nodded, not at all sure he was, in fact, ready. He gripped Will's shoulder with all his strength, glad that at least on this side of the man's body, there was no blood.

Then Cameron poured half the bottle of spirits directly onto the wound. Every muscle in Will's body jerked. His face contorted in pain, but he stayed in one place. "That's enough for now." Cameron spoke softly, with just a hint of his charismatic smile.

Percy exhaled. At least he'd been able to perform this simple task adequately.

"You're going to be all right, Will. Rest now. We'll get you into the carriage and to the hospital."

At the word *hospital,* Will's eyes widened. He vigorously shook his head, mouthing the word "*No*" with more desperation than Percy would have thought possible in his condition. Cameron stared down at him for a long moment, weighing the options.

"The bullet must come out. I could bring you to my house, but I'm only a student. Something could go wrong." Will had apparently accepted Cameron as his savior. He nodded once then closed his eyes.

What if this man was a hardened criminal, shot in a robbery attempt? Surely, the thought had occurred to Cameron, but still, he acted on an impulse to help. Percy would not argue.

Fortunately, Will was not a large man. Cameron bandaged the wound, and they managed to lift the man onto the blanket, so recently used for their picnic, and carry him up the embankment. The cheerful color of the carriage jarred with the reality of the situation. As they laid him on the bench inside the *landaulette*, it dawned on Percy that the blasted thing only had seats enough for two passengers—or one prostrate one—and the driver's box was only big enough for one man. There was no way they'd all fit for the journey home.

If the Stuart siblings could act courageously in an emergency, so could Percy Sommerbell. "You drive home and attend to Will," he said to Cameron. "We'll walk." He nodded to Jane. "We'll get a hack once we're in the city and meet at your house."

Cameron scrutinized his sister, silently asking her thoughts on the proposed course. She met his eyes and nodded. "He's right. Get him home. We'll follow." Her dress was smeared with blood. Her hair had come loose and damp locks, curled by the moisture, framed her face. She must be exhausted, yet her blue eyes held a determination that was tremendously beautiful. There was a song there . . .

"Are you sure?" Cameron's voice interrupted Percy's reverie. "I could come with you, and Sommerbell could drive him. I'm sure we'd—"

"He needs you," Jane cut him off. "We'll be fine." She darted into the carriage then returned, holding her cloak. Clever girl. She'd come prepared for this weather, even though the day was fine when they'd set out.

Cameron leapt up to the driver's box, taking the reins. He turned toward Percy, his eyes bearing down on him. "Keep to the main roads, and get her in a hack as soon as you can."

Percy nodded, hoping he looked much more sure of himself than he felt.

Without another word, Cameron urged the horses forward. Jane and Percy watched as the bright yellow carriage slowly faded into the mist.

TEN

"WE NEEDN'T TALK IF you don't want to." Mr. Sommerbell offered his arm and a tired smile. A *real* smile. Perhaps the first he'd ever given her.

Their quick lesson in mortality had changed everything. For once, she sensed no ulterior motive, just simple, easily decipherable emotions that mimicked her own—determination tempered with profound shock and fear. Jane hesitated for a moment, then gave in to what her body clearly wanted. The solid, reassuring warmth of another human being. She took his arm, and together they set a brisk pace toward town.

She had no desire to relive the horrific scene by the canal bank. Even now, her limbs were shaky and her breath came in shallow bursts. Apprehension and dread churned in the pit of her stomach. She hated the fact that Cameron was on his own. That man could die at any moment between here and home . . . But even still, something about confronting the life-or-death situation had restored her equilibrium. She was equal to the task in front of her because she *had* to be. Cameron would make it home. She would endure this walk with Mr. Sommerbell. Then she would assist her brother however she could, and life would continue as it had been.

Yes, she was equal to it . . . as long as they could avoid the subject of Mr. Sommerbell's proposition. She would just have to do her best to steer the conversation away from that topic and hope he understood her unspoken request for a truce.

"Do you think that man, Will, is a criminal?" she asked.

"It crossed my mind. But your brother was determined. Didn't seem right to question him."

"That's Cameron. It bothers me, though, that he didn't want to be taken to the hospital."

"Bothers me too."

A silence fell between them, fearful and unsettled, but not uncomfortable. For once, they'd agreed on something. That man *had* been vehemently against the idea of going to the hospital, but why? Perhaps he couldn't pay? That didn't make sense. The Royal Infirmary accepted charity cases. Maybe he was a radical, wounded in some sort of skirmish with the authorities. No. Though many in the city feared violence, as of yet, the strike was just words on paper. The most obvious answer was that Will was a criminal, a highwayman, shot in an attempted robbery. She shuddered. Whatever the explanation, she prayed her brother would be safe.

"Your brother isn't in any danger, you know." It was as if Mr. Sommerbell had read her thoughts. "That man's in no condition to hurt anyone."

"I know." But other things could go wrong . . . He *could* die in the carriage. Or one of his fellow highwaymen could have seen Cameron take him and followed? Jane took a steadying breath. There was nothing for it now but to get home as quickly as possible. She hastened her steps, tugging Mr. Sommerbell along with her.

"Cameron would bring home wounded animals, when he was a boy," she recounted, attempting to divert her mind from the dangers of the present. "A crow with a broken wing. A baby squirrel who'd fallen from its nest. That sort of thing."

"A stranger with a bullet in his shoulder is a far cry from a crow with a broken wing."

"Yes." Jane bit back her annoyance. Why couldn't he just agree with her? "But he cares for things. Maybe too much. It's his nature."

"He's got a knack for it," Mr. Sommerbell agreed. "*I'm* just pleased I didn't faint at the sight of all that blood." He wasn't exaggerating. She'd seen how white he'd gone just before Cam disinfected the man's wound.

"He's had practice. After he outgrew the curing of woodland animals, he'd often go with the doctor in Darnalay, to assist."

"And you? You seemed practiced as well."

"You may have noticed, Mr. Sommerbell, that my brother has a knack for knowing just what to do, and say. I do *not* share that talent, so I suppose I've become good at following his lead."

"I *had* noticed. It must be a trying quality at times, in a sibling?"

"It's infuriating. I assure you, though, he's *far* from perfect."

Mr. Sommerbell arched a brow. "In which areas is he less than perfect?"

She ticked the answers off on her fingers. "His bedchamber is a mess. The rest of the house would be, too, if Cori and I weren't there to pick up after him. He thinks he knows everything, which I assure you he does *not*. He tires himself out with too much working and studying. He's charming, but . . . he's *too* charming. He's never had to learn to fight, or stand up for himself."

She imagined her brother, in so many ways still just a vulnerable little boy, driving by himself through the rain. The man, bleeding in the back of the carriage. Would Cori be able to help get Will into the house? What if a neighbor saw and reported it to the Glasgow police?

"He's lucky to have you." Mr. Sommerbell's voice cut through her thoughts. "I'd wager following orders is not your forte behind closed doors. You keep him in check."

She took another breath, willing the frightening images from her mind.

"I try. He may be younger than me, but he's a *man,* Mr. Sommerbell, and I'm nothing but his spinster sister. I'm afraid my power over anything in this life is quite limited." *What if Will was a radical? Would the police think Cameron was his accomplice?*

Her nerves couldn't handle any more what-ifs. She would change the subject.

"Tell me about Italy."

"Italy." Mr. Sommerbell was obviously surprised by the question. "What would you like to know?"

"Something pleasant. How it's different from Scotland. What kinds of people you met. Foods you ate. Anything to distract us from *this.*" She gestured at the world at large. Cold. Wet. Terrifying.

He thought for a few moments.

"It was as different from *this,* as you can imagine. Venice was enchanting, with the canals and the lagoon . . . ancient stone. Twisting pathways that open onto lovely squares with fountains. Cats lurking in shadows. I used to enjoy wandering until I was completely lost. It was . . ." He searched for the right word. "*Otherworldly.* Excellent coffee. I met Byron, and others escaped from England. Artists, poets, musicians mostly, and their women. A rowdy lot, but entertaining in their way. We rented rooms over a coffee shop and we'd sit for hours at night drinking coffee and grappa, playing guitar. I can still smell the place ..." He closed his eyes and inhaled, transporting himself out of the Scottish rain.

"But you left Venice?" Images of Cameron bending over the injured man still flooded Jane's mind.

"It grew tiresome, once the novelty wore off. Too many wild parties. Contrived drama. We leased a villa on the Adriatic for the summer. Nothing very special, a run-down house about a half mile from the sea. Leaky roof, chipped tiles, crooked shutters. The floors creaked and the gardens were only weeds." He paused. "But it was *quiet*. Beau set up a studio and did some excellent work. I played guitar, swam in the sea, drank too much wine ... 'twas heaven.'"

His ability to escape the here and now in such obviously pleasant memories sent a wave of envy through her. She wished she could be like him. Forget the present and transport herself to a magical place and time. But it was *his* memory, not hers. *Her* pleasant memories all ended in death, anger and guilt. She dared not lose herself in them. Suddenly, she felt desperately alone, as if she were walking down this cold road entirely by herself.

He was still talking. "It was warm there, of course. 'Twould be hot if it wasn't for the sea breeze. The views were incomparable. But it was more than that. Something about it ... as if one were living in a dream, but also wide awake. I've wondered if it was the way the light falls at Southern latitudes ... or it may simply have been the distance from the familiar, I don't know."

"The air is pure and elastic..." She quoted the book Cynthia had been reading the day she'd met him. He looked at her sharply and opened his mouth to respond, but she cut him off. "What about the fruit trees?"

He chuckled. "I wish I'd met you before I went. I'd have paid better attention." He paused, thinking. "There were olive groves everywhere. But those aren't fruits, are they?"

"Well . . . yes. Olives are drupes, like cherries, or apricots."

"But that's not what you meant. There were vineyards, of course, but mostly for wine. I remember seeing fruit for sale in the market. Grapes, pomegranates, pears, oranges. Figs. I imagine they were grown nearby, but I really have no idea—" He broke off excitedly. "Now that I think of it, there *was* an old apple tree right behind the villa. It ripened just before we left at the end of the summer, and we ate some off the tree. Like children. They were huge, golden brown . . . not terribly attractive. Thick skin, but sweet and crisp. Very juicy, I think."

Finally, his words began to spirit her away from the wet gloomy present.

"I've only tasted dried figs. What are they like when they're fresh?"

He sighed. Clearly, he rated this memory in the same category as the coffee shop in Venice—able to be summoned with a breath. "I'm not sure what to compare them to. I've had figs grown in England, but they aren't ever very good. These were different. Better. There were several kinds, but the best ones were small. As big as a . . . a large strawberry. Green skin. The most surprising dark pink inside, almost the color of beetroot. They were soft, and had a thick, sweet syrup, like honey, but tangier. There was something decadent about them . . . sensual . . . like eating . . ." He paused, looking at her sideways, dark eyebrows raised evocatively. "I'm not sure, Miss Stuart, that you want to know what they remind me of exactly. Suffice it to say, eating a perfectly ripe fig is a pleasure of the senses."

Pleasure of the senses. The phrase echoed in her mind. She wasn't entirely sure what he was suggesting, yet suddenly all of her focus was drawn to four points of a rather lopsided rectangle—one where her hand lightly touched his arm, two more where each of her nipples brushed the inside of her chemise, and the fourth at the apex of her thighs.

His eyes remained fixed on her, blazing heat like two hot coals in the mist.

Certainly, she'd succeeded in taking her mind off of the dangers of the here and now, but this would not do either. It was once again time to change the subject

She opened her mouth and allowed a torrent of words to tumble out. "I'd imagine Cameron's home by now, and we're almost back to the city. There's no need for you to accompany me all the way. I can get my own hack, and you can go directly to your hotel. I'm sure you're tired after our . . . ordeal."

He said nothing for a long moment, just looked intently down the road that would lead them into the city. Then he unleashed a torrent all his own. "Your brother would kill me if I left you alone in the city tonight. I'll need to pick up the carriage to return in the morning any-how." He drew in a breath. "*Say you'll come with me. I'll take you to Italy. Or Greece. Or Spain . . . America, if you want. We'll sample the most exotic fruits. Or we can stay in England. I'll find a cottage that has everything you want, and I'll come to you, but only to be with you, nothing more . . . I just, I can't go back without you. Please. Say yes.*" The desperation, the vulnerability of his words made it clear. The sleek wildcat was gone. He faced her now as only a man, pleading for what he was sure he needed.

Her stomach twisted. Didn't he know they had an unspoken agree-ment not to bring up his blasted proposition? And to do it in such a way, with raw, exposed honesty that drew her in and pulled at her sympathy

. . . No, of course he didn't know. He'd made no such agreement. She'd been a fool to let down her guard, that was all.

"I told you I'm not—" And then they rounded a bend and all thoughts of figs and propositions and agreements vanished from their minds.

Less than a furlong in front of them, just visible by the flicker of torchlight, was a wall of men with guns. They all wore military issue red coats, but beyond that, their costumes were diverse. Some had trousers of black, white, or grey. Some wore kilts. A few wore the decorated hats of full military uniform, others top hats of various designs. One was bareheaded.

This must have been a hastily-formed militia, given red coats as a symbol of authority but left to their own devices for the rest.

Two men had disembarked from a waylaid coach that had been traveling out of the city. They were being questioned by one soldier as another climbed up into the carriage. Thankfully, none of them seemed to notice the two sodden figures walking toward them from the opposite direction. Jane steered Mr. Sommerbell off the road and behind some trees. There was no real danger for them in this blockade. They'd done nothing wrong. But even still, a pang of anxiety registered in her chest.

"They're searching carriages coming in and out of the city." They were too far distant to be overheard, but she lowered her voice nonetheless. "Is it to do with the strike?"

Mr. Sommerbell shrugged. He seemed unconcerned. "We've nothing to hide."

"No. But we need to agree on what we'll tell them. I don't think we should mention the injured man."

"Right." He thought for a moment. "We'll tell them we went for a drive in my gig when the weather was fine, and then our horse went lame, so we're walking into town for help. That's *almost* the truth."

"They'll think I'm your mistress. Or worse." Jane couldn't help voicing the fear, even though it hardly mattered.

"No. They won't. What they think doesn't matter anyhow. As long as we're not radicals or threatening to strike, it's no business of theirs who we are or what we're doing."

She sighed. He was right, of course.

They were both thoroughly soaked by now, and without the warming exercise of walking, she'd started shivering. "I would embrace you, just for the warmth, but I know better." He smiled, his real smile again. She liked that smile. It made her feel just a bit warmer. "It'll be fine, I promise. I'll do all the talking. Trust me?"

He winged his arm, and she took it. What choice did she have?

Eleven

PERCY HAD NEVER PUT much stock in traditional masculinity—guns, dogs, duels, things like that—but for the first time in his life, he understood the primal male urge to protect one's own.

It was true, what he'd said. The line of mismatched soldiers before them posed no real danger. They had nothing—well, *almost* nothing—to hide, and he *was* his father's son. Even so, there was something about approaching a heavily armed guard that put one on edge.

He willed his nervousness away. He must be steady for her.

Torches lit up the scene in front of them, a few affixed to long posts driven into the ground, some held by the soldiers themselves. The heavy mist caught the firelight, confining it into ghostly orbs that hovered around the torch heads. No light reflected. No shadows fell. A chill ran down Percy's spine, and he had the sudden urge to flee, to find another way into the city. But he had promised his protection. Gained her trust. He must see this through.

He could now see more detail of the carriage that was being searched. Two men, smartly dressed, were being questioned by a soldier outfitted in the full uniform of the British Army—red coat with long tails, an epaulette on one shoulder, tall boots and an ornate bicorne hat. This must be the man in charge. Another militiaman emerged from the coach, empty-handed. The two soldiers conversed for a moment, then the men were waved back into their transport and on their way.

Jane dragged him into the shadows on the side of the road as the carriage rattled past. She said nothing, just looked at him, eyes wide. Then they climbed back onto the road and resumed their march toward the barricade.

When they finally stepped into the glow of the torchlight, the commanding officer stalked toward them, trailed by a subordinate bearing a torch. He was heavily built, with a paunch and a face dominated by a coarse bristly mustache and narrowed, piercing eyes. There was something predatory about him, like a badger exiting its den, excited to become acquainted with its next prey.

"What have we here?" The man's words were clipped, yet slow. He was toying with them. "'Tis hardly weather for a walk, sir, 'specially with a *lady* on your arm."

It was at that moment that Percy finally understood what Jane had realized quite some time earlier. She was drenched, wrapped in a coarse woolen cloak. Her head was bare under her hood, and the moisture had caused her hair to break free of her chignon and form wild, wispy curls. Clearly, she was no upper-class lady. In comparison, though wet, Percy's coat was obviously expensive. His damp hair was covered with a fine beaver hat. His boots gleamed in the torchlight. Their difference in class and their lack of a chaperone made it clear. They were not siblings, nor spouses, nor betrothed. Indeed, to this man, the only plausible explanation for the pair in front of him was that Percy was a well-off man, and Jane his strumpet.

Hell and the Devil.

He squeezed her arm, hoping his touch would reassure her.

"Good evening." He used what he hoped was his most authoritative tone as he detailed the story they'd agreed to. Their horse had gone lame. They'd left his gig down the road. They were walking into town for help.

The man's face spread into a lewd grin, which he shot conspiratorially at Percy. "Out for a frolic, were you?" He thought for a moment, then nodded in Jane's direction. "Why dinna I take her off your hands?" His beady eyes turned hungrily to Jane. "I'll make it worth your while, lassie. I'll be done here in a wink, then just a quick romp and you'll be on your way."

Nervousness turned to white hot anger. Percy wanted, *needed*, to hurt someone, specifically the man standing in front of him, pointing that detestable, lecherous grin in Jane's direction. The rifle the man held, the line of armed men in his command, were of no consequence. He'd knock his teeth out, then kick him, hard, and repeatedly, in the bollocks— But as suddenly as it had arrived, the impulse to violence was stilled by the anchor of Jane's iron grip on his arm. Instead of striking the man, he drew in a breath, channeling all the fury into his voice and the intensity of his glare.

"How. *Dare.* You. Sir. This lady is my *betrothed.*"

The man blanched. *Satisfying, that.* But Percy was far from finished. "Do you know who I am?" The soldier just looked at him. "*Answer* me!" Percy barked.

"N-no, sir. I-I'm sorry, sir, I—"

"I'm Mr. Percival Sommerbell, owner of the Fulton Company mills, among other things. This lady, as I have mentioned, is my fiancé, Miss Stuart."

"P-pleased to make your acquaintance, Mr. Sommerb—"

"There is no *pleasure* in this acquaintance."

The man just stared at him. Dumbstruck.

"I do not think, *Sir*, that you have been assigned this post with orders to harass innocent citizens." Percy raised an eyebrow and paused, a long pause, just to watch the man squirm. "I'm quite sure your commanding officer will be interested to learn of our experience this evening."

Percy barely recognized his own voice. Who *was* this terse, commanding man? Surely, it wasn't Percy Sommerbell, guitar playing rogue and self-declared libertine? Whoever it was, the words had their intended result. The soldier stepped back as if he'd just had a shovelful of hot coals thrust in his face.

"I-I'm sure there'll be no need to bring him into this, sir. No harm done, eh?" He nodded in Jane's direction, not taking his eyes off Percy. "Please to be on your way . . . or, I can send one of my men down the road to pick up your gig." He was bowing now, or more accurately, nervously bobbing his upper torso up and down.

"That will not be necessary. Good evening." Percy made to walk by the man, then turned, as if remembering something.

"Your name, sir?" he asked. "I wouldn't want to sully some *other* man's name."

The soldier hesitated. He looked to the man holding the torch, as if for help, but the soldier just stared back at him. Finally, reluctantly, he spoke his name, "Devon Turner. Lieutenant Devon Turner."

Percy nodded, then they walked through the barricade, arm-in-arm, heads held high, eyes trained straight ahead, ignoring the curious stares of the militiamen. Jane's grip on his arm was so tight he was certain he'd find bruises in the morning.

They continued on in the same manner, well after they'd left the light of the torches behind. The rain had lessened, but it was cold and so dark now that they could see nothing beyond the road under their feet. They were in a world of their own, entirely adrift, yet together.

Finally, she spoke. He was glad—he'd been searching in vain for the right words. "You told him we were betrothed, yet you don't believe in marriage." Her voice was breathy, soft. It held a sense of wonder.

He managed a low chuckle. "The irony's not lost on me. I'd have hit him if you hadn't been on my arm . . . Jane, once again, I'm an ass. I should have listened to y—"

"Thank you." Her words were a soft caress. Without warning, she released his arm. He was caught off balance, reeling at the sudden loss of her.

She was angry. He must have misinterpreted her tone—

But then her gloved hand grasped at his, tentative at first, then warm and sure. She said nothing. He said nothing. They walked the rest of the way into the city, wrapped in darkness, fingers entwined, warmth and understanding flowing between them.

———— ◆◇◆ ————

It was half ten by the time they finally hurried through the threshold of the house on Balmanno Street. Every muscle in Jane's body yearned for rest, yet the emotional exhaustion was undeniably greater than the physical. She could scarcely remember the beginning of this day. The nursery, the kingcups, the slowworm seemed but a dream of someone else's past.

Cam met them at the door. Safe, but even more disheveled than when they'd seen him last. His waistcoat was gone, his sleeves rolled up to his elbows. Blood spattered his shirt. Intense weariness lined his face, mixed with obvious relief at seeing his sister home safely. He'd been stopped at the barricade, he confirmed, and had manufactured a story about an accident at a quarry where the injured man worked, stressing the emergency and the need to get him to the infirmary, quickly. Of course that did nothing to explain who *he* was, or his luxurious, bright yellow mode of transport, but this was Cameron, so of course he'd been believed and allowed through. Cam would be able to talk a hungry wolf out of attacking a calf.

When he asked if they'd gotten through the barricade unharmed, they simply nodded in assent. There was no reason to burden him with the details.

Cam reported that he'd given Will a wee bit of laudanum, and the man was now sleeping soundly. Cori had helped bring him in and attended to him while Cam successfully removed the bullet and bandaged the wound. He'd sent the maid to bed and gotten the man's address.

"He's a Chisholm, Janie." Cameron shot her a meaningful look. "William Chisholm."

"*Chisholm?*" She stared back at her brother, unbelievingly.

"Aye."

"What does that mean?" Mr. Sommerbell asked, clearly confused.

"'Tis a clan, in Invernesshire," Jane murmured. In her great-grandfather's time, Clan Chisholm had been one of the most powerful in all the Highlands. In recent years, they were better known as the victims of a brutal factor who'd resorted to incredible cruelty as he ran them off their land.

"Ah." Mr. Sommerbell nodded as if he understood, though of course he didn't. "If it's safe to move him, I'll take him home on my way back to the hotel," he offered.

"Aye. 'Tis a good idea to move him before daybreak," Cameron answered. "Less chance of being seen." He paused. Hesitating. "He's lucky.

The bullet wasna deep. If he takes care of it, it'll heal without trouble. He said he has a daughter at home who can look after him—" He broke off, running his hand through his tawny hair.

Something was wrong.

"Cam. What is it?" Jane asked.

"I asked how it happened." Cameron bit his lip nervously. "The wound, I mean. At first, he didna want to say, but I pressed him . . . He finally told me. Made me swear I wouldna tell a soul other than the two of you. I dinna know why he trusts us . . . I wouldna if I were in his place . . . 'cause we saved him, I suppose."

Her well-spoken brother was rambling. Her sense of foreboding increased. "Cameron. You're frightening me. *What has he done?*"

Her brother let out a long exhale. "He was part of a group that was planning to blow up the bridge with black powder. Block the canal. That's why he was there."

She was confused, and so, obviously, was Mr. Sommerbell. "Block the canal? Why?"

"In support of the strike. Coal for the factories comes by canal boat. Block the canal, the factories shut down."

Jane drew in a sharp breath. Mr. Sommerbell's eyes widened.

"Will and another man were surveying the bridge," Cameron continued, "making plans, when they were fired on. He doesna know by who. Police, militia, or someone in their employ most likely."

"And the other man?" Mr. Sommerbell asked.

Cameron shrugged. "He ran. That's the last Will saw of him."

Cameron was still biting his lip, eying them nervously. There was more.

"What else?" She reached out and touched Cameron's arm. She hadn't seen her brother this upset since the day they left Darnalay.

Cameron shrugged her off and sank into a chair, leaning forward with his elbows on his knees, hands cradling his chin. When he spoke, his voice was dull and emotionless. She knew that tone. He was warding off tears. "I asked him *why*, why violence. He's got two children at home. His wife died a year ago. Without her income, he couldn't make enough to feed his bairns, so they had to go to work with him in the mills."

Mr. Sommerbell shifted in his seat, his expression tightening.

Her brother continued, his voice wavering. "His daughter lost three fingers. She's only *seven*. She canna work now, but his son does, and wakes up at night gasping for breath."

"That's awful." Jane breathed. "But Cameron, if he's a radical, we need to get him out of—"

"He's angry, an' rightfully so." Cameron's head whipped up. He met her eyes. "They dinna have enough to buy bread, Janie. Barely enough to keep a roof over their heads . . . and Sommerbell—" Her brother directed his words toward Mr. Sommerbell, but did not meet his eye. "The factory where they work. Where his wee lass had her accident. It's a Fulton Company Mill. One of yours."

For a long moment, Mr. Sommerbell sat motionless, staring into space. Finally, his eyes focused. He looked at Cameron.

"Did you tell him who I am?"

"No."

"Thank you. For telling me." Mr. Sommerbell looked away again, lost in thought. Jane felt an urge to go to him, to hold his hand as she had on the walk. To soothe the pain. But with her brother near, she dared not show such affection. She would have to offer comfort through other, more domestic means.

"We need to warm up. I'll make tea and fetch some biscuits. Cameron, Mr. Sommerbell is soaked through. Take him upstairs and give him some dry clothes. We'll have tea in the sitting room while we wait for Mr. Chisholm to wake."

She quickly changed into dry clothes and heated water for tea. When she entered the sitting room, Cameron was bent over the grate, building a fire. Mr. Sommerbell was sitting in an armchair, a half-empty glass of whisky in his hand. He looked lost, and dreadfully weary. After the day they'd had, how could he not be? His hair was tousled, curling slightly from the moisture. His stocking feet were just visible in Cameron's brown wool pantaloons. They were too long, and his borrowed coat too big, but he was still overwhelmingly handsome. There was something about his vulnerability that tugged at her, and once again, she felt the urge to go to him.

They drank their tea and their whisky in near silence, too tired and overwhelmed by the day's events to attempt conversation. After a while, Cameron left to check on the patient. Jane hesitated a moment, but the impulse was too strong. She could never love this man, but that didn't mean she couldn't offer him the human comfort he so desperately needed.

She steeled her courage and rose to stand behind him, softly placing her hands on his shoulders and massaging, ever so gently. She'd sometimes done this for Father, after he'd been out all day visiting tenants, or when he arrived home after a long journey. He'd said she was skilled at it. Mr. Sommerbell snuck a glance at the door to ensure Cameron wasn't about to return, then leaned into her touch. She deepened the pressure, kneading the muscles underneath his coat. He closed his eyes, and . . .

This was nothing like massaging Father.

His cravat was loosely tied, and her hands easily slipped underneath it, touching his bare skin, working their way up his neck, smoothing away the tension. He let out a long breath, of contentment, she thought, or perhaps encouragement. Her hands took on a life of their own, and she watched as they moved back over his coat to the front of his shoulders, then slid around him, until finally her fingers met and clasped, enclosing him in her embrace.

His hands came up to hers, drawing her nearer to him, offering her comfort and warmth just as she offered it to him. She rested her chin on his head.

"Jane." His voice was soft but filled with an anguish that tore at her. "I . . . I don't know what to do. I never asked for this."

"I know." There was nothing she could say that would take away the pain, so instead she allowed her head to dip down and her lips to brush the side of his neck, just below his ear. It was the lightest of kisses—so light she almost wasn't sure she touched him at all. She must have, though, because she registered the smooth warmth of his skin against her mouth.

He sighed and tightened his embrace. She breathed him in, and for that moment, this was all there was, all that mattered.

She heard her brother's footfalls on the stairs and quickly jerked away.

"Mr. Chisholm's waking. Between you and I, Sommerbell, we should be able to move him safely."

Jane darted into the carriage to retrieve her bonnet, then watched as the two men helped the injured Mr. Chisholm into the coach. With a last word of warning to be careful—Mr. Chisholm's house was in Calton, where street gangs roamed at night—Cam nodded farewell and Jane did the same, unable to meet Mr. Sommerbell's gaze, afraid of what she might find there.

It was long past midnight. She was well and truly exhausted. Too tired to think, or even to *feel* . . . but there was one last thing she had to do. Along with her bonnet, she'd retrieved a small, crushed and very wilted

bouquet of kingcups from the landau. She opened the largest book she
owned, a botanical text she'd taken from the library in Darnalay, put the
blossoms inside, then very carefully, and very firmly, closed the book.
Finally, she fell into bed and slept. Thankfully, she did not dream.

TWELVE

A HALF HOUR LATER, Percy reined the horses to a stop in front of a dilapidated brick building that matched the address Cameron had given him. The rain had stopped long ago, but a thick mist still hung in the air. They'd left the carriage top up to obscure the injured passenger. It had, of course, also hidden Percy's view of the man, and he'd found himself unable to push away his fears of what might be happening inside the landau.

Was Chisholm bleeding again? If so, how would Percy explain bloodied seat cushions when it came time to return the carriage in the morning? Cameron had seemed confident the man was past the worst danger, at least for now, but what if he was wrong? What if Chisholm had expired during the trip through town? What the devil would Percy do then?

This part of the city had become somewhat familiar—he'd passed through it on each of his factory inspections—but he'd never been here at night. The larger streets were still bustling with activity. He passed what must be a brothel, still lit up and inviting customers, and a few pubs with rollicking crowds of men outside, drunk as dogs. Then he turned onto a smaller street and the noise fell away. Another turn took him onto a street so narrow it could hardly be classified as such. The coach wheels barely fit between the dirty gutters, and several times Percy had to duck to avoid being swept off his perch by the laundry lines strung between the buildings.

Now, without the noise of the horses' hooves on the cobblestones and the rumbling of the wheels, all was eerily quiet. The weathered brick buildings loomed on either side, making him feel closed in, trapped. The only light came from the two lanterns secured to the carriage, and he found himself looking around warily, half expecting the flickering shadows and fog to come to life.

Pushing away his unease, he descended from his seat, unhooked one of the lanterns, then opened the door to the carriage. He breathed a silent sigh of relief to see Chisholm's open eyes reflected in the light.

"Is this it?" Percy opened the door as wide as he could to allow the man a view of the building.

Chisholm nodded, shifting in his seat and wincing in pain. "You'll have to go in. Find Rose and Nat— Nathan. They'll get help." He took a labored breath. "Second floor. Fourth door on the left."

Percy gave the man a swift nod, then closed the door to the carriage and tied the horses to the rickety iron railing that bordered the steps leading into the building. He took one more look around, praying no footpads were lurking—Chisholm would be an easy target with no one to guard him—then, holding the lantern in front of him, he ventured up the battered stone steps and pulled open the cracked wooden door.

It was a good thing he had the lantern, for inside was as black as the backs of Percy's eyelids. The air was dank and stale. The scent of mold, dirt, and human filth flooded his nostrils. Every muscle in his body wanted to turn tail and run. To Italy. To Jane. To anywhere else than here.

Hell and the devil. He closed his eyes, taking a breath and willing himself to proceed. Then he opened them again and took a few shuffling steps forward. A staircase came into view, dim in the lantern light.

Second Floor. Fourth door on the left.

The stairs creaked as he ascended, and the smells increased. Finally, he reached a landing, and a door. He opened it and walked into a passageway, then past three doors till he was standing before the fourth door on the left. A dim light emanated from the crack underneath.

He knocked, and immediately heard a scurrying sound on the other side. Whispered voices. The door opened a crack, and a boy's pale face came into view.

"Are you Nathan?" Percy held the lamp up so the boy could see him.

The boy didn't answer, just looked at him with narrowed eyes.

"I'm Percy," he tried for a mixture of reassurance and authority. "A friend. I've brought your father home."

The boy's eyes widened. "Where's he?" He peered past Percy, looking for his father.

"On the street. He's been—he's injured. I need someone to help me get him up the stairs. He said there's a neighbor you might ask."

The boy opened the door further, and a girl—she must be Rose—came into view. She was standing close beside her brother. Neither of the children were in nightclothes, and Percy guessed they hadn't slept at all. He could just make out the shabby room behind them—a table with a single candle burning, three chairs, three pallets laid against a wall.

Rose's eyes darted to Percy warily. "What's happened? Who's this?"

"He's come with Da," her brother answered. "He's hurt, on the street." Nat's guardedness was quickly turning to authority.

"Hurt?" Fear washed over the little girl's face.

"He'll be fine," Percy assured her. "He's been seen by a doctor. He just needs some help to get up the stairs is all. Come see him if you wish."

The girl brushed past him and was at the end of the corridor before Percy even turned around.

"I'll wake Mr. Bara," Nat called after her. "Wait with him."

By the time Percy got back to the carriage, Rose was nestled close to her father on the fine leather seat. Her arms were looped around his neck.

Percy climbed up and took the seat across. That's when he first noticed the horrible empty space between Rose's thumb and pinkie finger. He quickly averted his eyes, unable to look, or even *think* of what it meant.

"I'll be fine, lassie." Chisholm was consoling her, patting her blonde head with his good arm. "I just need a little rest is all."

"I'll take care of you," she declared, with more certainty than should have been possible for a seven-year-old.

Chisholm's eyes moved from his daughter to Percy. "Thank you."

Percy found he couldn't meet the man's gaze. "There's no need," was all he could manage. His father's factory had taken three of little Rose's fingers. That was a debt Percy couldn't fathom how to repay. "You're from the Highlands," he said, in an effort to change the subject.

"How'd you know?" Chisholm asked suspiciously.

"Cameron," Percy replied. "He recognized your name. It's . . . a clan name?"

"Aye." Chisholm nodded. "Clan Chisholm . . ." His eyes wandered to his daughter as he continued to stroke her hair. "We're from Strathfarrer. Prettiest glen in all of Scotland."

"Da was a farmer," Rose supplied. "But a bad man made us leave when Nat was just a wee thing and I was in Mam's belly." She leaned forward, eyes wide. "*He burned down our house.* And our neighbor's too, *with her in it.* She was an old lady, and Da had to go in and save her."

"That's enough now, Rosie," Chisholm murmured. He was sitting back against the seat, his face lost to the shadows.

Percy gazed back at the little girl, unable to fathom what to say next. There were too many bad men in this world—men intent only on making as much money as possible. Percy and his father were two of them. "Your Da is a brave man," he finally stammered.

"Aye." Rose lifted her chin and sat back against her father's chest. Chisholm winced as she brushed against his wounded shoulder, then wrapped his good arm protectively around her.

"Do you know of the Banton estate? In the Highlands?" Percy directed the question to Chisholm.

"Mhm." The man nodded in assent. "I've family who live on Banton land."

"What do you know of the new Lord Banton? I've . . . a friend, who knew the old one." Percy didn't want to betray Cameron and Jane's identity without asking them first, but he was curious to hear what this man might have to say.

Chisholm considered for a moment "The old laird was better than most. One of the few who never intended to burn his tenants out." He paused, and even through the darkness, Percy could see the pain—a different kind of pain than the one from his shoulder—in the man's eyes. "But I dinna know about the new one. I've been away. I dinna get much news."

The sound of a door opening drew their attention. Nathan and Mr. Bara, a large man in a nightshirt, descended the steps toward them. Rose jumped down from the carriage and ran to meet them.

"Da's been shot, Nat. But don't worry," she put a hand on her brother's arm, "I'm going to take care of him. You'll still be able to go to work."

Nat simply nodded. Percy winced. Rose was seven years old. Her brother scarcely any older. They should not have to bear this responsibility.

"All right, then, let's get you upstairs." Mr. Bara asked no questions and wasted no time in heaving Chisholm out of the carriage. Percy supported his other side, Rose and Nat saw to the lantern and the doors, and within five minutes, the injured man was safely deposited onto the rough straw pallet that served as his bed.

Rose hovered over her father, covering him with a blanket and smoothing his brow with her disfigured hand. Percy found he couldn't look at her again as he gave her the directions for her father's care that Cameron had entrusted to him. Cameron himself would visit the next day, he assured her, and could answer any questions she might have.

"Thank you, Mr. Percy." She looked up from her seat. "I'll take good care of him. I promise."

"I've no doubt you will." Percy turned to leave, pulling Nathan aside as he did. "Take this." He handed the boy the few guineas he had on his person. "There's more if you need it."

Nat looked at the coins in wonder, then up at Percy. "Thank you, sir. I . . . we'll pay you back."

"No. It's yours," was all he could choke out, then he darted through the door and made his escape.

Thirteen

Jane woke to a headache and a note from Cameron saying that he had a long shift scheduled at the infirmary, then he planned to go see Mr. Chisholm. He wouldn't be home until late.

On a day like this, having a maid was really quite lovely. Before Cori's arrival, all the cooking had fallen to Jane. She'd reserved her efforts for meals shared with Cameron, making do with cold bits of leftovers when she was alone in the house. But this morning, she'd woken to a hot bath that had assuaged her aching head, then she'd come downstairs—not to a cold kitchen—but to a piping pot of tea, eggs, bacon, and a tray of fresh soda bread. The crumbly bread, flavored with currants, had become a staple in their house. The Irishwoman insisted it was leagues better than all the scones in Scotland. Jane wasn't in complete agreement, but topped with a thick spread of yellow butter, it was quite good indeed.

Cori pushed the newspaper at her as she settled herself at the kitchen table. Jane accepted it with a certain amount of dread. *Would there be anything about the shooting by the canal? Was Will a wanted man?*

"There's aught I could find about Will." Cori read her mind.

"Nothing?" Jane scanned the front page. There was news of the proclamation, though it seemed the newspapermen had not deigned to print the document itself, and the radical author was as of yet unknown. There was nothing of the blockades, or violence by the canals or anywhere else.

"*I'm* supposing the other man got away." Jane looked up from the paper to find Cori looking at her, brows raised meaningfully. "They wouldn't want us to know about that, now would they? Makes the lawmen look like saps." The maid rose from the table, clearing away her breakfast dishes. "And if he don't know they're looking for him, he'll be easier to catch."

"You *are* suspicious," Jane reproached. But, at the same time, she found herself wondering what other events might have happened that remained unreported.

"You think I'm wrong?" Cori shot her a level gaze from across the room.

"No." But if they were still looking for the other man, were they looking for Mr. Chisholm as well?

"I just hope Mr. Sommerbell got him home safely," Cori said. "That man was in no condition to be rattling about the city."

"There's no way to know now." Jane's eyes scanned the paper, but her thoughts were elsewhere. She *did* worry about Mr. Chisholm, but she found her mind more preoccupied with Mr. Sommerbell. How had *he* fared overnight? She wished suddenly that she could talk to him. Make sure he was all right.

"I'm off to the kirk then." Cori's voice invaded her thoughts. She looked up to find the maid staring at her, brows raised.

Though Jane and her parents had regularly attended the parish kirk in Darnalay, since coming to Glasgow, her anxiety had stopped her from venturing out on Sundays. Religion meant a great deal to Cori, and once she'd learned her employer was acting the heathen, she'd taken it upon herself to remind Jane several times a day just how much she was neglecting her Christian duty. She'd offered to accompany her mistress to Sunday services, even if it meant temporarily abandoning her Church of Ireland in favor of Jane's Scottish Kirk, and Jane had given in, partly to stop the constant scolding, partly because she knew Mama would have wanted her to go. They'd located a kirk nearby that suited them both, and for the last several weeks, they'd gone together on Sunday mornings. It really wasn't unpleasant. Cori was a cheerful companion, and the familiar service was comforting in its way.

But not today. She shook her head. "I'm sorry. I'm just too . . . weary this morning." *And confused. And afraid.* After the events of the previous day, she needed time and space to think things through.

"More's the reason to go." The disapproval in Cori's voice was clear, but thankfully when Jane didn't respond, she left it there. "There's water in the kettle if you need." Cori nodded, then she left the room. Several minutes later, Jane heard the front door close behind her.

She took a long breath. Finally, she was alone.

The weather had turned fine again, and a warm sun shone through the kitchen window, projecting the floral designs of the lace curtain onto the wooden table in front of her. She gazed absently at the swirls and blossoms of light as her mind wandered over everything that had happened the day before. *Could it truly have been only one day? Enough had happened to fill a month's time . . .* The proclamation. The slowworms. The tower. The bloodied man by the canal. The barricade. And that moment back at home when she'd kissed him, if one could call it a kiss. Somehow, after everything that had happened, they'd found peace with one another.

And desire. A feeling she hadn't known since Ken died. Had thought she would never know again.

She sighed and rubbed her temples. She could not—*would not*—accept his proposal and become his mistress. Her loyalty to Kendric prevented it. Her unwillingness to live Mama's life prevented it... But even still, the idea, the *vision* of what her life could be... Try as she might, she couldn't get it out of her mind. She felt as if she were standing in an open doorway. At her back, a dull, colorless world. Glasgow. Spinsterhood. And in front of her, just out of reach, a bright and colorful scene. A snug little cottage. An orchard, some chickens, and Percy Sommerbell, bent over his guitar, then looking up with a glint of desire in his dark eyes and that smile, his *real* smile, genuine and warm.

She shivered, pushing the vision away. Perhaps time to think was not as helpful as she'd supposed. Of course she *must* deny him. She must shut that door. And, in the meantime, she would distract herself with the newspaper. Perhaps there was something of more interest past the first page—

A knock sounded from the front door. Odd. No one ever called. Sometimes other students would drop by for Cameron, but not on a Sunday morning.

What if something had happened?

With unrest in the streets, it was entirely possible that Cam had come to harm and here was a messenger to tell her so.

Or perhaps the authorities had tracked Mr. Chisholm to this house?

Fighting panic, she rose and walked to the door, cracking it open ever so slightly.

Less than twelve hours after he'd walked out the front door of the house on Balmanno Street, Percy found himself standing again on that doorstep, knocking as loudly as he dared this early on a Sunday morning.

Please. Let her be home.

The events of the day before had raised the tension that had been building over the last week to an almost unbearable degree. He'd been pulled taut, like an overwound guitar string just. About. To break. Then this morning's news had been one turn too far. He'd been lying in bed, watching the sunlight stream through the crack in the drawn curtains, plotting his next excuse to see Jane while pushing away the memory of the squalor of Chisholm's room, the ugly scar on his daughter's hand. Then there'd been a knock. A message. He'd unfolded the letter, read it, read it again—and his entire world had broken in a percussive, twanging cacophony of sound.

His life would never be the same again. Yet, incredibly, the world around him continued as if nothing had happened. The peaceful silence in his room. The maid cheerfully delivering his breakfast. The church-goers of Glasgow smiling and laughing as they strolled to their kirk.

His only peace since coming upon the injured Will Chisholm had been with Jane. Her presence alone calmed him, and when she'd touched him—just the lightest of kisses on his neck—everything else, all the confusion, guilt and pain had faded, and he'd known in that brief moment, that he wasn't alone. It was unlike anything he'd experienced with a woman, or with *anyone* really. He desired her, surely, but it was more than that . . . not love, or at least not the same kind of love his mother seemed to feel for his father. Percy could never abide something so permanent. But even so, the word stuck in his mind. *Love.* What else could it be? Perhaps it *was* love, just . . . in a more transitory form.

He let his head rest against the door. Waiting. He closed his eyes, trying to recall the undulating minor arpeggios of Beethoven's fourteenth sonata—that always worked to sooth his nerves—but even his music had deserted him. All he could hear was a cacophony of noise. Now, more than ever, he needed her. She alone could help him find harmony in the dissonance.

And he must say goodbye.

She opened the door, just a crack, fear written on her face.

"Mr. Sommerbell?" Her alarm turned to confusion.

"Jane— Miss Stuart. I must speak with you. I'm sorry to intrude so early." Percy only hoped he didn't sound as unhinged as he felt.

"Of course." She opened the door, allowing him in. He caught a whiff of her rose scent. "I'm just breaking my fast. There's enough to share if you're hungry."

"Thank you, no. I ate at my hotel."

"Tea?"

"Yes. Please." He was practically shaking from all the coffee he drank at the hotel, but he could not say no to this woman twice. She wore a simple brown dress. Her hair hung loose down her back, still wet from being washed. With her stormy blue eyes fixed on him and her lush red lips drawn into a concerned pout, she was the most gorgeous thing he'd ever seen.

"Come." She took his hat, then led him to the kitchen where a small table was laid for one.

"Is your brother—"

"At the infirmary. We're quite alone." She sat, and he took a seat across from her. "You must try some of Cori's soda bread. She bakes it because it reminds her of home. There's more than we'll ever eat."

He accepted a cup of tea, no cream, no sugar—*she remembered*—and a piece of the crumbly bread. She pushed a butter dish at him. "Is it Mr. Chisholm? Did something happen?"

"He's fine. Or he was when I saw him last."

"You got him home?"

"Yes. His children were awake, and a neighbor helped."

Now. Now he must tell her. He opened his mouth to speak—

"You think the children will be able to take care of him?" Her question came as a reprieve.

"They seemed determined to do so." An image of little Rose flashed through his mind. So young, so small, yet she'd taken charge like a grown woman. "They kept thanking me. I gave them some coin, but I couldn't . . . I didn't tell them who I am."

"They had every reason to thank you." Then more gently. "You are not your father, Mr. Sommerbell."

Percy shook his head, batting away the comment, blinking away the tears. "Chisholm knows of *your* father, from the Highlands. He said Banton is known as a good man."

"He *was* a good man—or a good landlord, at least." There was pain in her eyes.

"They burned his house when he left. Chisholm's, I mean." Percy hadn't planned to tell her this, but it felt good to say the words out loud, as if speaking them took some of the burden of the man's fate off of him.

"Aye. That's what they do," Jane said softly, staring into space. "So the tenants don't try to come back." There was a long silence, then, "Why are you here, Mr. Sommerbell?"

He took up the knife and began to spread butter on the bread, keeping his eyes on the task as he said what must be said.

"I've come to say goodbye." He looked up then, quickly, half expecting her to cry out with relief. She didn't, but her eyes widened in surprise.

"I thought you had another few days in Glasgow."

"I did, but— Jane. My father has died. I've been called home."

"*Oh! Percy*, I'm . . . I'm so sorry." It was the first time he'd heard his given name cross her lips. She reached her hands toward him, and he took them, holding on as if his life depended on it.

"To be perfectly honest, I'm not sure which end is up at the moment. It's all just . . . too much." He met her eyes. "But there's one thing I'm certain of. I need you. Come with me. Please."

"I—"

"Not today. I must leave right away, and I would never expect you to leave your brother like that. But I can come back for you—"

"I've already told you, I can't—"

"If you can't say yes, just . . . don't say no. Not right now. Take your time. Consider my offer. Write to me—" His voice wavered.

She said nothing, just looked at him, blue eyes wide, pulling him in, deeper. And without thinking, he rose and went to her, sinking to his knees before her. He clasped her hands. "I'll inherit everything. The mills. Grislow Park, the townhouse, the accounts. I'll be lost, Jane. I already am. But when I'm with you . . . I can imagine all is well, or that it *will* be. *Please*. It needn't be forever, but . . . just *be* with me. Now. I *need* you."

He was on his knees in front of her, hands holding hers, eyes imploring.

She could not say no to this man. Not now. It would be more than he could bear. Of course she could not say *yes* either, but perhaps she could leave him with a bit of hope, even if she knew it to be false. It might help him through the trials that stood before him, and then, when she finally gave him her answer, he would be past this crisis and better able to cope with it. Probably he only felt this need for her *because* of the crisis. He was overwrought. Soon, when he was gone from Glasgow and the shock of his father's death had faded, he would find another woman. He'd forget all about her.

"I will think on it," she murmured.

His eyes flashed with relief, and pain. And despite everything he'd been through, everything that was to come, she spied a familiar, smoldering desire—desire that perfectly reflected her own.

She would never see this man again. There was no one else in the house and would not be for hours. It was true that she did not love him, could never love him, but she *could* allow herself this one last moment of connection to remember for the rest of her lonely days. And if it would help ease his torment, well, that would be good too.

She'd never known that so much could be imparted in a meeting of the eyes—a deep, unspoken connection where everything was said, yet nothing was said, because what was communicated was deeper, more primal than language. Or perhaps she preferred to think of it that way. Perhaps she was afraid to attach words to these feelings. The only ones that would suffice were words she could never use. Words that brought with them a crushing load of guilt.

No, she would not think in words. In this moment, she would cast language aside and simply allow herself to be lost in this man's eyes.

Without looking away, he brought her fingers to his mouth and kissed each knuckle, softly, reverently. A deep seated need to be closer to him overtook her, and she extricated her hands from his grasp, then used them to push his coat from his shoulders, down his arms. It landed on the floor with a soft swish.

His eyes widened as he registered her escalation of the moment.

Spurred on by the heat in his gaze, she gently unwound his loosely tied cravat, allowing it to join his coat as she looped her arms around his neck, feeling the softness of the hair at his nape, the smoothness of his skin, inhaling his now familiar scent.

She lowered her head, breaking eye contact to close her eyes as she kissed him. With the loss of sight, all her other senses were magnified. His scent, his fingers running through her damp hair, the whisper of his breath. And his lips. *His lips.* Soft, yet firm. Yielding, yet demanding. Sensual and warm and so . . . so . . . *him*. She registered the familiar ache between her thighs. Her body anticipating what it could not have.

She must be careful not to let things get out of hand.

FOURTEEN

SHE. KISSED. HIM. NOT because he desired it. Not because she was lost in a fit of passion. But because she wanted to. Perhaps she would regret it—*she was certain she'd regret it*—but even still, she would take this moment of pleasure for herself, for him, even as she knew it would be their last.

To be lost in this man's eyes was like losing one's way in a well-designed maze garden, where the hedges were rigorously pruned and just low enough that, if you stood on your tiptoes, you could see over them and find your way out. His kiss, though, his kiss was like being dropped in the middle of a vast wilderness of mountains and trees, rivers and lochs, and knowing beyond a shadow of a doubt that you could never, ever escape. She tasted the astringency of black tea, the fruitiness of currants, and the musky, intoxicating sweetness that was his alone. The kiss deepened. She welcomed his tongue with her own and they danced, light and teasing. Then all at once serious. Urgent. Desperate for more. Her last bit of control slipped away as her grip on him tightened. She frantically explored him, memorizing his teeth, his lips. Losing herself to the sensation.

She had no idea how long they kissed. At some point, she came up for air long enough to notice they were both sitting on the floor, she on his lap, wrapped in his arms. The warm, throbbing between her legs was more insistent now, and she could feel his hard length underneath her. She was grateful she had enough experience in these matters to know what that meant.

These were dangerous waters.

"I canna—I can't allow you to make love to me." She panted.

"I would never ask that of you. Not now." He pulled her even closer, stroking her hair, then whispered softly in her ear, "But there are other ways . . . Would you let me show you? Give you a proper farewell?"

She pulled away just enough so she could see him. His mouth was quirked into a small, wicked grin, but his eyes gave him away. The brittle, desperate plea she saw there undid her, and though she was quite sure there would be nothing at all proper about what came next, she wanted him, wanted this. She had thought this part of her, her bodily desire, had been buried with Kendric along with her heart, but it had sparked back to life and she yearned to experience it—to experience *him*—just one time before she said goodbye forever.

"Not here." She lifted herself off his lap, gathering his discarded clothes and offering her hand as he rose from the floor. He took it, and she led him upstairs to her little room, her own private refuge.

Though she didn't expect anyone home for hours, she locked the door behind them. The lock slid easily into place, but she didn't turn around to face him. *What should come next?* That perfect afternoon under the apple tree with Ken, just before he fell ill, had been the moment their hearts truly fused into one. But, in the physical sense, it had been the fumbling love of two innocents. She'd also learned, alone in her bed at night, that she could give herself pleasure by touching certain parts of her anatomy in certain ways. But this . . . this was a different matter entirely. She took a breath, then slowly turned around. *She wouldn't know what to do. He would change his mind. Push her away.* But all misgivings vanished when she met Percy's gaze. There was still pain there certainly, and desperation, but there was also blistering desire. Desire that left no possibility of doubt, or judgement.

She went to him, gave herself up to his embrace. He drew her close and kissed her. There was no softness in this kiss, nothing tentative. Only need, solid, forceful and unwilling to be denied. His hands worked at the buttons of her dress, and she found herself raising her arms so he could lift it over her head. She hadn't bothered with stays this morning, and she was glad. Her chemise was the only thing that remained between them.

"Bed." There was no smoothness to his voice now, only simple words, commands. All else was superfluous.

She complied, lying back, gazing up at him in wonder. Her rational mind had floated away. There was only him.

"Bloody boots." He sat on the bed and pulled them off. One at a time, fumbling, and much too slowly, then he was next to her, over her, his mouth once again on hers. He broke the kiss and began to explore with his mouth, licking, kissing, nibbling her neck, her ear, her collarbone . . . . His hand cupped her breast, and he growled like a hungry animal. His fingers found her taut nipple underneath the thin linen, then he gave it a gentle pinch, sending a hot spark straight to her already aching core.

She whimpered. She would not be able to stand this much longer . . . . She would . . . she would . . . In truth, she was not quite sure what she would do. *Good Lord, she really was losing track of her own thoughts.* But he mustn't stop.

"Don't stop."

She must have said that out loud because he looked up at her and chuckled, a deep, dark, gravely sound that only increased the longing within her. "Wouldn't dream of it, love." He pushed her chemise down, exposing her breasts to his view. She held her breath, suddenly self-conscious, but all nervousness evaporated as he moaned at the sight of her, eyes wide in appreciation.

"My God. You're perfect."

She exhaled. She was adored. Beautiful. Powerful.

He took her nipple in his mouth, gently circling it with his tongue, then he drew back and blew on it. The cold air hitting her sensitive, wet flesh sent a wild chill through her, then he lowered his head again and suckled her, hard, and wet, and hot, and suddenly her blood was fire. She was nothing *but* fire, mindless in her need. Her hips ground against him, aching for release.

"Please. Now. I need—"

Were those truly the best words she could come up with?

He grinned at her. Wicked, wicked man. He knew what he'd done to her, he knew what she needed, but still he refused to give it to her. "Patience." He directed his attention to her other breast and then—*finally*—moved down to the foot of the bed and pulled her chemise up to expose the little thatch of curls between her thighs. She was thoroughly exposed to him, yet she felt no shame. She was past that now.

Kneeling between her legs, he slowly kissed his way over her stomach, her hips, the tops of her thighs . . . tenderly, as if he were trying to memorize every contour of her body, the taste of her skin. It was the most excruciating, beautiful agony she'd ever known, and she couldn't help it. It was too much to bear. She opened her legs and gently ran a finger over her cleft, parting it, touching herself where she needed to be touched. She was slick with desire, and she groaned with the pleasure of it.

Percy sat back and gazed at her hungrily. Watching. She could feel the heat of his eyes on her most sensitive flesh, urging her on. "Yes. Show me."

Her fingers found her clitoris, that little collection of nerve endings at the top of her labia that was the center of her pleasure. She circled it, closing her eyes and moaning at the sensation. Then he was touching her again, his fingers lightly tracing their way to her opening, dipping one finger into her, then two. Her hips rose off the bed to take him deeper.

He groaned. "I want to taste you. Will you let me?"

How could he expect her to speak? And yet, she *did* want him to taste her. More than anything in the world.

"Yes." The word was somewhere between a gasp and a sob, but she got it out, and in an instant, she felt the warmth of his mouth, teasing her clitoris with his tongue, nipping at it lightly, sucking. Pleasure overtook her in powerful waves as his hot, wet, beautiful mouth moved over her. He plunged his tongue into her, devouring her, drinking her in as his fingers again found her clitoris, stroking it in rhythm with his tongue. Her hips strained toward him, moving to his rhythm, and she felt the pressure she'd been sure was at its peak build inside her again. She was racing now, racing toward . . . toward . . . and suddenly, she'd arrived and he gripped her tightly to him, his tongue still deep inside her as her muscles convulsed around him and she shouted his name and the world exploded in pulsing golden light.

When she finally returned to her body, he was there beside her, holding her as the last tremors of her release shuddered through her. She felt heavy. Even the slightest movement seemed an impossibility. Jane thought she'd understood what sexual release was, but this was a thou-

sand times more than anything she'd felt from her late night self-explo-
rations.

He watched her with a wide grin. *He was proud of himself.* "Welcome
back, love."

"I'm sorry, I don't know what—"

"No. No regrets. Not after— Jane. You are the most beautiful thing .
. . *that* was the most beautiful thing I—"

The distinct sound of knocking—loud knocking—came from downstairs.

Jane discovered that she *could* move after all as she sprang up from the
bed, smoothing her chemise back in place as she went to the window.
"You can see the front steps from here," she said, then she pulled back
the curtain.

He followed, and together, they peered out.

"My coachman." She breathed a sigh of relief, and it seemed he did too.
"I told him I'd be twenty minutes, but it seems I've been a bit longer." He
smiled, but she could sense his anxiety returning. They'd both managed
to forget for a brief time, but real life was encroaching. "I must go." He
sat on the side of the bed, pulling on his boots. She silently handed him
his cravat, then his coat. There was still a noticeable bulge in his trousers.

"Do you not need . . .? I could give you— like you gave me—" More
awkward words had never left her lips, but she meant them. He had
just given her so much, and she had given him nothing. His body quite
obviously still craved release.

"You would do that, wouldn't you? My kind, generous, beautiful
Jane. He reached out to smooth her hair. "I'll be fine, I assure you.
It won't be the first time I've taken myself in hand in a carriage." He
laughed at her shocked expression, then grew suddenly serious. "*Devil*

it. I miss you already." He took her hand and kissed it, just as he had in the tower. "But we'll be together soon."

The hope in his eyes threatened to tear her in two. They would never be together. She would never see him again.

He picked up her dress, and she lifted her arms as he brought it down over her head, smoothing the fabric over her body, touching every curve, lingering over her breasts, her hips—then he abruptly stood back, taking a deep breath. "I must stop, or I'll have to reconsider my answer." He offered his arm. "Walk me to the door?"

They walked out of her room and down the stairs, arm and arm. When they reached the bottom, he turned, once again the desperate, distraught man who'd knocked on her door. "I'll find a house in Northumberland, with room for an orchard. And I'll have a contract drawn up, just as I said. A thousand pounds, no conditions . . . But Jane." He took her hands, looking deep into her eyes. "This isn't about money, not for me. It's about . . . *us*. I need you. Please just . . . just think about it. Say you'll write to me?"

The painful pleading in his eyes was more than she could bear. She did not say no. She did not say yes. She simply said, "Go. Go now." And he did. The last thing she saw of him was when he turned to look at her one last time, just before he shut the door of the carriage that would take him to England. He met her eyes, and a flash of recognition flared between them.

Write to me.

. . . then he was gone.

FIFTEEN

Grislow Park. 1st May, 1820

MY DEAREST JANE,

THEY DANCE the maypole in the village today. My mother adores the custom, and any other year, she would be out in the sunshine with flowers in her hair, and she would insist I come with her, which I would pretend to be loath to do. But instead, we remain cloistered in this depressive house where black mourning and gloom abide. Forgive me for waiting so long to write. I hope you do not interpret my silence as apathy, or begin to think my devotion to you diminished. You are constantly in my thoughts, and my memories of all we shared during our brief time together have sustained me through the interminable weeks since we said goodbye. In truth, I've been holding out hope that I might receive a letter from you, and that my first to you would be in reply. But no letter has arrived, and I can wait no more.

I have been constantly preoccupied since my arrival a month ago, first by the funeral arrangements and the hosting of relatives, then the settlement of Father's will. Anyone who ever called him friend has come to call, and I couldn't leave my mother and sister to receive them alone, so I've endured hours of tedious conversation, drunk gallons of tea, and eaten a hundred pieces of cake in solidarity with them. Mother's grief is overwhelming. She loved him, more than I ever understood while he lived. I miss him too, Jane, though I never would have thought it possible that it be so. My father was a man of remarkable abilities. I see that now, and I regret that I did not take the initiative to know him better while he lived, or to learn from him how I might bear the great responsibility that has been laid upon me as his heir. I'm certain I don't have the ability to do half of what he did, but for now, I am pretending for the sake of my mother. In my heart, I simply want to run far away. To you, my Jane. I have visions of escape from this sad house, of rescuing you from that foul city and fleeing together to some Mediterranean clime where we would eat oranges on the shore and then swim together, laughing in the warm sea. Alas, that is not to be, at least not today.

I have an appointment tomorrow to view a house that I hope will prove perfect for you. I won't say more about it as I don't want either of us to have inflated hopes, but I will write to you again if it proves to be so. In addition, I've given my solicitors instructions for a contract and will have it sent to you as soon as it's finished. I endured many raised brows and pointed questions when I explained the nature of the document. My man of business could not understand why I would want him to write something so unfavorable to my own interests, but I insisted, and so it shall be.

There's one more thing that needs telling, something that's been eating at me since I last saw you. I don't suppose it matters terribly now, but

I feel I must be honest, because that's how I want things to be between us. Nothing held back, no secrets. The truth is I lied to you when I described my sojourn in Italy, or rather I omitted a critical fact, which is just as deceitful as a lie. It was not just myself, Beau, and Mauro in that villa on the coast. Our number included three courtesans, from Venice, whom we engaged for their services and company. I have had many lovers, Jane. I'm not ashamed to have known pleasure, but you must understand that none of these liaisons amounted to anything beyond a fleeting excitement and an indulgence of the senses. They meant nothing. I swear to you now that I have never made such an offer to another, nor felt toward any other what I feel toward you. You are as different from all those others as a rose is to a thistle. How eagerly I await your answer. *Please let it be yes!* As I have said before, you are not your mother, I am certainly no earl, and we need not repeat their mistakes. We could forge something new, a life all our own. At your word, I shall send my coach and it will deliver you into my arms.

I trust all is well in Glasgow. I have heard no recent news of strikes or violence, and my managers have not reported a disturbance in production, which leads me to believe things must be peaceful. I will likely need to travel there again in the coming months to officially take over my father's holdings. I hope by then you will be here with me, but if not, I will look forward to seeing you. Give my regards to your brother, and send me news of Mr. C and his family. Has he recovered? Write to me, Jane! Until then, I shall remain

Yours. Adoringly.

PERCY SOMMERBELL

Rosehill Cottage. 4th May, 1820

DEAREST JANE,

I write to you today from the desk in the study at Rosehill cottage. *Your* cottage! A cherry tree is blooming just outside the window. Perhaps this paper will become infused with its sweet scent and you will smell it as you read these words. In my imagination, you are on your way to me now, riding away from the cesspit of a city called Glasgow. I would herald your arrival by filling the house with cherry boughs, daffodils, hyacinths and primrose, all blooming in colorful profusion in your own little garden.

I've taken Rosehill on a ten-year lease, which allows me to be patient as I wait for you, though I confess it to be a reluctant patience. It's but a short ride from Grislow Park, and it's the most picturesque place you can imagine, built in the style of our great-grandparents. Grey stone with ivy climbing in abandon, tile to keep out the English rain. The latest occupant was an elderly woman, and the rooms are furnished in the style of forty years ago, bright but busy with too much formality and gold ornament for my taste. I shall leave all as it is, and when you arrive, I'll take you to town to procure whatever furnishings you desire. You have a breakfast room, a dining room, a drawing room in the front and a morning room that faces to the south with doors that open onto the garden. This little study where I now sit is next to that, with a wide arched door between. I can just see you there, reclining in a pool of sunshine, reading the most recent edition of some botanical magazine while I sit at this desk dealing with the tedious business that has been foisted upon me. These new responsibilities would be so much more bearable had I the opportunity to look up and see you there, my sweet Jane!

We'll get a dog, my love, when you get here, and he shall keep you company when I am away. Or a cat if you prefer. Or a parrot. Or whatever pet your heart desires. Except perhaps a snake. I do not think I could abide a snake.

Your bedroom faces east to let in the morning sun, and there's a window that overlooks the stretch of land where we will plant your orchard. It's large and airy and private from the room I've claimed as my own. I will have no expectations of you when you arrive, only that you will be as happy as I can make you, and though it is true my desire for you burns as hot as the sun, your sweet beautiful presence here will be enough. I will not press you for more.

There are two more rooms on the second floor. Your brother can have his pick when he visits. I've hired a caretaker who sleeps off the kitchen, and there's plenty of room for a maid or two, a cook, even a butler and a footman if you desire. But I haven't told you of the grounds yet! There's a formal garden surrounded by hedges. Spring flowers bloom there now, and there are roses and other plants that I'm sure you would know the names of (and someday you will teach them to me). The kitchen garden is in some disarray, though it will not take long to put things to rights there, I'm sure. It's bordered by a picket fence and, beyond that, the empty meadow that will become your orchard. I've gained permission from the landlord to plant whatever you see fit. It is a canvas awaiting your brush!

I can barely contain my joy at this place, and my excitement for the happiness we will find here. I miss you more than I can say, my Jane, but I will be patient. You are understandably circumspect, as it is no small thing to leave the life you know and join me, but you have a home here, if you choose. At your word, I shall send my carriage, and I remain

Yours. Exuberantly.

PERCY SOMMERBELL

Glasgow. 20th May, 1820

Dear Mr. Sommerbell

I received yours and wish to again extend my deepest condolences for the death of your father. I know what it is to lose one's parents and feel suddenly alone, and it is not a feeling I wish upon anyone. I'm sure your mother has been glad of your company in her time of need.

As you have likely read in the papers, though the mood in the city was quite tense for a time and some violence resulted, the planned rebellion never materialized on the scale that was called for. Many of Cameron's friends have come to believe the entire episode a ruse manufactured by the government with the intention of inciting violence, which would, in turn, supply grounds for convictions. If this was the case, it seems to have worked. The authorities have detained dozens of men said to be violent radicals (thanks to God Mr. C is not one of them). The arrested men will soon be brought to trial and likely transported or hanged. Cameron despairs at this. As you know, he has great sympathy for the working classes. I find myself torn, as I suspect you must be. It is, of course, terrible to see the plight of the souls living in the wynds, but I am relieved that I need no longer fear violence on my doorstep.

Mr. C has healed well under Cameron and Rose's care. It is a small miracle that he escaped the events of that terrible day with both his life and his freedom, and he has promised me he will not resort to such action again. He is a good man, and I believe he will keep his word. In turn, I have offered to take his children on as pupils. Rose is the sweetest little thing. I have not yet found the key to opening her up to me, but she is bright and eager to learn. I have hope that my tutelage will give her the opportunity to make something of herself, even with the loss of her fingers. She has started coming to our house three afternoons a week, and it has proven a welcome distraction. Nathan comes on Sundays, along with his father. Mr. C himself was lucky to attend a parish school as a youth. He can read, write, and he knows basic figures. With a little more tutelage, I believe he could pass for a clerk.

Forgive me, I know it was not my place, but I told Mr. C of your family ties to the factories. It seemed dishonest to keep it from him. He does not hold it against you. He says that you have already settled a good sum of money on him in respect to Rose's accident, and for that he, and I, are most grateful. I pray you, in your new situation, do not forget families like theirs. Your inheritance gives you an opportunity to do good that most of us never aspire to. I urge you not to waste it.

I appreciate your honesty regarding your situation in Italy, although you did not need to tell me as it is no business of mine. It is not your past that makes it impossible for me to accept your offer. As you mention honesty between us, there is something I must tell you. A thing that is somehow easier to put to paper than to speak aloud. When I was nineteen, I was betrothed to a boy. The son of my father's groundskeeper. He was my heart, and I his. I wanted nothing more than to be his wife. Just two weeks after our betrothal, he died, of a hectic fever brought upon by a small wound on his leg. My heart is buried with him, and this is the true reason that I cannot accept your proposal.

You say you would have no expectations of me if I accept your offer. I believe you mean it, but, to be quite honest, I do not think it possible to be near you and to remain friends only. I suspect the spark between us would prove too strong for either of us to resist. I do not regret our time together, but that time is over. We must both move on. I am and shall remain

Your friend. From afar.

JANE STUART

Rosehill Cottage. 9th June, 1820

My Dearest Jane

I've waited several weeks to respond, because I did not want to seem overeager, but it is a lie. I think of you every hour of every day. I once supposed that my longing for you would fade with distance, but I find I miss you more with the passage of time, and though you did not say yes, and in fact you continued to list your reasons for denying me, you also did not give a definitive no. You called me a friend, and so I continue to carry the hope that you will someday come to me.

I am once again writing to you from Rosehill. I've spent a good deal of time here in the last months, because it's pleasant, private, and, though you've not ever been here, it reminds me of you. It's late in the day now. A storm blew through an hour ago, and the sun has just come out with the most glorious golden light. I wish you could see it! The roses are blooming in your garden, along with a profusion of flowers of the most brilliant blue, which I'm told are called delphinium. I've written a song for them—an ode to the delphiniums in my beloved's garden. I hope one day to play it for you.

Thank you for confiding in me the tragedy of your betrothal. It pains my heart to hear of yet another loss you've endured. You have my love, that has become clear to me in these last months, but I do not need, nor do I expect, to be loved in return. I only ask for your companionship and your friendship. Nothing more.

The reality of my inheritance, and how to square my family's business interests with my conscience, continues to plague me. You may know that I've written to your brother, requesting an introduction to the man whose father owns New Lanark, as it is my intention to visit the place when I come North in the fall. I have also written to my managers in Glasgow, directing them to do away with the employment of small children in my mills. They argue that in addition to lost efficiency, this change will further impoverish the children's families, as the income they bring in is necessary. Therefore, to their dismay, I've directed them to continue paying the children's wages. It's a temporary solution to a difficult problem, but I could not stomach the thought of those children working under my employ. I very much appreciate your tutelage of Mr. C and his children. It is a comfort to know that his daughter will have skills to rely on in future life. If you decide to come to me, I will see to it that they are able to continue their education in Glasgow. Do not cease to remind me of my duty to those in need, Jane. You are so good and so kind, so quick to help others. You make me want to be better than I am, and your presence convinces me I have the ability to do so. I only wish, with all of the beneficence you show others, that you would give your own happiness more weight.

The sun is setting now, and I wonder if you are watching it too, in that city to the north?

Farewell for now, love. I am

Yours. Hopefully.

PERCY SOMMERBELL

London. 5th July, 1820

My Dearest Jane

I've been in London these last weeks, attending to business that my father left undone. I find I am becoming more accustomed to the burden that has been foisted upon me, but even still, I struggle to know how I may right the wrongs I find myself the overseer of. I am continually wracking my mind for the answers, but the injustices I face all seem too large for one man to set right. I understand now, why so many men ignore or justify the ugly truths of modern industry while at the same time reaping its benefits. It is a hard truth to face, and there are no easy answers, but nevertheless I am determined to find them.

I no longer think, my Jane, that I need you for my own survival, and I see now it was unfair of me to put that burden upon you. But I do not *wish* to live without you, and it saddens my heart to think of you imprisoned in that befouled city when you could be happily ensconced at Rosehill.

I trust you've received a copy of the contract, sent from my solicitor in Newcastle. If there's anything that would make the arrangement more amenable, do not hesitate to ask. There is very little I would not give you, just as there is very little I ask of you, simply your companionship and your happiness.

I thought the diversions of London might distract me from thoughts of you, but alas, I was wrong. It has been raining constantly. My friends have found me a wearisome bore. I miss you dreadfully. I return to Northumberland the day after tomorrow. My dearest wish is to find a letter from you awaiting me there. I am and will continue to be

Yours. Tenderly.

Percy Sommerbell

Rosehill Cottage. 2nd August, 1820

MY DEAREST JANE

I've heard nothing for so long that I begin to despair you may never write again, and yet I wait, faithfully. The choice is yours, and I am patient. Words are not my medium, but because I cannot send you my music through the post, I send you a poem by a man who shares my name—Percy Shelley, a fellow Englishman whom I met in Italy.

The fountains mingle with the river
And the rivers with the ocean,
The winds of heaven mix for ever
With a sweet emotion;
Nothing in the world is single;
All things by a law divine
In one spirit meet and mingle.
Why not I with thine?—

See the mountains kiss high heaven
And the waves clasp one another;
No sister—flower would be forgiven
If it disdained its brother;
And the sunlight clasps the earth
And the moonbeams kiss the sea:
What is all this sweet work worth
If thou kiss not me?

Write to me, Jane! *Come to me*! I am yours.

PERCY

Glasgow. 18th August 1820

Dear Mr. Sommerbell

I received your recent letters, and must apologize for my silence. I have no good excuse. I simply have not known what to say.

Cameron tells me that you will be journeying here in a month's time, and that you have arranged a tour of New Lanark. I am gladdened by this news, and I hope your investigation of that place yields some of the answers you seek. As you may have heard, several of the men arrested in the spring have been sentenced to hang. Their executions are imminent. The mood in Glasgow is grim, with many despairing that the current situation will ever be changed.

The children are coming along in their studies. Mr. C is progressing quickly as well and will soon be past my abilities as a teacher. I wonder if you might consider him for a clerk or secretary in one of your factories? I continue to visit your aunt regularly and have just finished a book she lent me—The Interesting Narrative of the Life of Olaudah Equiano. Have you read it? The author details the trials of his life as an enslaved man before the turn of the last century. It is appalling, what our race has inflicted upon another, and I found myself wondering if any of the cotton used in your factories comes from American slave plantations?

To be quite truthful, I've found myself quite morose these last months. My mind is too often preoccupied by imagining what life at your Rosehill might be like, and it has made the world around me seem more grim than it was before. I am so tired of the foul odors and smoke of this city. It gives one a sense of hopelessness, not just for this place, but for mankind as a whole. Even still, all the reasons I have to refuse your answer remain. I simply cannot sign the contract you sent me, as tempted as I might be.

It is very forward of me to suggest it, but I wonder if you might reconsider the idea of marriage? As I have said, I can never give you my heart, but marriage does not require such things. I could perform in all other aspects as a wife. I could be a friend to you, and a support. I could help you establish a school in Glasgow if you so desire, and ensure your households run smoothly. I could provide you with legitimate children who would bear your name. You have said you do not believe in marriage. I understand your reasons for this belief, and I do not, in theory, disagree with them. However, theories of how life *should* be must sometimes be tempered with the practicality of life as it is. I fully expect that your answer will be no. If this is the case, then I pray you preserve my dignity and never mention it again. If you would consider such a thing, perhaps we may speak of it more when you arrive in Glasgow. I remain

Your Friend

JANE STUART

Sixteen

Jane quickly folded the sheet of foolscap, with each crease obscuring more of the words she'd just foolishly committed to writing. Better not to give herself the opportunity to reread it. If she did, she'd surely lose her nerve and decide not to send the letter at all. She held a stick of red wax to the lighted candle before her, watching as it turned to a shimmering liquid that pooled onto the paper, then she stamped it with the small ring she always wore—a simple spray of roses. It was the ring Mama had used to seal letters, and had been on her finger when she died. Wearing it made Jane feel closer to Mama somehow, as if she were here now, lending her strength.

For a long, hesitant moment, she held the folded paper up to the flame. She could still burn the whole idea to ashes, but once she'd posted it, there would be no going back. Was it foreboding that churned in her stomach, or anticipation? Both, she suspected. She'd just written a letter to Mr. Sommerbell—*Percy*—proposing marriage. The thought both terrified and thrilled.

If she was being honest, there was a third feeling in the pit of her stomach, or perhaps a bit lower than that. Lust. In the months since he'd left, the sensations of desire, the throbbing awareness in her sex, the acute sensitivity of her skin, her breasts, her lips, had become almost unbearable. Some days, she felt as if she were walking in a dream, removed from what was happening around her, lost completely to fantasies of his dark eyes, his beautiful fingers as he traced fire on her skin, the warm wool, cedar and citrus scent of his embrace, his hot lips soft upon her . . . She saw, smelled, heard, felt him every day, every night.

That Sunday morning in her bedroom had been a disastrous mistake. She'd thought she could satisfy the desire building inside her then snuff it out like a candle, but, instead, the fire had raged hotter than she'd imagined possible and now it was beyond her ability to control. Almost every night, she resorted to touching herself, thinking that perhaps if she satisfied herself this way she would be able to banish him once and for all from her thoughts, but it didn't work. Even after bringing herself to an exquisite release, when she woke the next morning, there he was, behind her eyelids, with that seductive smile . . .

Knowing he waited for her, in a dear little cottage all her own. Knowing he wanted her as badly as she did him. Knowing she could be useful to him and so many others by helping better the lives of those he employed. That she did not, in fact, have to resign herself to life in Glasgow. That there was another path open to her . . . It had all become more than she could bear, and when the idea had come, the realization that there was one thing—*marriage*—that might make it all possible, she'd had no choice. Either she would go mad with wanting, or she would gather up all her courage and propose. He *knew* she did not love him. She was not, therefore, breaking her vow to Kendric. *Was she?*

Ken's face flashed before her. Her beloved. The key to her heart. *What was she thinking?* Her betrayal was clear. She could not send this—

"I'm off to market." Cori ducked into the room, dressed to go out. Suddenly self-conscious, Jane jerked the paper away from the flame. "There's some cheese and bread for Miss Rose when she comes." The maid reached a hand toward her, gesturing to the letter. "I can post that if you like?"

Jane stared at the Irishwoman for a long moment, then nodded and held her breath as Cori crossed the room to retrieve the missive. And, just like that, it was out of her hands.

"A letter to a friend?" the maid asked.

"Something like that."

Percy raced up the steps and through the front door of the cottage. He'd had only one message from Jane in the months since he'd left Glasgow. One precious letter that didn't exactly give him hope but spoke of friendship and contained a delicious admittance of her desire for him. Now, *finally*, a second letter had arrived.

Late afternoon sun slanted through the windows as he made his way to the study and slid behind the desk. He'd received it this morning, and it had been an excruciating wait, but he'd finally been able to slip away to the privacy of Rosehill. It felt right, somehow, to read it here, in the place he felt closest to her.

The house was quiet, as if it, too held its breath.

He pulled the letter from the pocket of his waistcoat, along with a missive from Beau who was apparently still in Greece. He set the message from his friend aside, Beau could wait, and examined Jane's letter.

There was his name, carefully addressed in her now familiar hand. Clean, graceful lines with no unnecessary embellishment. He turned it over. A simple spray of roses stamped in red wax. The same seal she'd used for her last letter. He pressed the paper to his face, breathing in the scent, then finally, he broke the seal and unfolded the foolscap, praying for good news and not heartbreak.

Hours later, he was still sitting behind the desk, clutching her letter, staring unseeingly at the rising moon. His thoughts tossed one way, then another, until finally, just after midnight, he rose and went to the stable to collect his horse.

<hr />

"Cybil?" Percy knocked lightly on the door to his sister's study. It was ajar, but he knew better than to barge in unannounced. Cybil often stayed up all night writing—it had been her habit since she arrived back at Grislow Park seven years ago—and she'd always made it quite clear that she did not wish to be disturbed. But tonight he would risk her wrath. He needed to talk to her. Alone.

His sister was wrapped in an old dressing gown. A long braid hung down her back. She was hunched over her escritoire, quill in hand. Her spaniel lay sleeping at her feet. A stack of paper sat on the desk on either side of her, one comprised of blank sheets, the other filled with lines of her cramped, angular script. Two candles were her only source of light. The drapes were drawn, blocking whatever moonlight might have filtered into the room.

"What?" She looked up at him, eyebrows raised in an obvious sign of annoyance.

"I need to talk."

She put the quill in its holder, sighed and sat back, arms folded. "Yes?"

He cleared his throat and entered the room. There was nowhere to sit that wouldn't leave him in complete darkness, so he stood in front of her desk. He was suddenly nervous. He didn't know what to do with his hands, so he stuffed them in his pockets like a schoolboy.

"What is it?" Cybil was clearly irritated.

He cleared his throat again. "I'm . . . I'm thinking of getting married." There. He'd said it.

"*Married*?" Cybil's brows remained elevated, but their angle changed ever so slightly to register surprise rather than annoyance.

"Yes." Percy licked his lips.

"To whom?"

"A woman."

She rolled her eyes. "*What* woman?"

"Jane. Stuart. I met her in Glasgow. She's . . . she's the daughter of an earl. A Scottish one."

"Mother will like that."

He shook his head. "The *bastard* daughter of an earl."

"Oh." Cybil shrugged. "There are worse things." There was a long silence, punctuated only by the dog's soft snores. "Percy. What are you trying to say?"

He took a long breath. "You—or I mean, your marriage, to Ernest . . ."

Her expression tightened. "What of it?"

"Well. You're not exactly a happy couple."

"Couple? I haven't seen him in years."

"Right. Well. I've always thought . . . since then, that I would never marry. Because of what it—what he did to you. Marriage is *forever*, and now you're stuck, legally." He paused, searching for the right words. "How does anyone know what they'll feel in a year, or five years, or ten?"

"You're talking about love?"

"Yes. Love. I mean, I love her, I'm certain I do. But you loved Ernie, and then—"

She held up a hand to stop him. "I never loved Ernie. Not for one second."

"You didn't? But everyone said it was a love match. You were so happy."

"I *acted* happy," she corrected him. "You were a twelve-year-old boy. Easily fooled." She pinched the bridge of her nose. "If you must know, I married Ernie because he had a title, and Mother and Father wanted me to, and because . . . because I'd be able to live in London. Not here." She sighed. "I knew he was a bully, but I thought I could handle him. I thought it would be worth it. I was wrong."

"Oh." Percy was stunned. "I always thought—"

"It wasn't because of some fool notion about love. I can assure you of that." Cybil looked down at her hands, massaging one with the other. Then she raised her gaze again and glared at him over the candles. "You need someone, especially now Father's gone. If you've found a woman mad enough to marry you, you should do it, especially if you love her." She leaned forward. "But be honest with her. Be kind. And let her be who she is."

"Of course." An image of Cybil's face the night she'd arrived home after leaving Ernie flashed through his mind. The dark bruise on her cheek. The cut on her lip. "I would never— I *love* who she is."

"Good." Cybil nodded. "I must admit I'm surprised. I thought you had a new mistress."

"What?"

Cybil leveled her gaze. "You really think no one's noticed how often you've been gone?"

"Well, I did ask her to be my mistress," he admitted. "She said no."

"Clever woman. I like her already."

"You *will* like her." It was only as he said the words that Percy realized they were true. He smiled at the image of Cybil and Jane conspiring together. Then the smile fell away as realization hit—he *wanted* that future, wanted Jane to be part of his family. Forever. He'd been so intent, so *sure* that marriage was some great evil, that he hadn't been able to see what was right in front of him. Jane. Love. Always.

What a bloody idiot he'd been.

"Percy?" Cybil's annoyed voice cut through his epiphany. "Are we done?"

He shook his head to bring himself back to the present. His mind felt clearer than it had in months. Years perhaps. "I'll be gone for a while."

"Glasgow?"

"And other places." A plan was formulating. Going to Glasgow wasn't enough. He needed to show her just how much he cared. He turned and walked to the door, then pivoted back to his sister. "Thank you, Cybil. I hope you find a way . . . someday, to not be stuck."

His sister sighed. "Not bloody likely," she muttered. Then she picked up her quill and continued writing.

Percy left her to it. There was much to do, but for the first time since Father died, he felt peace.

⚬

"*A fine new house. May now be seen. With a larg-ee—*"

"Large," Jane corrected gently.

"Large park. Fit for a king," Rose finished, then looked up with a wide grin—an expression that had taken Jane months to coax from her. Rose's smiles were still rare, and precious.

"Perfect." Jane smiled back at her. "Continue."

The lass read on, slowly, but clearly, *"A lar— large pond too. With stock of fish. And choice of fruit. Which may be eat. Be a good child. Then you shall see. A flock of sheep. A sh— show—"* She looked up at Jane questioningly, pointing to a word in the book with her good hand.

"Shoal of fish." Jane finished for her.

"What's a shoal of fish?"

"'Tis a group, swimming all together in a jumble," Jane told her. "In the ocean, or a loch."

Rose nodded, knowingly. "I've never seen an ocean, or a loch. That's why I didn't know."

An aching tenderness formed in Jane's chest. By all natural rights, Rose should've been enjoying a childhood amongst the most beautiful lochs, rivers and glens of the Highlands. The lass had no idea what she'd lost. But perhaps her ignorance was a blessing.

"There's a loch near Darnalay." She pulled the girl closer to her on the sofa. "Just a wee little one, but it has so many fish. Trout, and pike, and salmon. I used to go fishing there with Cameron, and our friends. We'd get up when it was still dark and ride to the loch with our poles to watch the sunrise over the water. It sparkled, like magic. And then we'd spend the day, eat a picnic lunch on the shore and bring fish home for supper." She smiled down at the girl, who was listening with rapt attention.

"Will you take me there?" Rose's eyes were wide and bright with imagination.

A sudden lump in Jane's throat prevented her from answering right away. She swallowed it down. "No, lassie. I can't. 'Tis no longer my home."

The girl nodded. She was used to disappointment.

Cori bustled into the room. Rose's attention was drawn to the maid, and Jane quickly dabbed her eyes with her sleeve. What a simpering ninny she'd become. She could no longer pretend numbness to herself, or anyone else. Percy Sommerbell had seen to that.

"A letter for you, Miss." Cori handed Jane a sealed missive. "The rest were for your brother. I left them in his chamber."

Jane turned the letter over, and in a breath, her melancholy was replaced by a potent mixture of panic and excitement. She stared at the paper for a moment. The sloppy script was unmistakable.

"Miss?" Cori's voice. Jane looked up to see two faces eyeing her expectantly.

"Rose. I'm afraid we'll need to be done for today," she choked out. "Cori, will you give Miss Rose something to eat before she goes?"

"Yes, of course." A look of concern crossed Cori's face. "Is aught wrong?"

"No . . . I . . . No. All is well." Jane attempted a reassuring smile.

Cori nodded, her brows still lowered questioningly. "Very well. Come along, Miss Rose."

As soon as the maid had ushered Rose from the room, Jane raced to her chamber and bolted the door. She sank down onto the bed and, with shaking hands, broke the seal.

Grislow Park. 22nd August 1820

My Dearest Jane

Yes! Yes! Wait for me. I am coming to you. Look for me in a fortnight.

All my Heart.

Percy

She read the message over and over, searching for whatever meaning lay in between the twenty-three words scrawled in Percy's looping, anarchic hand. Finally, she let the paper drop to her lap, allowing her eyes to close and her head to rest on the hard oaken headboard.

There was no doubt these twenty-three words answered her proposal in the affirmative. He'd said yes not once, but twice. But the brevity was perplexing. His previous letters had not been brief. He must have been in a hurry, but if that was the case, *why a fortnight*? The trip from Glasgow to Northumberland was no more than three days by coach . . .

Excitement glowed inside her, pulsing with every breath. The message was puzzling, true, but *he'd said yes.* She would be his wife. She spoke it aloud to test the feel on her tongue.

"Mrs. Sommerbell. Jane Sommerbell." The words sounded more foreign than French or German.

She'd never contemplated what came next if he were to say yes because, until this moment, the possibility hadn't seemed real. Once the idea of marriage had come to her, she'd known she had to ask him, but in truth, she'd expected him to say no, or perhaps she'd *hoped* he would.

Questions and doubts raced through her mind, far faster than she could answer them. Did he mean to remain faithful to her after they married, or would he be courting a mistress in a matter of months? What if his devotion to her waned before the wedding and she was left humiliated and alone? How would she tell Cameron? Who would take *care* of Cameron? What would Cynthia and her husband think? They'd opened their home to Jane as a friend, but would they be as welcoming to a bastard marrying into their family?

What about his mother?

. . . and oh sweet, sweet heaven. Was she breaking her vow to Kendric?

Her body pressed into the mattress, heavy, still, eyes closed.

Breath pushing out.

Drawing in.

Pushing out.

It seemed impossible that her physical form could be so entirely still while, at the same time, her mind exploded with fear and excitement, guilt, relief, doubt.

A fortnight was an eternity.

SEVENTEEN

THE SUN WAS SETTING over the thatched rooftops of Darnalay Village when Percy finally reined his gelding to a halt in front of the inn. For seven excruciating days, he'd traveled north by post chaise, stopping only to eat, change horses and stretch out for a few blessed hours of sleep. When he'd finally reached Inverness, the innkeeper advised him the last leg of the journey would be faster on horseback, so this morning, he'd requested a horse be saddled, and traveled the last fifteen miles on his own. He'd left most of his belongings at the inn, but Jane's letters had been too precious to leave behind, so he'd tucked them into his saddlebags, along with a change of clothes. His guitar was strapped securely to his back, though now he regretted bringing it. His back ached. In truth, every part of him ached.A boy appeared to take the reins, and Percy strode—every step a painful reminder of how long it had been since he'd undertaken such a lengthy ride—toward the heavy wooden door of The Rook & Rabbit. Its name was proclaimed in both words and pictures on the worn sign hanging above the entrance to the inn.

In all, he'd traveled less than the distance from Grislow Park to London, but the journey over the wretched Scottish roads had taken a full day longer. Had he been in a different frame of mind, Percy would have likely found the trip enchanting, but his thoughts continued to be plagued by that constant, looming anxiety of the mills—the unsolvable puzzle of how to maintain his family's wealth without losing his very soul. He'd thought he might escape these thoughts here, in the wilds of the North, but the landscape was marred by too many blackened ruins of farmhouses and barns for that. He'd asked one of his drivers about them and been told that, yes, these were the remains of the houses of people who'd been evicted to make way for the enormous flocks of sheep that now dominated the landscape. The man seemed to sympathize with the plight of the tenants, so Percy pushed the conversation a bit farther, repeating the story Rose Chisholm had told him about the old woman who needed to be rescued.

The coachman shook his head sadly. "Aye. That's happened, an' worse. I've seen the whole sky black from the smoke. Hundreds of houses at once. People screaming. Bairns crying." He shuddered at the memory.

"And the people . . . they all go south? To the cities?"

"Some do." The man conceded. "The young and the strong mostly. The *lucky* ones go to America. But those who are old or sick, the widows with their bairns, they go to the crofts on the coast that the lords send 'em to. There's nothin' there. No way to make a living. They starve."

The knowledge that the empty glens he traveled through had so recently been populated gave a haunting, eerie feel to the wild beauty and isolation. Once upon a time, Percy would have found it inspiring. He'd have composed some sweeping, melancholy piece to commemorate the trip. But it was all too real now, after meeting Chisolm. To write music about it would have justified it somehow, made it into something beautiful, when, in truth, there was nothing beautiful about it.

As it was, the lonely landscape only made Percy feel the distance between himself and Jane more keenly. He'd told her to expect him in two weeks, and he'd been *hoping* to surprise her much sooner than that, but he was now hopelessly behind schedule. One day spent settling things at home. Seven long days on the road. It was another four days at least back to Glasgow from here, leaving him little time to convince the new Earl of Banton to give him what he sought.

He'd tried to make good use of his journey, using the time to read and reread a book on the particulars of grafting, which he'd found in the library at Grislow Park. Probably it had once belonged to his uncle. He was now fully prepared to harvest not only whatever early fruit he could find, but also sticks from Jane's small trees that could be grafted onto other trees—*scions,* they were called—and transport them safely, wrapped in damp paper, back to Glasgow and then Rosehill. How fantastical that one could simply insert the wood of one tree into another and expect it to start growing as if nothing at all had changed. It was no wonder Jane was so drawn to this science.

Darnalay was not much different from the other Highland villages he'd journeyed through, but it seemed somehow more vibrant and well kept. A weathered stone kirk dominated by a square tower, a forge, one small shop, the inn, and a group of thatched cottages, their gardens overflowing in a tangle of vines and flowers. Chickens roamed freely. The road led through the village and over a bridge, and he could just see the turrets of a stone tower—*it must be the castle*—in the distance. Instead of the sheep Percy had become accustomed to seeing, shaggy Highland cows grazed peacefully in meadows between. The setting sun cast a golden glow over the scene, giving the place an air of peaceful enchantment. He could imagine Jane walking toward him, just this side of the stone bridge, a basket of apples swinging from her elbow and a smile on her lips. This was her home, and though her physical self had departed more than a year ago, her heart, he knew, still resided here.

A young girl answered his knock. She eyed him warily, then showed him to a room on the second floor. It was sparsely furnished, but clean. Better than most of the inns he'd stayed at in the last week. He splashed some water on his face, then wandered downstairs to find sustenance and perhaps a dram of whisky before retiring for a much needed night's rest.

The bar room was empty save two hostile-looking men, farmers from the looks of them, drinking ale at a nearby table. Percy offered them a smile but received only scowls in return. The innkeeper—a tall woman of middling age, as cold and unfriendly as the men—stalked over, introducing herself as Mrs. MacPhearson. She brought him whiskey, followed by a succulent dinner of mutton and boiled potatoes, and though the meal was by far the best he'd had in days, her manner betrayed no hospitality. He tried to thaw her ice with an innocent jest, but her only response was a disapproving frown, so he gave up and allowed himself to descend into brooding silence. He had no idea what was wrong with these people, but he was too exhausted to care. Anyway, if all went as planned, he'd be gone from here by midday tomorrow.

He finished his meal and asked for another whiskey, intending to drink it quickly then retire to his room. His eyelids were heavy, his thoughts blurred. Surely he'd never looked forward to a clean bed and soft pillow as much as he did right now.

As the innkeeper set the glass down, a whim took hold of him. "Do you by chance know Miss Jane Stuart?" he asked.

Mrs. MacPhearson stiffened. She scoured him with a searching glare. "What's it to you?" Her eyes dared him to give the wrong answer.

It didn't feel right to refer to Jane as his betrothed, not to this woman with her obvious distrust of him, so he replied simply and honestly. "I've come to collect apples and scion wood for her. I wondered if you knew her."

His words inspired a veritable key change in Mrs. MacPhearson, from a threatening harmonic minor to something much more pleasant—*D major*? The stiff, unfriendly matron was gone. In her place, a genial woman with twinkling eyes and a warm, welcoming smile. "A friend of Miss Janie's? God save us, laddie, why didna you say so sooner? I thought you were here to do business with the laird."

"I *do* plan to visit the castle to ask permission for the apples. But I'm no friend of his. I'm here for Miss Stuart."

Something in his face or tone must have betrayed him. A knowing look lit up the woman's face. "You're sweet on her, arnna you? I canna blame you. Janie's a bonny lass." She turned to the men sitting nearby and said something in Gaelic, motioning for them to join the table. Percy thought he heard the word *Janie* in between the foreign words.

Whatever she said elicited a similar change in them. The men's scowls were replaced by curious grins, and they strode over to Percy's table, drawing up chairs. "Na, but that beats the whole world allthegither. Do you know Cameron, too? How do they do? Where're they livin'?"

Two hours later, Percy had still not found sleep. He remained in the bar room of the Rook & Rabbit surrounded by a small crowd of village folk, his fifth wee dram of whisky in hand, his head swimming from the combination of alcohol and fatigue. Word had spread quickly that a friend of the Stuart siblings had arrived at the inn, and it seemed the entire village had come out to learn the particulars of Jane and Cameron's situation.

The two men who'd glared at him were indeed farmers, one of whose daughter, Ainsley, was a friend of Jane's. They'd taken their lessons together in a school set up at the castle by Jane and Cameron's mother. Ainsley's father went to fetch his daughter. When she arrived, she pushed her way up to the table, then shyly asked after Jane. Ainsley was to be married in the fall, she told Percy, to Todd Fraser. Could he give Janie the news?

The blacksmith, a burly white-haired man called Mr. Birnie, told a guffaw-filled story about the time a young Cameron asked him to forge a set of iron wheels, which the lad intended to strap to a dog that was born with only two legs. He'd done as the young man asked—*The wee lad was so solemn. I couldna say nay*—but to everyone's amazement, the dog had no use for the wheels. He learned to walk on two legs, and had been attached to Cameron for the rest of his short life.

Between remembrances, the villagers bombarded Percy with questions—many of which he had no idea the answer to—in their almost incomprehensible brogue.

Do Cameron's lungs still give him trouble? Percy had no idea Cameron had anything wrong with his lungs. Does Janie have trees to tend to in town? No, she does not. Are the bairns well taken care of? Well fed? Yes, he believed so. Are you plannin' to woo our Janie with the apples? Yes. He hoped to show her just how much she mattered to him. What a fool he'd been not to propose till now.

Perhaps he should not have answered the last so honestly, but after four whiskeys, the truth just slipped out.

Being with these people, *her* people, he understood for the first time just how painful it must have been for Jane and her brother to leave Darnalay, just as they were grieving the loss of their parents. What a lonely and hostile place Glasgow must have seemed after a lifetime spent among these close-knit Highland folk.

He remembered the pain in Jane's eyes the first time he'd met her.

The crowd began to thin as, one by one, the villagers went to seek their beds. The blacksmith was the last to leave, giving Percy a wink and a slap on the shoulder. "Good luck, laddie. 'Tis well known a faint heart never won the fair lady." Then only Percy and the innkeeper remained.

Mrs. MacPhearson sat across from him, legs stretched out before her, whisky in hand. "I remember it like it was yesterday . . . wee Janie comin' through the backdoor for the first time with a basket of apples over her arm, looking so proud. Was just a wee wisp of a thing, but she kept us in apples through the winter, she did." She looked to Percy "You're a lucky man, Mr. Sommerbell, if she settles on you."

She rose from the table and started gathering up dishes. Pushing in chairs. Percy took his cue and stood, handing her his glass. He yawned. *Damnation, he was tired.*

"Thank you, Mrs. MacPhearson. For everything. I only wish Jane and Cameron were here with me. They miss this place."

The woman's expression clouded. "But they must never come back, Mr. Sommerbell." She glanced around, as if afraid of being overheard. "'Tisn't safe. The new laird's accused them of stealin' from him when they left . . . money and such. Though, of course, it was only what belonged to them." She paused, her voice lowering to a whisper. "He's nay a good man, Mr. Sommerbell. He's to burn the tenants out. To make way for sheep."

Percy's stomach clenched. It should come as no surprise that Jane's cousin would do as every other English lord inheriting a Scottish title had done. It was a good business decision, one Father would have approved of—but to think of this place, *these* people, joining the ranks of workers in Glasgow, or starving on the coast. To think of the well-kept cottages he'd passed, this inn, being reduced to ashes . . .

An image of Rose Chisholm clinging to her father in the landau flashed through his mind. Will had been one of the lucky ones, strong enough to travel south—and look where he'd ended up.

Percy pushed the image away. The mills and the injustices he'd inherited from Father were already more than he could bear. He couldn't do anything for these people anyhow. He would simply collect the apples, then he would leave.

"Good night, Mrs. MacPhearson."

Instead of answering, the woman's eyes narrowed. "You love her, dinna you?"

"Yes." He was too tired to lie.

Mrs. MacPhearson nodded, as if he'd passed some kind of test. "Bide a moment, laddie. I have somethin' for you." She turned and disappeared into the kitchen, returning several moments later with a folded piece of paper. A letter. The seal was broken. Intensity sparked from her dark eyes as they met Percy's, and a sense of foreboding overtook him. Whatever this was about, he was not at all sure he was ready to take it on.

"Freya Riley gave this to me, before she left for America. She worked in the castle. A dear friend of Janie and Cameron's mother, God rest her." Mrs. MacPhearson sighed, as if remembering better times. "Freya was cleanin' early one morning in the library, and this was just sittin' there, on top of a pile of opened letters. It must've been delivered after the bairns left."

"She took a letter that was not addressed to her?"

"Michael Dunn had no business with it." *Michael*. That must be the new Earl's given name. Funny he'd not known it till now. "Na. 'Tis addressed to Miss Janie and Master Cameron." The innkeeper raised her brows meaningfully. "And Freya recognized the seal of course. No one knew where the bairns went, so she brought it to me before she left, for safekeeping."

She pressed the letter into his hands, her eyes boring into his. "You must get it to them, Mr. Sommerbell. I've not told a soul. No one. But the laird knows. After Freya took it . . . he looked everywhere, then turned them all out of the castle. Ransacked every house in the village, and the farms too. But he's not found it. I made certain of that." She smiled.

"He turned out . . . the servants? From the castle?"

"Aye. 'Tis just Mrs. Brodie there now. The cook. And the laird's new factor and his men that came with him from London . . . as loyal as dogs, they are. Caitiffs, the lot of them." The disdain in her voice was clear. "Tavish still looks after the horses, and Clyde—Mackinnon—he keeps the gardens in order. But neither of them stays in the castle. They're forbidden to go inside."

"I don't—"

"Just read it. You'll see." She passed Percy a lit candle from the table. "An' take care. 'Twould be better if you didna go to the castle at all. The laird's men—"

"I'll be fine. I can pay whatever he asks."

"You're determined to try. I can see that." She moved closer, leaning in. "Just be careful, Mr. Sommerbell. Michael Dunn isna to be trusted." With that warning, she turned and disappeared into the kitchen.

Alone in the dining room, Percy held the letter close to the candle's flame. The simple elegant script reminded him of Jane's hand, but of course it wasn't. It was addressed to her and Cameron. The postmark was from March of the previous year, sent from Edinburgh. He turned it over to examine the seal, shining red in the candlelight.

A simple spray of roses.

Thinking his eyes were playing tricks on him, he brought the flame closer.

It was identical to the seal on Jane's letters.

He raced up the steps to his room, all traces of fatigue vanished. The siblings had left Darnalay in the spring, late April or May. This letter must have been delayed in the post, not terribly surprising given the remote location. With shaking hands, he unfolded the foolscap and began to read.

Castle Hotel, Edinburgh. 14th March 1819

MY DEAREST CHILDREN

It is quite possible that we will return to you before you receive this letter, but I am filled to the brim with happiness and cannot help but send you word of our news. Your father and I have been married! I would have thought at age four and forty I would be too old to elope, but that is what's come to pass. What I believed to be a shopping excursion was in fact a wedding trip, planned and executed by your dear father. We were married yesterday in a small kirk outside the city, and are now ensconced in luxury at the Castle Hotel. Despite my protests and my excitement to return home to you, your father insists on pampering me a few days yet—and I have promised him I will not complain.

I am a countess, my dear children, and you are legitimate in every way. I never pondered this even as a possibility for us, but due to some particularities of Scottish law, children can, apparently, be claimed as legitimate even if born before a marriage takes place—as long as both parents were not married at the time of birth, which, as it happens, neither I nor your father were. And so, your father intends to claim you, not only in his heart

where you have always been, but in the eyes of the law. I cannot tell you how
happy this makes me, and how dear your father is to me, as are you both.
His reputation will suffer for this marriage I fear, but he insists it is more
than made up for by the love of his family. We depart in four days and
will fly home to you as fast as our carriage will take us. Adieu, my loves! I
will hand the paper now to your father, who wants to pen a few words.

My Dears
Your mother has given you the particulars of our news, leaving me only to
say how pleased I am at finally being able to claim you as my own. I do
not rejoice in the death of my late wife, but it allowed this union to take
place, and I feel for the first time in many years that I am free. My time
in Edinburgh shall be devoted only to the adoration of my new wife, but
directly upon our arrival home, I shall write to London and the Lyon Court
and direct my solicitors to adjust my will as necessary. Cameron, as heir,
there is much for you and I to speak of, and Jane, if you wish it, we shall
immediately begin the preparations for your debut in London next season.
There is much to do, but for now, you must know that I am
         your adoring father, and husband to your beautiful mother.
                                                          ROBERT DUNN

Cold shock pierced Percy's stomach as he watched the foolscap slip from
his grasp and flutter to the planked wooden floor. All thoughts of scion
wood and apples were gone. His interview on the morrow with the Earl
of Banton took on an entirely new purpose.

EIGHTEEN

NEVER HAD A FORTNIGHT lasted so long. Eight days had elapsed since she'd received his letter. Eight never-ending days, seven even longer nights, and still there were six more to wait—if he came at all. Jane lay awake, as she had every night for the last week, looking up at the cracks in the ceiling. The same room, the same bed where he'd—

No. She wouldn't think of it. Thinking of it only made things worse.

She stared into the darkness, watching her thoughts race in familiar, endless circles. Imagining where he was at this moment, what he was doing, what could possibly be keeping him away for an entire fortnight. Probably, this whole thing was a mistake. Probably, he'd gone to London and was indulging in the pleasures he was accustomed to. Probably, he'd realized that he did not, in fact, wish to marry an exiled bastard spinster. It was for the best. She should never have sent that letter in the first place. He was a rogue. A seductive, wickedly handsome rogue with eyes as hot as coals gleaming through smoke . . . She closed her eyes, and there he was, arms outstretched, drawing her to him. Promising passion. Promising purpose. Promising a home. Promising . . .

The insistent, quivering sensation in her core was all too familiar by now, and she knew there would only be one way to find sleep tonight. She sighed with resignation and desire as her hand found her nipple, erect and sensitive under the thin cotton of her shift. She pinched it between her thumb and index finger, savoring the painful pleasure that surged from her breast to her sex. She continued the pressure, squeezing, rolling her hardened nipple, as her other hand pulled up her shift, the soft cotton sliding seductively over her thighs.

Every nerve in her body awakened as sensation coursed through her. She imagined he was here with her, as he had been that morning. She imagined the hands that caressed her were not her own but *his*, sensitive and knowing and warm. Her breath caught as her fingers found her clitoris, the source of her need. Then they found her opening—hot, wet, smooth as silk, inviting exploration. Behind her closed eyelids, she saw only him, eyes locked with hers, lost, together, in their shared passion. His thumb circling her. His fingers delving into her, drawn in deeper, deeper. Her breath rising and falling. Her hips undulating to his rhythm. Faster, deeper still. His eyes dark as ebony, burning with desire, drawing her into himself just as she drew him in . . . Until sensation overtook her. Her body was awash in pleasure, drowning in it, and for that moment, all doubt was gone.

She bit her lip to keep from crying out.

Her body relaxed back onto the bed, limbs heavy, shift bunched up over her waist. She was still in her room. Still alone. Still staring up at that unchanging ceiling. The acute desire was sated, but still, she wanted. Wanted him in the flesh, not just in her mind.

This was madness.

What if he never came? What if he rejected her? What if she did not live up to his fantasies? What if he did not live up to hers?

Six more days. She took a deep breath and finally found sleep.

Nineteen

Percy could scarcely make out the distant edifice of Darnalay Castle as he rode the short way from the village. Fog shrouded the tower and upper levels of the stone structure, reducing the surrounding woods and pastures to an impenetrable curtain of grey light and shadow. There were gardens, he knew, and Jane's orchard, of course, but they were lost to his view.

It was early. Too early for a polite call, but he needed to be back in Inverness by nightfall to collect his belongings and begin the journey south to Glasgow and to Jane. He'd said goodbye to Mrs. MacPhearson when he left the inn. His scant belongings were packed in his saddlebags, and his guitar was, again, strapped to his aching back.

Anyway, this was not a polite call. He would rouse the imposter Earl from his bed if necessary.

Just after he'd left the Rook & Rabbit, a thought had come to him, an overly apprehensive thought perhaps, but one he could not shake. Beyond a kirk register somewhere in Edinburgh, the letter the innkeeper had given him was his only proof of Jane and Cameron's legitimacy.

There was a risk, slight though it may be, that if he took it with him to the castle, it would somehow fall into Michael Dunn's clutches. Giving in to his anxiety, he'd stopped by the stone bridge just outside the village, climbed underneath—making sure to avoid getting his feet wet in the shallow, fast flowing burn—then crammed the letter behind a loose stone. He'd breathed a sigh of relief as he restarted his journey toward the castle. The letter would be safe in its hiding place until he returned to retrieve it in an hour or so.

He rounded a bend, and suddenly, the weathered stone facade loomed above him, ghostly white in the mist. The lowered drawbridge was flanked by rounded bartizans that connected to a high stone wall. The wall must have encircled the entire keep. It stretched away on either side, then disappeared into the fog. The portcullis was up, giving him an unobstructed entrance. All was still and eerily quiet. No groom or footman came to greet him. No dog barked. Even the birds were silent.

A chill shivered through him. Perhaps Mrs. MacPhearson had been right when she'd advised him not to come.

No. Jane and her brother had been through too much already. If there was even a sliver of a chance that Michael Dunn might step down voluntarily, that the siblings could be spared the torment of a drawn-out court case, Percy wanted to try.

He dismounted his gelding, tying the reins to a tree branch. He debated, for a moment, if he should leave his guitar. But there was nowhere safe to put it, so he kept it strapped to his back.

How did one call upon a medieval castle? There was no door to knock upon, only a drawbridge lying flat over a grassy trench that must have once been a moat, but did nothing now to prevent intruders such as himself from invading the keep. Two gnarled old trees sprouted up from the abandoned moat and loomed on either side of the drawbridge, like ghostly sentries in the fog.

In the silence of the mist, all sound was amplified. His boots crunching over the small stones of the drive, thudding with a hollow echo as he crossed over the wooden drawbridge, then dull and muted as he strode onto the weathered stone floor of the castle itself. He passed under the portcullis. The sharp iron bars hung down like bared black teeth. He couldn't help but imagine them dropping suddenly, crushing him underneath.

He stood in a small courtyard. To his left and right, three stone steps led downward through wide archways, mirroring each other, then opening into larger yards. The entire space was barren, no furniture, no decoration of any kind, just ancient grey stone walls and floor open to the sky. Spectral white swirls of fog drifted in from above. Directly in front of him, the tower house rose four imposing stories, crowned by a parapet and bartizans at the corners. Mother would love this place. It could have been the setting to any number of the gothic novels she adored. He wondered if the same sense of foreboding had existed when Jane's father was master here.

"Ho, there!" The abrupt, sonorous shout startled him, even though it came from his own throat. The sound echoed off the thick stone, then receded, and silence fell once again.

Was it possible no one was here?

After several long moments, he heard the sounds of a door opening, then closing. A man appeared through the arch to his left, flanked two other men, large and menacing. *Bodyguards?* The lead man was thin and tall, balding, with a sharp, pinched face. The two behind weren't in uniform, but they walked with an air of authority that left no doubt they were armed. All three were slightly disheveled—hair askew, cravats untied, coats only half buttoned—as if they'd been roused unexpectedly. They did *not* look pleased to be receiving a visitor.

"What's your business?" The lead man's bearing and clipped tone betrayed him as a servant of some standing. The estate manager perhaps, the man Mrs. MacPhearson had referred to as the factor?

"I need to speak with the Earl." Percy held out his card. "It's a matter of the utmost importance."

The man didn't even glance at his outstretched hand. "His Lordship does not entertain visitors."

"And yet, I must see him." Percy met the man's gaze.

The factor took the card gingerly, pursing his lips in distaste. He peered at it, then scoured Percy with a long, searching glare. "Come." He turned and began walking away.

He should not have come. But he had. He was here. With a resigned sigh, Percy followed, being careful not to show any apprehension as the two guards fell in behind him. The factor led them down the right-hand steps and across the courtyard, then through a doorway that led into a wide room that once must have been the great hall but was now set up as a kind of sitting room. The high ceiling was crossed by impossibly large beams. An enormous hearth served as the focal point of one wall. It was taller than Percy, with an elaborately carved stone mantle. Large paintings, portraits mostly, and mounts with antlers decorated the walls. The hall was furnished lavishly, yet it had an air of abandon to it. A thick layer of dust covered the expensive furniture, and a musty, damp odor stuck in Percy's nose. Obviously, this room was not much used. Odd that no one had even bothered to cover the furniture.

The servant stopped and turned toward him. "Wait here." Then he disappeared through a doorway on the far side of the room.

It was not a short wait. The guards took up their station at the door, but Percy did his best to ignore them. He set his guitar down on a settee that stood before the mantle, then sat beside it, staring at the cold hearth. After a time, he grew restless and stood to examine the portraits. Several hundred years of Earls of Banton and their families stared back at him. Each bore some resemblance to Jane and Cameron—a smile here, a nose there. There was one that could have *been* Cameron. The same brown eyes and affable grin, the same red hair, but the style of dress was dated. It looked to be from around the turn of the century, twenty-odd years ago. The man was outdoors, sitting on a rock ledge. Trees framed the picture. Two hunting dogs looked up at him admiringly.

This must be their father as a young man.

Percy's eyes met the mirthful gaze of the late Earl of Banton, and a silent, determined understanding passed between them. He *would* right this wrong. For Jane. For Cameron. For the people of Darnalay.

It shall be done, sir. He projected his thoughts at the man in the painting. *I swear it.*

How he wished he could have met this man, could have asked for his daughter's hand . . . which led his mind to the question that had been hovering at the edge of his consciousness since he'd read the letter. The question he'd pushed away every time it drew too near—once she knew the truth, would she still want him?

The sound of a door closing jolted him back to the present.

"His Lordship will see you now."

Percy followed the factor through a doorway—thankful that the armed men did *not* follow—then up a dark staircase to the second floor. They took a series of turns, then passed through a long corridor. He looked out a window and realized they were crossing into the second story of the tower house. The servant opened a heavy wooden door to reveal a beautifully furnished room, clean and warm, a stark contrast from everything he'd seen of the castle so far. The walls were filled from floor to ceiling with bookshelves. Thick red and gold carpet covered the floor. A large mahogany desk dominated one side of the room. Delicate end tables flanked a damask settee, which was set cozily between two matching chairs in front of a crackling fire. There were windows on three sides of the room framed by gold velvet drapes. A grandfather clock stood sentry next to one of them.

A man sat behind the desk, scribbling at some papers. This was Michael Dunn, the Earl of Banton or, more accurately, Michael Dunn, the usurper.

"Mr. Percival Sommerbell." The servant read his name as if it were the bitterest of poisons.

Dunn gave the servant a curt nod. "Thank you, Bevin. Leave us." The door clicked shut and they were alone.

Silence. They appraised one another, sizing each other up as before a fight. Michael Dunn looked nothing like his cousins, though he was of a similar age. His high cheekbones, hawkish nose and strong chin were framed by curling light blonde hair. Had his expression not been drawn into an intensely hostile glare, he, too, would have been handsome.

The imposter earl's piercing blue eyes met Percy's. "You are here, to steal fruit from my orchard. A gift for the bastard who calls herself my cousin." He spat the words out, every syllable a carefully aimed dagger thrown in Percy's direction.

Percy resisted the urge to round the desk and strike the man, but he would not be baited into anger so easily. "Word travels quickly. You have spies in the village?" He kept his tone exceedingly polite.

Dunn ignored the question. "Go back to where you came from. You do *not* have permission to set foot anywhere on this estate. Good day." He looked back to the desk, dismissing him.

Percy strode closer and positioned himself directly in front of the imposter, so that he could look down on him. "I'm not here to collect fruit. And you are *not* the Earl of Banton." Dunn's eyes widened. He opened his mouth to speak, but Percy wasn't finished. "I'm here to give you an opportunity to step aside, *willingly*. Acknowledge the rightful inheritance of your cousins."

"My cousins? Those basta—"

"If you refuse, I'll take my proof to the courts in Edinburgh." Percy took a breath, then continued more slowly, emphasizing each word. "I am a man of means. I will hire the best barrister in all of Scotland to take the case. I will win."

Dunn seemed stunned, but he quickly recovered. His eyes narrowed. "You have the letter."

"I have in my possession a letter from the late Earl of Banton, and his wife, to their children. Their *legitimate* children."

Michael Dunn stared at Percy for a long moment, then he broke eye contact. His face contorted into what was probably meant to be a reassuring smile. "Give it to me. I'll have my solicitors examine it. If it's deemed authentic, I'll step aside."

"It *is* authentic. And you may examine it. On my terms."

"Which are?"

"We'll send for Cameron Stuart, his sister, and *my* solicitors. Only in their presence will I produce the letter."

"Nonsense. Just give me the letter." Dunn's color was rising. "If it's real, I will step down. *You have my word.*" The cold ice of his stare declared him a liar.

"Step. Aside. Now. I will not ask again."

"*Where is it*?" The imposter stood. He was shouting now. All pretense of civility had evaporated.

Percy pressed his lips together and stared back at the man.

"I don't believe you have it," Dunn challenged.

This was not a game Percy intended to play any longer. "I have my answer. I'll leave you to your business." He raised a brow. "I will warn you, though, if you attempt any evictions before this is settled in court, you *will* pay." He moved toward the door, relieved that he could now, finally, be on his way to Glasgow and Jane. "Good day—"

"Wait."

Percy pivoted, halfway to the door.

"*This* may change your mind." Dunn had sat back down. He beckoned, holding out a piece of paper, the same false smile stretching his lips. Percy was itching to be gone from this place, yet he could not show fear, nor give the impression that he was running away.

He strode back to the desk. "Don't waste my time. I will try this case, and I will wi—"

Time suddenly broke free of its regular confines as the next few seconds stretched and then condensed into flashes of awareness. A loss of balance. The floor giving way beneath his feet. A cry of terror—his own. The light and color of the library disappearing from view.

Falling.

Darkness.

An excruciating pain in his ankle, and the impact of hard stone against his elbow, his back, his head. Then stillness. Dark.

He was lying on his back, gasping for breath, pain ricocheting through his body. Far above, he could see Michael Dunn's blonde head peering down at him through what must have been a trapdoor in the library floor—a fuzzy halo of golden daylight.

"The late Earl was a beetle-headed fool." The man's voice floated down to him, as if in a dream. "But *I* am not. You have two choices, Mr. Sommerbell. You can tell me where that letter is, *or* you can sign your name to a document declaring me the rightful Earl of Banton."

Percy's vision blurred. Two rectangles of light swam in front of him now.

"You will remain here until you've made your choice."

Then a heavy thud and everything was black.

TWENTY

RAIN PELTED THE WINDOWPANE, then trailed downward to pool on the sill. Jane stared dully at her breakfast, the plain oatmeal porridge a perfect representation of her future. Bland, grey, uninspiring. The desolation was so much worse now after the chimera, *Mrs. Jane Sommerbell*, had appeared before her, then vanished.

The fortnight deadline had come and gone. He had decided that freedom trumped marriage and was on his way to the Continent, planning to pass the winter with his Italian courtesan. Or he was in London, pursuing a new attachment. Or maybe he was still in Northumberland and had realized the truth—that marriage to a woman such as her was beneath his station. Whatever the reason, he had not come. Would *never* come. She'd been a fool to believe anything else.

At least Cameron didn't know. She'd put off telling him, and she was glad of it now. Her despondency was bad enough without the added humiliation of his sympathy, or disapproval or her actions.

She shook her head to clear away the errant thoughts. She must get on with it. Finish her breakfast, prepare for today's lesson with Rose, make the best of the life that lay in front of her.

Rose. Her lessons with the girl were the one thing that still brought meaning to Jane's days. A bright spot of color in her otherwise dreary existence. It had taken the lass some time to open up, but once she had, she'd blossomed into a cheerful, winsome girl, full of curiosity and eager to experience the world. Her resilience was a marvelous thing, and Jane was confident Rose would be able to make something of herself.

But Jane herself had no resilience left. No energy for life at all.

"Morning, miss." Cori poked her head into the kitchen, her wet hair plastered to her face. "I brought the post." She pulled a small bundle of letters from the pocket of her cloak and handed them to Jane. "I tried to keep them dry, but 'tis a lashing rain this morning."

Jane flipped through the letters. Most were for Cameron, but there was one addressed to them both. She examined the neat scrawl. The handwriting looked familiar somehow, yet she couldn't place it . . . Yes, she could. It reminded her of the tidy, square hand of Mrs. Brodie, the cook at Darnalay castle. Jane used to sit in the kitchen on days such as this, eating Mrs. Brodie's warm oat cakes with clotted cream and watching her write in the ledger book. This looked just like that, but of course it was not. Mrs. Brodie would have no idea where she and Cam were. They hadn't left an address when they'd left Darnalay—hadn't even told anyone they planned to settle in Glasgow for fear their cousin would try to find them and contest ownership of the money they'd taken. She broke the seal and flattened out the damp paper.

Darnalay Castle. 3rd September 1820

MY DEAR CHILDREN

Forgive me if I skip over the niceties for I have important news and I daren't take long writing it. There's a man came to the village Thursday last, a Mr. Sommerbell. He spent a night at the inn & told the folk there he planned to call on the new Laird. Said he'd be asking to collect apples and scions to bring to you, Janie. In love with you, he is, or so they say in the village. The next morning, Tavish found a horse tied up in front with the man's belongings in the saddlebag, but no sign of the man, nor did he ever come to claim the horse. And since then, the factor's been asking me for a plate of cheese and dry bread twice a day, but he'll give me no reason why or who it's for. It must be Mr. S is still in the castle and the food's for him? The Laird went and searched Mr. S' bags in the stable, but he didn't take anything, just stomped back to the castle all red in the face. But then Tavish looked himself and found some letters—from you, Janie, with your address in Glasgow, so God be praised, we knew where to find you.

There's no saying why the man's been detained here, but we fear that's what's happened & we must do something, but we don't know what. The Laird's got six men as guards & the factor & he's dismissed all the staff save myself, Tavish and Clyde—& those two not even allowed inside the castle walls. He keeps all the rooms locked & he's got all the keys & anyway we don't even know where poor Mr. S is. I fear he's locked in the pit. We thought you might know his family and could send word to them?

Ach, my lovies. How I've missed you! I pray this letter will arrive to you. Tavish's waiting now to take it direct to the post in Inverness. Please send us help if you can.

Your devoted servant

NESSA BRODIE

The clock on the wall ceased ticking. The fire ceased crackling. Jane and everything around her sat frozen, as if the contents of Mrs. Brodie's letter had shocked time itself. He was in Darnalay. Had gone to collect apples. For her. *And was now held captive*? That beautiful man who'd declared his love with no hope of reciprocation. The wildcat whose lithe grace and devilish grin were the very definition of freedom—locked up *in the pit*?

Jane's ancestors had built the pit prison in the base of the tower house in medieval times, to hold their enemies and break them using the torture of darkness and isolation. There was no way in or out, save the trapdoor in the library floor. She'd played down there as a child, with Cam and Tavish and Kendric. The small, dark chamber was, of course, strictly forbidden, but that made it even more appealing to four children in search of adventure. It had been a wonderful place to play, but to be *actually* imprisoned there, with no light, no air . . . Sick dread roiled her stomach.

Time started again suddenly, and she couldn't move quickly enough. There was no time to wonder why her cousin would have done such a thing, or why he'd turned the servants out in favor of armed men. No time to carefully plan the next steps. Jane sprang up from the table and flew to the door, shouting over her shoulder for Cori to cancel Rose's lesson. She had to find Cam. They must depart immediately for Darnalay.

Percy huddled in the small circle of light, slowly chewing the last bite of cheese. He would not swallow until he absolutely had to, for when the last bit of flavor was gone, he would once again be left with nothing but the terrifying contents of his own mind.

The only accounting of time available to him was the arrival of Michael Dunn's men. Twice a day, they opened the trapdoor, leaving two men to guard the entrance while a third descended the stone stairs to deliver a flask of water and a plate of stale bread and cheese. Every other visit included an empty bucket for Percy to relieve himself into. On the second day, they'd brought him a flint, and twice, he'd been left with the butt of a candle. If he'd kept count correctly, which he wasn't entirely sure he had, he'd been imprisoned for six days. Twelve plates of food. Six buckets of his own waste stinking in the corner. The fortnight he'd promised Jane had expired yesterday.

Did she think he'd forsaken her?

Several times, Michael Dunn's blonde head had appeared in the rectangle of light above. He'd repeated his demand—hand over the letter, sign a document declaring his legitimacy, or continue to reside in the dungeon. Each time, Percy had found the strength to say no, but defiance was becoming harder as his sanity slipped away.

At first, he'd been angry, blisteringly so. Then a sense of quiet determination had come over him. He'd been sure he could hold out for weeks, months if needed. He'd always valued time alone with his thoughts—perhaps here, with no distractions, he'd finally be able to think up a solution to the puzzle of his inheritance.

But then the hallucinations started.

They'd begun subtly. Geometric shapes pulsing in the periphery of his vision. A soft humming that seemed to emanate from the walls. Then a crowd of children stood in front of him dressed in rags and staring at him with accusing eyes, blood dripping from their hands. Cotton floated in the air, and it was hot. Too hot to breathe. Then the children screamed in panic. The flames! The flames were spreading. Burning everything. Then they were gone and Father was there, glaring his disapproval then turning his back on his son. Percy had been desperate to see Father's face. To explain everything—his regret, his love—but no matter how he begged and pleaded and cried, Papa would not turn around. Then Father was gone and a pile of rotten fruit appeared. Grapes and pears and figs and lemons oozing and putrid, writhing with maggots. Then a nest of snakes hissing and biting at his feet. A high-pitched scream that came from everywhere at once and would not stop . . .

Each illusion was worse than the last, and Percy blessed Michael Dunn's men for the few moments of light, the grunts and clipped commands, the flavor of dry cheese and stale bread—for they were real.

He'd found that even in his worst moments, when he was diminished to a crying, screaming lunatic ready to give in to Michael Dunn's demands, that if he could force his thoughts back to *her*, to his Jane, and cling to her with all his strength, she would guide him back to himself. He could conjure her with a breath, in through his nose, eyes closed, and there she was. Steady, solid, beautiful, fresh as a wild rose after a storm. She was his anchor. His guiding light, and he knew in those moments that even if she rejected him, even if she refused to ever see him again, even if he rotted in this hell for years, he would not betray her.

But, all too quickly, her image would fade, and he was alone once more.

On the third day, he'd discovered apples, thinly sliced and carefully hidden beneath the food on his plate. The next day, he'd found honey smeared to the underside of the bread. The meal he finished now had contained gooseberries, cleverly embedded in a hunk of cheese. He couldn't be sure of anything in this dark prison—the food could be just another invention of his own mind—but perhaps, *perhaps* it was a small kindness by whomever was preparing it. A rebellion against his captor. He dared not hope, yet could it be that he had a friend in this castle?

Reluctantly, he swallowed the last bite of cheese, then sat for a moment, savoring the echoes of salt and brine on his tongue. When there was nothing left, he rose and began to walk.

His ankle had buckled beneath him when he fell, twisting painfully. At first, he'd not been able to put any weight on it and he'd feared it could be broken, but gradually it had improved and he'd begun walking. Just a few steps at first, then more, until he was circling the room, counting the laps as he went. Ten, fifty, one hundred, two hundred. It still throbbed, but he'd learned to appreciate the pain. If he could focus his mind on the sensations in his ankle and the rise and fall of his breath, he could, for a while at least, avoid the terrors that came with the silence and stillness.

He held the candle in one hand, letting the fingertips of the other trail along the wall, feeling for any loose stones that may portend a possible escape route. Of course there were none. He'd felt every stone in this place, but he pushed himself on because to stop meant giving in to despair.

But then his fingers curled around the edge of a stone, more pronounced than any he remembered. His pulse quickened as he dug his nails into the loose mortar. Abruptly, the stone came away in his hand and a shout of joy escaped his lips. But no. There was only a small opening beyond, not big enough to climb through, nor deep enough to provide an escape.

Worthless.

Then he noticed the box.

He hesitated. This *could* be another illusion. He might open it to find it full of imaginary spiders, or rotting meat, or some other nightmarish thing. Even if it *was* real, who knew what horrors could be found in a place such as this? It was a small box, not large enough to hold a human body. Unless the body was of a child . . .

Hell and the Devil. He really was losing his mind.

Unwilling to let a simple wooden chest get the better of him, he reached for the latch. It felt real enough. Cold metal. Hard wood. He drew in a deep breath and held it as he lifted the lid.

A woolen blanket. A knife. A book of some kind. *A journal?* A charcoal pencil. A flint. A glass lamp. An earthenware jug. He pulled the stopper and sniffed. *Lamp Oil.* Three wooden sticks, sharpened to points. Four pieces of thick fabric. Cloaks. But they were small, as if for children. He choked back a sob as he recognized the last object in the bottom of the chest.

Salvation. Music.

A slender, unassuming wooden flute.

TWENTY-ONE

THEY TOOK THE MAIL coach to Inverness—two days and two nights of grueling travel, stopping only to change horses. Jane closed her eyes for stretches, but between the crush of people, the constant jouncing of the carriage, and the sick dread that had settled in the pit of her stomach, real sleep was impossible. Cameron suggested they stop at an inn for a night, as they had when they'd made the same trip in reverse a year and a half ago, but Jane wouldn't consider it. Her brother might be able to sleep soundly with the knowledge Percy might be imprisoned in the dungeon, but she could not.

She'd told Cam the whole truth, or the relevant parts at least, before they left Glasgow. He'd bristled when she'd recounted Percy's proposition, but softened when he learned of her refusal and her marriage proposal.

"You're a brave lass," he'd said.

"I dinna feel brave."

It was mid-afternoon when they arrived in Inverness. Cameron was insistent now that they stop. They needed rest before confronting what lay before them. Every instinct urged Jane to push on, to keep moving until she knew with certainty that Percy was safe, but the steely look in her brother's eyes made it clear that any argument would be futile. He was resolved, and like it or not, she needed him.

Their limited funds allowed for only one room in a cramped, dirty inn on the outskirts of town. As soon as they were in the door, Cameron found a pillow and stretched out on the floor, not even bothering to take off his boots. Jane fell onto the bed, the last of her resistance crumbling as she pulled the blanket over herself. They were both asleep in a matter of minutes.

She awoke to a soft knock on the door and Cameron's voice.

"Come."

A young girl carried in two covered plates and a bottle of wine and set them on a small table. It was dark outside.

Cameron was sitting by the fire, staring blanky at the flames. Jane suspected if she looked at his pillow, she would find evidence of drool. Her brother had slept soundly.

He nodded to the girl. "Thank you. We'd like a bath brought up as well."

"Very well, sir." She dipped a quick courtesy and was gone.

Jane sat up in bed, shaking off the haze of sleep. They had to make a plan. Had to get to Darnalay.

Her brother was ahead of her. "I'll ride at first light. Try to reason with the Earl. At least get more information." He used the same uncompromising tone Father had taken when giving a directive. There was to be no argument.

So, of course, she argued. "We're both going."

"Janie, that's not—"

"That's what we agreed to."

"We never agreed."

Jane glared at her brother. Now that he said it, she realized he was right. She'd *assumed* they would both go on to Darnalay. But they'd never actually talked of it.

"What if he puts *you* in the pit?" she challenged. "You'll need me. I can defend myself if that's—"

"Defend yourself how? *How?*" He ran a hand through his hair. "If you stay here, you'll be safe."

"I'm a grown woman, Cameron. I don't need your permission. Besides—"

"He's got guards, Jane. Six men, Mrs. Brodie said. If you go and we're both captured . . . then the *three* of us will be locked up, and there'll be no one in the world who'd even know where we were."

She hadn't thought of that.

"If I dinna come back," Cam continued. "You'll need to post a letter to Sommerbell's mother. It'll be up to you to get help."

"But . . . I dinna *want* to be safe. You stay. I'll go and talk to the new Earl. Just because I'm a woman doesna—"

"There's a better chance of me reasoning with him, man to man. Besides, you're clever." A hint of a smile crossed his face. "I'll need you to rescue me if I get myself chained up next to Sommerbell. And it willna be easy."

She sighed. There was reason in his argument. She hated the idea that a man would be more receptive to another man than to a woman, but she knew it was true.

"All right. But I willna wait longer than a day. If you're not back by midnight, I'll post a letter to his mother then ride to Darnalay myself." She rose from the bed. The food smelled good. "Thank you for ordering the bath. It'll be good to be clean."

He snorted. "The bath's for me. Dunn's *sure* to throw me in the pit if I dinna rid myself of the stench. You can have yours in the morning after I leave."

◆

Cameron was gone when Jane awoke the next morning. Riding hard, he would be in Darnalay by noon, then back to Inverness for a late supper. She ate, had her bath, then started pacing. The small room could not contain her restlessness, so she walked the streets of Inverness, carefully avoiding the shops she'd frequented with Mama—the modiste, the milliner's, the bookshop, the cafe. The memories were too sweet, and too painful. Especially today.

Afternoon sunlight slanted through the window when she arrived back at the inn, illuminating the dust motes and forming them into columns of floating golden light. For a moment, she was back in the enchanted tower, and she could see him standing before her, reaching for her hand— But no. He wasn't here. He didn't see the sunlight, or feel its warmth. He was alone, at the mercy of her cousin. In the pit.

Suddenly, and without warning, it all came rushing at her—the pain, the guilt, the fear. She'd managed to avoid it by pushing herself into unceasing forward momentum, but now, in this silent room, all by herself, she could no longer hide. Every minute he was down there was a stabbing pain to her heart.

The sobs came, soft at first, then loud and angry. She cried for the horror of whatever her cousin had done, for the anguish Percy must be feeling right now, for her foolishness in not simply accepting his suit at the very beginning.

He did not deserve this. It was her fault. *Everything* was her fault.

When she had no more tears to shed, she rose and ordered tea, and coal for a fire. Crying had not made anything better, not really, but the restlessness was gone. There was nothing to be done now anyway, not until Cameron got back. She got out her book. It was the same one Cynthia had been reading the day Percy first arrived in Glasgow—a travelogue of Italy. Cynthia had lent it to her, but Jane had put off reading it, afraid it would remind her of him. On a whim, she'd tucked it into her valise on the way out of the house on Balmanno Street. She was so engrossed in the book she didn't notice the door behind her opening and softly closing.

"Janie." Her brother sounded tired. He sank into a chair and started pulling off his boots.

She dropped the book. "You're back soon. What happened? Did you see the Earl?"

"Aye."

"And . . . ?"

"And nothing. He received me in the great room, under guard. I asked him if Sommerbell was in the castle. He said no. Said he'd never heard of him. Then he left. The entire interview lasted two minutes."

"You think Mrs. Brodie was wrong?"

"No. Sommerbell's there all right." Cameron rested his head on the back of the chair, closing his eyes and letting out a long, weary sigh. "Tav met me on my way out. He didna want to be seen talking to me, so he waited in the woods. He said Sommerbell's horse is still there. Dunn's posted guards at all hours . . . and he took Tav's hunting rifle. Mr. Mackinnon's, too. He doesna trust them." He lifted his head to meet her eyes. "And his guitar. I saw it. 'Twas in the great room on one of the sofas. The blue one by the hearth."

"You're sure that's what it was?"

"Aye." Cameron shook his head as if attempting to rid himself of the memory. "Ach, it was bleak, Janie. Everything was dirty. The gardens overgrown. It was home, but it . . . it wasna." He ran a hand through his hair. "You'll have your way anyway. We're to ride tomorrow to Mr. Mackinnon's. We'll stay there. Tav'll meet us. And Mrs. Brodie. We'll find a way to get him out."

Mr. Mackinnon. Jane's chest tightened. "Surely we can stay at the Rook & Rabbit? Mr. Mackinnon's is so small . . ." Of course she'd never admit it to her brother, but just hearing the name of Kendric's father, let alone the idea of staying with him while plotting to save Percy, was unsettling. Then another thought occurred to her. *Perhaps Mr. Mackinnon already knew of her betrayal.* Perhaps he'd read her letters. Certainly, Tavish had read at least one. Same with Mrs. Brodie.

"The Earl has eyes in the village. Tav said most of the folk hate him, but some are willing to take his money." Cameron let his head fall back against the chair, closing his eyes again as he talked. "We're to go through the woods so we're not seen. We've a better chance if he doesna know we're there."

She'd known Tavish as long as she could remember. His father had been the stable master before him, and along with Kendric, Tav had been their constant playmate when they were children. She trusted him.

"What's he like?"

Cameron looked up. "Tav? Same as always, but more . . . worried."

"Not Tavish. Michael Dunn. Our cousin. What's he like?"

Cameron shrugged. "I only saw him for a minute. He hates us, I think. I dinna know why. We're no threat to him." Her brother stared into the fire, eyes dull and haunted, his voice suddenly cold. Detached. "He plans to burn the tenants out, Janie . . . Tav said it's just a matter of time.

There's already been men out surveying the land, marking off the new parcels for the shepherds."

Her stomach churned. *Why hadn't she thought of this before?* Of course, her cousin would want to make as much money as he could. Father had been an oddity amongst his peers. He'd considered his responsibility to his tenants to be a sacred duty, and the Banton estate had been an oasis, one of the only large landholdings in the Highlands to avoid the *improvements* that had brought devastation to so many. It was unimaginable that the people of Darnalay—Ainsley and her father, Widow Grant and her five bairns, Old Man Fraser who relied on his neighbors for almost everything and could remember back to the days of Jane's great-grandfather—were all living in fear, waiting for the day their homes would be burned.

"Surely, there's some way to stop it. Father would never have allow—"

"Father's *dead,* Janie. It's the new Earl's land now. He can do whatever he wants with it." Here was the bitterness and anger that lay beneath her brother's carefree facade. Under it all, Cameron was still the little brother she'd always known, needing love, needing assurance.

She touched his arm. "This isna easy. Thank you."

For a long moment, neither of them spoke.

"You love him, dinna you?" Cameron asked.

Did she? Loving Percy Sommerbell was the ultimate betrayal of Kendric. It would mean a lifetime of guilt. But she could no longer deny the truth. Not to herself. Not to her brother.

"I wanted to marry him because I hoped to be of help, with the mills. I could be useful." She spoke slowly. "But, yes. I do love him." The admission slipped out. A whisper. A weight of stone around her neck.

"Cam?"

"Aye?"

"Dinna tell anyone."

"I won't." Cameron met her eyes. "But . . . 'Tis nothing to be ashamed of, Janie. You of all people deserve love." He paused, then added softly, "Ken would agree with me, you know, if he were here."

She nodded, blinking back the tears. But she said nothing, just busied herself with packing their things and preparing for their departure in the morning.

TWENTY-TWO

"Good evening, Mr. Sommerbell." Michael Dunn's voice came from above, piercing the quiet.

Percy ignored him. It was easier that way.

"You had a visitor." The imposter earl was undaunted by the silence. "Cameron Stuart came to see you." *Cameron was here?* "Nothing to worry about. He won't be back."

"*Jane*?" Her name came out as a whimper. Percy had long ago given up his facade of bravery.

"Jane . . .?" Dunn feigned ignorance. "Oh, yes, the sister. The one you're in love with." He paused, allowing time for hope. "He didn't mention her."

Percy growled up at his captor. He was more animal than human now.

Dunn chuckled. "You *could* go to her, you know. 'Twould be quite simple . . ."

Percy said nothing. If he opened his mouth, it would be to confess the location of the letter.

His captor waited a few moments, then sighed. "Have it your way." The trapdoor shut with a familiar thud.

Percy lay back on the straw pallet, closing his eyes. It was dark either way, but he'd learned the blackness behind his own eyelids was infinitely safer than the black of the dungeon.

Had Cameron really come, or was it just some trick to get him to capitulate? He'd probably never know. Better not to think of it.

Had it not been for the chest of treasures he'd uncovered—*when? He couldn't be sure . . . sometime in the past*—he'd surely have told Michael Dunn where the letter was by now. The box must have been left behind by Jane and Cameron and their band of playmates. The journal entries were dated 1808 and '09 and were written in four distinct hands, all childlike, one that looked very much like Jane's. There were treasure maps, poems, drawings of animals and plants, a fantastical story of dragons and knights. They'd *played* down here.

The twenty or so blank journal pages were responsible for the little bit of sanity that remained to him. For hours—*days?*—he'd focused all his attention on creation and filled the little book with musical compositions. Hymns to sunlight, to Jane's eyes, to the cause of justice. The Irish flute and his voice gave him melody, the drumming of sticks against the wooden box was his percussion. But he'd used up all the pages now. The jug of lamp oil was nearly empty. And the hallucinations were back, worse than before.

Father had returned, but this time, he'd been a rotting corpse risen from the grave, moaning, dripping and putrid. Reaching out, as if to attack his son. Later, Percy's guitar had appeared, floating before him. Percy had been overjoyed to see it, had reached for it, but the moment he grasped it, it morphed into a snake that wrapped itself around his throat, hissing and strangling him for air. He'd been sure it would kill him. Sure it was real . . .

But even worse than any of that—it was becoming harder to conjure her. His Jane. His love. Even *she* was slipping away. Surely, she hated him by now. And who would blame her? He'd written two ridiculous sentences, promised to come to her, then disappeared. Even if he did somehow manage to prove her inheritance, why would she *want* him? She'd be Lady Jane Dunn, sister to the Earl of Banton. She'd have no cause to settle for the likes of Percy Sommerbell, the industrialist. Hell, even *he* despised Percy Sommerbell the industrialist.

Was she even real? He could no longer be certain. Mayhap it was just a dream he'd had.

Of course she was real. Why else would he be here, locked in this dark hole?

He thought of Mother, still grieving her husband. Was she now to grieve the loss of her son as well? For even if he returned to her sound of body, what good would he be if he'd lost his mind?

What was Cameron's inheritance worth to him anyhow, or some peasant farmers' lands?

Did he really want to give Jane the means to rid herself of him?

A humming began, just inside his head. *No. Not again.* He closed his eyes, forcing a breath and searching desperately for Jane's image, but she wasn't there. The noise was louder. Nothing he did could stop it, and now it was a shriek, ripping through his thoughts, taking over his consciousness. He clawed at his hair. Pulling. Desperate to be rid of the awful sound.

Then, suddenly, it was gone, leaving only the sound of Percy's ragged breathing echoing through the silence.

TWENTY-THREE

JANE WOKE TO THE smell of wood smoke. It reminded her of home. Then she opened her eyes and remembered. She *was* home. She was in Mr. Mackinnon's cottage, wrapped snugly in a thick tartan in Mr. Mackinnon's own bed. The groundskeeper had insisted she sleep here, claiming he'd be content to bed down in the loft with Cameron. She'd argued that she'd be perfectly fine on a straw pallet next to her brother, but the old man wouldn't hear of it.

In the end, she was grateful for the bed. She'd slept incredibly deeply, and she felt more refreshed than she had in days, months perhaps. A part of her felt guilty for it. Percy certainly didn't have a feather bed. Could he sleep at all, down there in the dark? *What must it be like?* She shut her eyes, took a breath. In truth, being rested was a good thing. She'd need all her wits about her today.

She started to rise, then sank back down again when her upper legs and buttocks screamed with pain. She hadn't once been on a horse since leaving Darnalay, and yesterday's journey had taken its toll. They'd arrived in the afternoon, diverting from the main road well before they reached the village so as not to be seen. Mr. Mackinnon hadn't been home—he'd been working near the castle and didn't want to attract suspicion by leaving earlier than usual—but he'd come in time to prepare a rabbit stew for their supper. Tavish and Mrs. Brodie arrived after dark, slipping silently in from the woods, then the five of them had sat around Mr. Mackinnon's table until nearly midnight, concocting the plan that was to unfold today.

It would work. It *had* to. Percy would be freed. They would put all this behind them and, if he still wanted her, they would marry. But she couldn't stop thinking of the tenants, the villagers, the people her father had held so dear, whose welfare he'd seen as his greatest responsibility. Was freeing Percy enough?

No. It wasn't. But even still, Cameron was right. There was nothing else they *could* do. Their cousin was laird now. The fate of Darnalay was in his hands.

She shut her eyes, recalling the faces around the table last evening, illuminated by the dim glow of rush lights. She'd known the cook, the groundskeeper, and the stable master for as long as she could remember. They'd been as close as family, and though it was good to see them again, there was little comfort in it. Everything had changed. There was a desperation in their eyes that had never existed before. Perchance they saw the same in hers.

Her thoughts drifted to Percy. Eleven days he'd been alone in the pit. And for what? Why was her cousin holding him? Did his wickedness go so far that he'd detain an innocent man just for the crime of loving her? Was it retaliation for the money they'd taken? Or was there something else . . .? Anyway, Percy likely wanted nothing to do with her now, if he ever really had. As soon as he was free, he'd retreat to his secure life in England and his aversion to marriage. How could she blame him?

She rose, painfully, then dressed and combed out her hair, tucking it into a tidy bun. No need to look anything other than plain for the role she'd be playing today.

The front door was open, allowing a shaft of sunlight into the dark, windowless room. Mr. Mackinnon sat just outside the door, mending a shirt. A kettle hissed on the fire. Though pleasant, the scene of quiet domesticity seemed all wrong. Ken had been so boisterous, constantly in motion, constantly making noise. She could imagine him even now, swaggering through the front door, whistling a tune, that golden smile bright on his face . . . Was Ken's father used to the silence by now?

Jane had been just a wee thing, no more than three years old, when Mr. Mackinnon had first noticed her interest in plants. He'd shown her how to watch them and how to discern what they needed. Later, he'd taught her how to prune the trees in the orchard, to fertilize them and thin the immature fruit so the remaining apples and pears grew to their full potential. She'd looked up to him, seen him as a mentor. Then, when Ken died, the bond between them deepened. She and Mr. Mackinnon were the two people in the world who'd loved Ken the most, the only ones who'd been able to understand the depths of one another's grief.

How could she face him if he knew she'd betrayed his son?

Did he know already?

She would simply have to avoid the subject.

She poked her head out into the sunshine. Mr. Mackinnon looked up, warming her with that same golden smile. "There you are, lassie. I was just thinking of waking you. 'Tis half nine."

She'd agreed to meet Mrs. Brodie at half ten.

"I slept so soundly. Better than I ever did in the city." Jane breathed in the familiar outdoor smells of damp earth and rotting leaves. "It must be the quiet."

"This is your home. You always sleep better at home."

Soon, it would no longer be his home, or Tavish's, or Ainsley's . . .

Mr. Mackinnon rose and passed into the house. "Let's get you somethin' to eat."

She forced herself to sit, ignoring the screams of protest from her aching legs and backside. She couldn't afford pain today. If Mr. Mackinnon noticed her wince, he didn't let on. He set a bowl of porridge in front of her, oats with yellow butter and a thick drizzle of honey, *wildflower honey*, fruity and rich. It tasted of Darnalay itself.

She blinked back tears. Mr. Mackinnon poured tea.

"Where's Cameron?" she asked.

"Off to the stables with Tav. Said he wanted to be sure everything's ready for tonight." Mr. Mackinnon's lips twisted into a small, knowing grin.

Cameron and Tavish had been born only six months apart. Tav's mother had died in childbirth, so Jane's mother cared for the baby while his father was busy in the stables. The boys had grown up as close as brothers, and though he never talked of it, Jane knew that Cam missed his friend dearly. They were probably happily hidden away in a dark corner of the loft, regaling each other with tales of their lives in the last year and a half.

She sighed. "As long as they're not seen."

"Those two? They're sneaky as thieves. Pulled the wool over your father's eyes often enough, didna they?"

"Aye. I just worry is all."

There was a comfortable silence. Mr. Mackinnon sipped his tea. Jane ate her porridge. A thrush sang just outside the open door. Then, casually, in the same tone he'd use to ask if a tree she'd grafted was taking, or when she thought a crop would come ripe, Mr. Mackinnon said, "Tell me about your Mr. Sommerbell."

The honey sweetened oats turned to paste in her mouth.

"He's . . . the nephew of a friend. Cynthia. In Glasgow."

"Do you care for him?"

She dared not look up. Instead, she kept her eyes focused on the bowl in front of her. *Not now.* She wasn't ready, would never be ready for this conversation.

"You've read the letters?" she asked weakly.

"Nae. Tav read enough to know that Sommerbell's a friend of yours and Cameron's. But to come all this way, just to get apples and scions for you. And for you to be here, set on rescuing him. It leads this old man to wonder . . ."

The silence stretched. The thrush's song was anxious now, grating. She searched frantically for the right words, then realized—there *were* no right words. Only the truth.

She stared at her porridge. "I dinna *want* to love him. I tried not to. It's just . . . I was so desperately alone, and then he came and, it was as if . . . as if I was living in a shadow and all of a sudden the sun came out." Tears stung her eyes. It took all her energy to raise them and meet Mr. Mackinnon's gaze. "I loved Ken. *So much.* I still do—" She broke off, unable to continue.

"It's all right, Janie." A tender smile played on his lips. His eyes crinkled at the corners.

How did he not understand what she'd done?

"But it's *not.* I've betrayed your son, Mr. Mackinnon. He *died.* And I *lived.* I dinna deserve to, any more than he deserved to die. And what if . . . what if I forget him? What if I'm too happy and I . . . I forget . . .?" She was crying in earnest now.

The groundskeeper rose and came to crouch beside her, wrapping her in his arms. The scent of woodsmoke, leather, and clean air was so familiar, so dear.

"There, lassie. You willna forget. Ken's *in* you, just as he's in me, right next to his dear mam." He drew back, looking her in the eye. "Do you really think he'd want you to be miserable the rest of your life? Think on it. If it'd been the other way 'round, what would you have wanted for him?"

If she'd died and Kendric lived . . . She would want to be mourned, remembered, of course, but she would want him to be happy. The thought resonated through her like the reverberations of a great bell.

She would want him to be happy.

"I'm glad you've found love, Janie. You deserve it."

His words, so similar to what Cameron had said when she'd finally admitted her love for Percy . . . She'd disregarded her brother, assumed he was just trying to lift her spirits, but what if . . . *What if they were right?*

Mr. Mackinnon kissed her forehead, then rose and strode toward the door, lifting his coat from its hook. His shirt was wet with her tears.

"Your shirt. It's soaked through. I'm sorry—"

"Shirts dry, lass. Finish up now. Nessa'll be expecting you." He shrugged into his coat and flashed her one last golden Mackinnon smile. "Good luck, Janie. God be with you." And he was gone.

He didn't say goodbye. It would have been too painful, for they both knew they would never meet again.

It was a half mile from the groundskeeper's cottage to the castle. The trail ambled through woods, wound around the edge of a meadow purple with heather, then dipped back into the cool shadows of the forest before following Darnalay Burn to where it flowed behind the castle. Jane walked slowly, the conversation with Mr. Mackinnon still echoing through her.

There was a spot, right as the trail came upon the burn, where the bank smoothed out and formed a muddy little beach. Jane and Ken used to come here when they were small. They'd put twig and leaf boats in the water, then run as fast as they could back to the castle to watch their little crafts bobbing down the current. It was never a race. They'd cheer both boats equally as they dodged rocks and evaded the eddies.

Ach, how she'd loved that boy. How he'd loved her.

She stopped, staring at the wee stretch of mud, and in her mind's eye, Ken appeared. Not as a boy, but the man he'd grown to be. Her lover. Her best friend.

He was standing with his back to her, then suddenly, he turned. She braced herself, preparing for his angry accusation, but it never came. Instead, his lips quirked into a small smile as he gazed at her with those beloved hazel eyes.

He didn't speak. He didn't need to. It was all there in his eyes—acceptance, and peace, and deep, undying love—love that she needn't ever fear the loss of because now, finally, she understood. Ken was inside her, as Mr. Mackinnon had said. He was part of her. Her joy was his. Her happiness, her love . . . they were his, as well as hers. And there was no guilt, or shame, in loving another because it was through her love, her happiness, that he would find peace.

His smile grew into a wide grin, as if confirming her thoughts. Then he turned away to look out over the burn, and was gone.

Tears streamed down her face. She was free.

TWENTY-FOUR

"THE MEN FINISHED MARKING the last of the new plots yesterday."
Bevin stood at attention in front of Michael Dunn's desk, his hands
clasped behind his back as he made his daily report.

"The new tenants?" Michael asked.

"No reports. Assuming they adhere to the timeline we gave, they'll be
leaving Dumfries within the month and arriving here before the snow
falls."

Bevin had grown up in the borderlands and had contracted with four
shepherds of his acquaintance to take over the new leases. One hundred
and seven inefficient and unprofitable tenant farms turned into five
lucrative sheep operations—four for the new lowland tenants, the fifth
and largest for Bevin himself.

"Very good." Michael nodded.

Bevin hesitated. "My lord, about the man in the dungeon . . ."

Michael raised a brow, "Yes?" He kept his face carefully blank.

"We need a plan." Bevin's words cut through his thoughts.

"A plan."

The factor nodded. "What will we do if he doesn't yield?"

Michael swallowed down the traitorous guilt that rose like bile every time he thought of the man in the pit. His face, pale and drawn in the darkness, the screams that filtered up through the library floor . . . He'd assumed the man would relent after a matter of hours, but his captive's resolve hadn't wavered in eleven days. There was no doubt Mr. Sommerbell knew where the letter was—he'd said as much the day he arrived—and so, though the situation was less than pleasant, as long as he refused to capitulate, Michael could not let him go free.

"There *is* no other plan." Michael sent Bevin a look that made it clear he would accept no argument. "We will simply have to *ensure* he yields." *Hopefully before he's driven entirely mad.*

"Yes, my lord." Bevin nodded. He didn't ask exactly what Michael meant him to do. It was better that way. Michael trusted his factor, but he prefered not to know what lengths the man would go to to secure Mr. Sommerbell's cooperation.

Bevin turned to leave, then stopped short. "I nearly forgot. The cook has asked for an audience."

"The cook?"

"Yes. A girl, her niece, I believe, arrived this morning. Mrs. Brodie has asked that she stay on as an assistant."

"I see." Michael allowed a trickle of annoyance into his tone. "I want no more servants in the castle than absolutely necessary. You know this."

"Yes, my lord. I told her as much, but she insists on speaking to you herself."

Michael sighed. Sometimes being a laird was a wearisome business. "Very well. Send her up, but she must be brief."

"Very good, my lord." Bevin bowed and left the room, closing the door behind him.

Michael sat back in his chair, steepling his fingers. Why the cook needed a bloody assistant was beyond him. It wasn't as if she would be here much longer. He hadn't given them notice, but he had no doubt the cook, and the tenants too, knew what was coming. Michael himself had planned to be gone from this desolate wasteland months ago. He'd only come to inspect the property and ensure his uncle's bastards vacated the place before setting Bevin and his men to the messy task of evicting the tenants. But then the letter had turned up, and disappeared, and he'd been forced to stay, to dig it out, wherever it might be.

Suddenly restless, he rose and strode to the window, surveying the empty courtyard below, the endless forest beyond. How he longed for his return to London and to civilized life. No longer would he be the easily overlooked Mr. Dunn, son of a second son, forced to live on the charity of the uncle he despised—the uncle who'd mismanaged the family estate and put fidelity to his mistress and bastard children above responsibility to his lawful wife and rightful heir.

As a child, Michael and his parents had frequented the Banton townhouse in London, but only to call on Lady Elinore. The Earl himself was nearly always absent, ensconced in this Scottish hellhole with his harlot, while his countess withered, and finally died alone, in London. They'd never spoken of it directly, but he'd caught the glances and innuendos that passed between his parents and his aunt. He'd noticed the flashes of pain on Aunt Elinore's face at the mention of her husband. His mother's looks of pity. Engaging a mistress was one thing—Michael himself intended to employ such a woman upon his return to London—but his uncle had taken things entirely too far. A mistress was to be kept on the periphery of a man's life, to shield his spouse from his baser needs, but Robert Dunn had married his countess only to abandon her, and the ton had taken notice. Elinore had been humiliated.

The few times Michael had met his uncle, he'd found the man distracted and distant, unwilling to be bothered by the boy who would one day inherit his Earldom. He'd never even invited Michael to Darnalay to view the land that would one day be his. This estate that had been allowed to lag behind all the rest in its archaic notions of land management. Darnalay under his uncle's rule had been the laughing stock of Scottish landholdings. Robert Dunn himself had been a disgrace. A worthy politician perhaps, but otherwise a stain on the family name. And the man's last act—to marry his whore in a mad attempt to usurp his rightful heir—only proved the point. It was up to Michael to avenge the wrongs done to his aunt, to bring the family estate into the modern age. He'd be damned if he let a paltry letter, or his bastard cousin, or the man languishing in his dungeon get in the way.

Soon, he would leave this place in Bevin's capable hands. He'd build his factor a new, modern house, befitting the manager of a great estate. The castle—this antiquated stronghold that had, for far too long, sheltered his treacherous uncle's by-blows—would be left to crumble. A picturesque ruin . . . just as soon as the matter of the letter was cleared up. And until then, Michael and his men would need to eat, which meant he needed a cook, and apparently the cook needed an assistant.

Bloody nuisance is what it was.

A knock sounded at the door.

"Come," Michael barked, not bothering to keep the aggravation out of his voice.

The cook, he couldn't remember her name, came into the room, a younger woman who must be the niece in tow. Michael kept his place by the window, watching as the old woman bobbed a curtsey then proceeded to put on a show, complaining at length of the pain in her back.

Her *poor* sister had passed on, leaving her niece with nowhere to go, and couldn't he *please* take her on as a kitchen maid to help her auntie?

The niece, Jaimee, cowered behind her aunt, eyes lowered, face pale. But every so often, she peeked up at him through her thick lashes . . . *Trying to tell him something?* She *was* pretty, in an innocent, Scottish kind of way . . .

The old woman was still talking. "Please, my lord. She'll be no trouble at all. You'll not even know sh—"

"Look at me, girl."

Jaimee lifted her eyes and met his gaze. Full lips, nice-sized bosom. But what was that behind her eyes? Something fierce, and heated. *An invitation?*

Michael was out of practice at reading the female sex—he hadn't had a woman since he'd left London. It was quite possible he was misinterpreting the girl's stare. But did it matter? If there was even a chance this chit would be willing to make his last month in this detestable castle more enjoyable . . .

"She may stay," he declared. "She'll have room and board, but any payment will come out of your wages." He gave the cook a severe look.

The two women exchanged glances. The older one nodded.

"Thank you, laird." They both curtsied, then turned to leave.

Michael watched Jaime's enticing backside as she walked away. Tonight. He would go to her tonight.

TWENTY-FIVE

JANE LAY ON THE narrow bed in the small bedroom in the servant's quarters. Her stomach was churning. Excitement? Fear? Whatever it was, it was threatening to cast up the few bites of dinner she'd managed to choke down.

The majority of her day had been spent in the kitchen with Mrs. Brodie. The cook's back truly did ache, and though Jane's mind had been clouded by thoughts of Percy, she was glad to relieve the old woman of her most taxing chores, even if it was for only one day. She'd heated water, lugged firewood, scrubbed pots and performed a myriad of other chores. Amazing how much work was required to sustain so few men.

Just before dinner, Mrs. Brodie sent Jane out to harvest whatever early apples she could find. The windows of the servants' hall—where the Earl's six burly guards had been ensconced all afternoon, drinking and playing cards—overlooked the orchard. Jane felt their eyes on her as she picked the fruit, and she didn't dare cross to the far side to see how her stand of small saplings had fared the last year and a half. It didn't matter. She had more important things in front of her today.

She'd returned to the kitchen with a basket of green apples for a tart, along with one beautifully ripe Swan's Egg pear. Mrs. Brodie cut the pear into impossibly thin slices, laid them out on a plate, then carefully concealed them under a rind of cheese and several pieces of stale bread. One of the Earl's men came and took it away, along with a flask of water. As she watched him go, it felt to Jane as if her heart was on that plate, hidden away with the slices of pear.

She closed her eyes, willing her pulse to slow, her stomach to settle. Mrs. Brodie had left an hour ago. The cook's complicity would be obvious in the morning, so she'd decided to leave. She'd packed as many of her belongings as she could carry, then quietly slipped out into the night. Jane had embraced her old friend, then watched her mount and ride away. Mrs. Brodie would go to her sister, who was very much alive, where she would wait for word that Percy was safe. Jane had promised the cook he'd finance her passage to America in thanks for her part in the rescue. She prayed her promise would be fulfilled.

Of course he would pay. Providing she was successful in freeing him.

On the way back to her chamber, she had made a quick detour into the housekeeper's room. She'd opened the top left drawer of the sideboard, carefully lifted out the false bottom and almost cried with relief at the sight of the metal ring with its profusion of keys, the extra set Mama had kept hidden away for emergencies.

It was after midnight now. Everything was silent. It was time.

She rose from the bed, undressed, then donned the clothing Mr. Mackinnon had given her the night before. The linen shirt, black wool trousers and coat had been Kendric's. Last night, the thought of wearing Ken's clothes had seemed unbearable, but now his nearness was reassuring, as if he were here, lending her strength. She tied on her own sturdy half-boots then took a deep, steadying breath. She was ready.

She crossed the room with sure, steady steps, pulled the bedroom door open—and found herself looking at dark blue stripes in silk. A banyan that clothed a—*oh sweet heaven*. She tilted her head up and confirmed that the man standing before her was, in fact, her cousin. Lord Banton. He smelled of whiskey.

"Where are you going." It wasn't so much a question as a command. Ordering her back. She retreated. He followed.

She withdrew to the far side of the room, desperately grasping for some plausible reason why she might be exiting her bedchamber in the dead of night, clad in men's clothing, and— *What was he doing here? Did he know who she was?*

"I beg your pardon, my lord," she mumbled. "I couldna sleep. I . . . I thought to explore the castle."

"Come now, Jaimee. I'm not naive as all that." He smiled at her knowingly.

He *knew*. She'd soon be in the dungeon beside Percy.

"I *thought* you might be a naughty wench." Her cousin's smile grew. "Only one day here, and already you're tupping the locals. Who is it? The stable master? Some boy from the village?"

He *didn't* know—but the heated glint in his eyes left no doubt the true reason for his midnight visit. Her breath froze. *This couldn't be happening.*

"There's no need to leave." He paced slowly toward her. "Everything you need's right here, lass." His hand went to his falls, stroking himself through the woolen fabric.

She backed away. "Heavens, my lord. I never . . . I just wanted to see the castle. Truly." The words may be lies, but they were laced with honest panic.

Her cousin stopped his advance. "There's no need to lie, lass. We could have fun, you and I." He cocked his head to one side and lifted his brows. "There's coin in it for you, if you like."

Jane stared at him, eyes wide. She couldn't talk. Couldn't even breathe.

"I'm a generous lover, Jaimee. You wouldn't regret it."

Another long silence, then slowly, with as much certitude as she could manage, she shook her head. *No.*

"You're sure?"

She nodded. *Yes.*

The Earl's face fell.

Relief flooded her. Her cousin might be a villain, but at least he wasn't base enough to force himself on a servant girl. She couldn't just let him leave, though. Cameron and Tav were already waiting outside. The man was foxed. It might be hours before he retired, and what if he never did? What if he returned to press his suit? She couldn't afford to lose that much time.

"I apologize." The Earl's face flushed. He turned and started toward the door. "I—"

"Wait." The word stopped him, but she had no idea what she'd say next. "I . . . I wonder if *you* might show me the castle."

"Tonight?" He turned around slowly, hope sparking in his eyes.

"Aye." Jane moved her gaze to the floor, then looked up at him through lowered lashes. At the same time, she slipped her hand in her coat pocket, wrapping her fingers around the keys.

"Of course." Her cousin walked back to where she stood and offered his arm. She smiled, a saucy, innocent smile, but instead of looping her arm through his, she raised both her hands to his chest. For a second, his grin broadened—he thought she was going to embrace him—then she pushed, hard. The Earl lost his balance and fell backward onto the bed. Before he could even hit the counterpane, Jane was through the still-open door, slamming it behind her. She frantically searched through the keys. *Where is it?* There. The small silver one that worked on all the servants' rooms. It turned easily in the lock. At the same moment, a heavy pounding sounded on the other side of the thick wooden door. Michael Dunn howled in fury.

There was no time to stop for breath. It was only a matter of time before his shouting alerted the guards.

It was dark, but Jane could navigate the castle with her eyes closed. Down the steps, past the stairway that descended to the kitchen, past the meat larder, the pantry, the still room, up the servant's stairs, past the morning room, the dining room, then finally up the winding staircase that led to the library.

Again, she fumbled with the keys, then finally, the door opened and she burst into the darkened library.

It was warm. The thick walls retained the heat from the embers still burning low on the grate. It smelled so familiar. Once this had been her favorite room in all the world.

Was that music? It seemed to be coming from below her feet.

The desk had not been moved since Father's time, and the small button on the floor by the desk was easily found. She pushed it, and the trapdoor opened.

———◆———

Percy lay on the pallet, eyes closed, the flute held to his lips. His thoughts were of her—her face, her hair, her scent. He played the haunting melody that had come to him after meeting her for the first time. This would keep the terror away for a while, then, if he was lucky, he would find sleep.

The door opened above him, but— That wasn't right. It hadn't been that long since his last meal. He could still feel the bulk of it in his stomach, still taste the sweet juice of the pear that'd been hidden under the crusts of cheese and bread . . . Although it was entirely possible the feelings, the flavors, even time itself was unreal.

He tucked the flute under the pallet, obscuring it from view. Most likely it was Michael Dunn or his factor, here to demand Percy's surrender. Dunn had been absent the last few days, and the factor had become increasingly threatening. The last time he'd delivered Percy's food, Percy had been sure the man intended to strike him.

If it *was* Dunn, so be it. It was time to give in. Time to go home . . .

"*Percy.*"

A hushed whisper. Feminine. Definitely not Dunn, nor the factor or any of the other men. *Had they sent a maid?* Percy kept his eyes closed so he could imagine it was Jane, coming to him. In his mind's eye, he could see her face hovering before him, wreathed in the faint light of the world above.

Footsteps descended the narrow stairway that led into his hell. They drew closer, closer than Dunn or his men had ever come. The treads were almost silent. The whisper of leather soles on stone. The faint smell of wild roses. Certainly, this was not real, but as he had no desire to see whatever gruesome apparition stood before him, he kept his eyes closed. It was much better to continue with the pleasant illusion he'd settled on. That it was her, come to him.

Breathing . . . quick, steady, slightly out of breath. The light touch of a palm to his brow.

The warmth of her skin.

A sharp intake of breath.

A tremor shuddered through him. This was the cruelest delusion he'd suffered so far. It felt so *real* . . . Bracing himself for the worst, he opened his eyes.

A dark silhouette. Black on black.

"You aren't real," he whispered, reaching out to touch the face that hovered over him.

His hand landed on the smooth flesh of her cheek. He could hear the smile in her voice. "I'm real, love. I've come for you." She stroked his hair, then lowered her face and lightly brushed her lips against his. The physical sensation was too much, like a cacophony of sound, or a mighty ocean wave.

He pulled away. His whole body was shaking.

She clasped his hands. "Are you well? Can you walk?"

"Well enough." His voice sounded all wrong, like metal grating against metal. He sat up and fumbled for his coat, then reached for his boots and started pulling them on.

He was deranged. A madman. He knew very well that this was just another illusion. Any second now, it would unravel and he'd be left alone in the dark. With his boots on.

"I'll fetch a light." She disappeared into the darkness.

He counted three breaths. Four.

She was gone. She was not coming back. He was no longer simply going insane. He had officially arrived.

"Confound it." Her voice came from the corner of the room where he'd found the chest. "I thought it would still be here."

She must have been looking for the cache of treasures. The lamp.

Reflexively, he reached out and his fingers touched the smooth glass shade, the cold tin base. He'd found himself unwilling to burn the last of the oil. There was just a tiny bit left. He grabbed for the flint lying next to the lamp and, after several tries, lit it. A soft glow filled the space.

"You found it."

Their eyes met, and he knew. This was real. *She* was real.

She was dressed strangely in black trousers and coat. Wisps of hair escaped her long braid. Her cheeks were flushed from exertion, her eyes bright with curiosity as she took in the lamp and all the other contents of the chest that were arranged neatly around the pallet.

"Jane, how did y—"

"Hush. There's no time. I'll explain everything once we're—"

She was cut off by his body colliding with hers. He crashed into her, and her arms came around him. Her fingers threaded through his hair, pulling his face toward her. She kissed him again, but not softly this time. This kiss was hard and fast, a kiss that put all doubts to rest. He wrapped his arms around her, breathing her in, clinging to her as if she were the only thing that mattered. Because, in truth, she was.

They stood for a moment, holding each other in a fierce embrace, until it seemed they were forged together, a column of strength. Inseparable.

Percy could feel the wetness on his face. His eyes stung. She broke the hold, and the lamplight glistened on her tear-streaked cheeks as she gazed into his eyes.

Her eyes. How he'd missed her eyes.

"We must go." One hand holding the lamp, one hand holding his, she guided him up the narrow staircase and into the world above.

Twenty-six

Jane stopped for a moment at the top of the dungeon stairs, listening. Only thick silence, punctuated by the slow ticking of a clock. Then she led him out of the library, down a corridor and through a small door he never would have found had he been by himself. He had to duck to keep from hitting his head. Then a claustrophobic set of stairs. A twisting series of corridors. Percy had the distinct feeling she'd brought the lamp only for him. Several times, he stumbled, but she glided on, never hesitating, stopping only to point out an obstacle or a creaky floorboard.

Finally, she opened one last door, then hand in hand, they stepped out into the night. She extinguished the lamp. There was no moon that Percy could see, only starlight shrouded by wisps of clouds. It was plenty of light to navigate by, and in truth, he was glad for the dark—for as much as he longed to see the light of day, he feared the sudden brightness would burn his eyes.

The rocky ground dropped off steeply before them. The sound of flowing water betrayed a creek lost in shadows below, and beyond that the faint outline of trees. Percy inhaled deeply, allowing his senses, heightened after being starved for so long, to take it all in. The metallic chirp of insects. The smells of damp earth and rotting leaves. The gurgle of water splashing over rocks. The chill air rushing into his lungs. The warmth of Jane's hand grasping his.

An owl hooted in the distance.

Life.

Reality.

"Come." She led him down the embankment, then upstream a few yards to where a series of stepping stones spanned the burn. They crossed, then entered the forest behind the castle.

The great fortress of stone loomed behind them. No light shone from any of the windows. Jane kept to the forest, skirting around the south side of the building. He could make out the high wall of a garden just on the other side of the stream, then the wall fell away, replaced by trees too evenly spaced to be the work of nature. *Her orchard?* She pulled him farther into the woods.

"Cameron." Her voice was a hoarse whisper. "Where are you?"

"Here." Jane's brother appeared out of the shadow. He held the reins of two saddled horses. They moved closer, and in the dim light, Percy could see another man—dark hair, similar age to Cameron—and two more horses. He recognized one as the gelding he'd ridden from Inverness.

"Sommerbell." Cameron clasped Percy's hand and grinned "You made it." He turned to the other man. "Tav, meet Percy Sommerbell. Sommerbell, this is Tavish. He's coming with us t—"

"We have to go," Jane cut in. "*Now.*" Her words were rushed, shrill, and for the first time, Percy realized just how panicked she was.

"What—"

"There's no time, Cameron." She was already on her horse. "The Earl's awake. I locked him in the room, but it's only a matter of time before—" As if on cue, shouts sounded from the castle.

Cameron shot his sister a confused look, then turned his focus to Percy. "Can you ride?"

"Yes." Thank goodness for all the walking he'd done in that dungeon. Otherwise he'd be too weak.

Tavish tossed him the gelding's reins, and they both mounted. Then Cameron swung himself into his saddle and they were off.

They rode south, away from the castle, Cameron in the lead, Tavish bringing up the rear. There was a path, Percy realized, barely perceptible in the dark. *This must be a shortcut to the road that led to Inver—*

Hell and the god-damned devil.

The letter.

He urged his horse forward. Ferns brushed against his legs as he came up beside Cameron.

"We must go back."

Cameron's head whipped around to look at him, eyebrows raised in disbelief.

"Not to the castle. To the village. The bridge. There's something—"

"No." Cameron glanced over his shoulder. "We're to Glasgow. There's a shortcut. We'll bypass Inverness and be on the road south by tomorrow night."

"You don't— It . . . it's why he locked me up. Your mother, she—" *Damnation. There was no time to explain.* "Just give me the direction. I'll go. I'll catch up."

Cameron looked at him sharply, then shook his head. "No. My cousin's men willna find any horses in his stable. Tav and I saw to that . . . but they could *walk* to the village."

"It's worth the risk. I'll just be a minute, then I'll join you—"

"We'll all go," Cameron announced. He nodded in Jane's direction. "But *you're* the one who'll be dealing with Janie when she realizes where we're going."

———◆———

Why the devil was Cameron cutting back toward the village?

"Cameron," Jane hissed at her brother. He glanced back, then motioned toward Percy with an exaggerated shrug.

They'd risked so much rescuing this man, and now he wanted to go *back to the village*? That was the *opposite* direction they should be riding. Of all the foolish—

She spurred her mare to catch up to Percy's gelding.

"What's going on?"

"It's *important*." His eyes caught hers. "*Trust me.*"

Something about the way he looked at her . . . She sighed, and followed.

———◆———

There were men with torches in the village. She could make out the lights bobbing and moving from house to house, hear the shouts as they woke the villagers and searched their homes. The Earl would never have gone to such lengths for her sake alone. He must know that Percy escaped along with her and had his men searching for him in the village. Thankfully, the forest path ended only fifty yards from the bridge, on the castle side. Jane, Cam, and Tav stayed hidden in the trees, Tavish holding Percy's horse, while Percy dismounted and crept through the darkness toward the bridge. Jane held her breath as he carefully climbed down the bank and disappeared into the shadows. After a few moments, he emerged, tucking something into his waistcoat.

"Hold."

A voice rang out. Panicked, Jane searched the darkness until she spied the figure striding over the bridge toward Percy. Her cousin did not hold a torch, but he was fully illuminated by the starlight, and she could see the pistol, gleaming in his hand, trained on her love. They were less than ten feet from each other.

"Give. Me. That. Letter."

Percy stopped mid-stride. "No."

"I *will* shoot you."

"Go ahead."

Percy's defiant tone left no doubt in Jane's mind. He would be mad enough to let himself be killed for whatever fool thing it was he'd gotten from under that bridge.

She looked around wildly for something, *anything*. Her eyes fell on a cluster of hazelnuts that were just in reach, not ripe enough to eat, but perfectly suited to her purpose. She plucked them from the tree and threw them, one after another, toward her cousin. One pelted him on the shoulder, one on his temple, the next his thigh. His concentration was broken as he looked around for the source of his attack, then he grunted as something else careened into his gun and knocked it to the ground. Jane looked up and was surprised to see Tavish, his slingshot—the one he'd used as a boy—in hand. But she was even more surprised by the sight of her brother with a pistol—*where on Earth did he get that?*—drawn and pointed at their cousin. Cam had moved out of the shadows. He was clearly visible to the two men standing by the bridge.

"Come along, Sommerbell," Cameron called, his gun trained steadily on the Earl. "My cousin willna hurt you."

Percy began to walk slowly back toward his horse.

"*Cousin?*" The Earl peered at them, then growled when he realized who the men on the horses were. Who she was. "*You.*" He glanced toward his gun, just a few feet away on the ground, then grunted in pain as another rock from Tav's slingshot struck his hand.

"I wouldna try that." Cameron remained steady, pistol still trained on their cousin.

"Bevin. Here!" The Earl shouted, finally seeming to remember that he had men searching the village. But it was too late. Percy had reached his horse. He mounted, then they turned and galloped back into the wood.

A single gunshot rang after them. It hit a tree a few yards off.

———◇———

They rode through the night, first on forest paths that Cameron and Tavish knew from their hunting trips with Father, then on a cart track that wound its way through fields planted to wheat and oats—fields that, next year, would be nothing more than pasture for sheep. Jane pushed the thought away. They'd succeeded. They'd rescued Percy. There was no more they could do.

Slowly, the sky turned grey, then brightened the white of the thin clouds that obscured the sun. They'd left the Banton estate behind and come into a narrow glen with steep, heather-covered slopes on either side. A stream meandered through, slow flowing and deep, flanked by birches and some of the largest white willows Jane had ever seen. The trees towered over them, their long boughs trailing in the water, obscuring the mossy bank. Cameron dismounted and led his horse to the burn to drink. Tavish followed suit, and the two men conferred then climbed back up the bank toward Jane and Percy.

"We'll rest here," Tav said. "Cam and I will take the horses, find them some grass."

Cameron grinned at his friend, then turned to Jane and Percy. "*Be good*. We'll be along soon."

Heat rose in Jane's cheeks at her brother's suggestive eyebrow raise, but there was no use denying it. They all knew she and Percy craved time alone.

They found a smooth expanse of ground hidden between the trees. It was damp, but moss-covered and soft. A welcome relief after the breakneck pace they'd kept all night. Percy took off his coat and folded it up for a pillow, then stretched out his legs and reclined, gazing up at the willow boughs and the milky white morning sky.

He was a stranger. A pale, silent stranger, with the beginnings of a beard and tired, dull eyes.

She remembered how he'd looked when she'd found him in the dungeon. Terrified, shaking, as if she were a ghost come to haunt him. He'd shrunk from her kiss. Once he lit the lamp, though, he seemed more himself. He allowed her to kiss him and followed her to freedom . . . But perhaps his first reaction had been the truthful one. Perhaps his time in the pit had changed things.

She sat with her knees drawn up to her chin, feeling the distance between herself and the man beside her.

He reached for her hand, and a tiny bud of hope formed. He opened her fist, kissed the pad of each finger, her palm, then brought it to rest over his heart. His two hands settled warmly on top, binding her to him. The bud inside her burst into bloom.

Percy spoke first. "How did you—"

"I love you." She interrupted him because this was the most important thing. All else could wait. He didn't respond, so she said it again, "I love you. I thought I couldna. But I can. I *do*."

A slow smile spread across his face, but there was something else. A pain she didn't understand. "Jane. I saw things, in the dark. Terrible things. But when I thought of you . . . 'twas what kept me sane." She could feel the steady beat of his heart beneath her palm. "The treasure chest. It was yours? That flute saved me in the end."

She chuckled at his use of words. It was hardly treasure stowed away in that box. "We used to play down there when our parents weren't looking. The flute was Ken's. He tried to play, but he was hopeless, terrible really . . ." She smiled at the memory.

"Ken. Your betrothed?"

"Aye."

A long pause. She lowered her hand, laced her fingers through his.

"How long was I down there?"

"Eleven days . . . Percy, *why*, why did he do it? I can't—"

"In time, love. When your brother comes back, I'll tell all . . . but tell me now, how did you find me?"

She told him of the letter they'd gotten from Mrs. Brodie, of their journey to Inverness, of Cam's visit to the castle and the rescue plot, and how she'd locked her cousin in her room just before she'd come to find him.

He listened intently. "The cook, Mrs. Brodie. She sent me food. Good food, hidden under the rest. Isn't she afraid for her position? Surely she'll be dismissed, or worse?"

"She left for her sister's last night, just before we did. I told her you would pay her passage to America. You will, willna you?"

"Of course. I'll give her money, too, to make a start, if that's what she wants. But perhaps—" He shook his head, thinking better of what he was about to say. "What of Tavish? He can't go back."

"No. He'll come with us to Glasgow, stay with Cam and me for a while. Find work. He's good with horses . . . He'll find something."

Cameron's head poked through the willow boughs. His eyes were closed, his face scrunched up dramatically to accentuate the fact.

"Is it safe? You're not . . . you know . . ."

"No, Cameron. We're not."

He heaved a mock sigh of relief. "Tav's finishing with the horses. He'll be along in a bit. I brought the food."

He began to lay out the breakfast Mrs. Brodie had packed for them—apples, cheese, oat cakes, flasks of water.

"Cam. Where did you get that pistol?" Jane had to know.

Her brother shot her a sly grin. "'Twas Father's. He kept it hidden in the big carriage, in case of highwaymen. Tav didna even know it was there."

Incredible. The escape would never have been possible without Mama's keys, Father's pistol . . . In the end, her parents had been there when it mattered most.

Jane swallowed down the lump in her throat. How she missed them.

Tavish appeared, and they ate hungrily. After a long moment of silence, broken only by the sounds of chewing, Cameron finally asked the question that was on everyone's mind.

"Now's the time, Sommerbell. What was under that bridge that was so damn important?"

"This." Percy pulled out the folded piece of foolscap. "The innkeeper, Mrs. MacPhearson, gave it to me the night I stayed in the village. 'Twas delivered to the castle after you left. A maid found it on a pile of opened mail. Freya something . . ."

"Freya Riley," Jane supplied. Freya had been Mama's dearest friend. *What could this be about?*

Percy nodded. "That was it." He continued. "Freya went to America. No one knew where you were, so Mrs. MacPhearson kept it. She gave it to me, to give to you." He held the paper out to her. "She kept it a secret, but Dunn knows. It's why he dismissed all the staff. He knew one of them had taken it. I suspect it was the only reason he remained in Darnalay. He hoped it was still there somewhere, and he couldn't leave till he knew it'd been destroyed."

Jane looked at the letter in her hand. She squinted. Looked again. *Mama's handwriting.* She turned it over. *Mama's seal.* It was post-marked from Edinburgh. Her stomach lurched.

"Read it."

Heart pounding, she unfolded the paper and read her parents' words.

The world around her tilted. She was dizzy. A humming sounded in her ears, and she found she couldn't draw breath. Everything she thought she knew—about her parents, herself, her brother—it was all wrong. All the pain, the loss of the last two years . . .

Father had loved them. Really and truly. Had made them legitimate . . . *And the tenants.* If Cameron was the rightful heir, he could stop the evictions.

With shaking hands, she passed the letter to her brother. She still couldn't draw breath. The world began to ripple around her. She was going to faint . . .

Percy's hand found hers. His touch was an anchor, and mercifully, she could breathe again. Their eyes met. There was love written on his face, undeniably, but it was clouded by that same pain she'd seen earlier, when she'd told him she loved him. *Did he think she would reject him, now that she knew?*

She squeezed his hand in reassurance.

Cameron read the letter, then silently handed it to Tavish. Her brother was expressionless, staring blankly at the brown water flowing by, but she noticed that his hands, too, were shaking.

The pain of their parents' death was suddenly raw again. This was such a joyful letter. They were so excited to come home, but when they did, they'd been in coffins.

Percy kept hold of her hand. He filled the shocked silence with the rest of his story. "I never asked Michael Dunn for apples. I'd intended to, but like a damn fool, I confronted him, and he locked me up. He demanded I hand over the letter in trade for my freedom, or sign a statement affirming his legitimacy. It's lucky I had the sense not to bring it to the castle." He nodded toward the letter. "He'd have destroyed it by now."

Percy had endured eleven days in the pit for this. For her. For Cameron. For the people of Darnalay.

"Cam." Jane kept her voice soft. She really wasn't sure what was going through her brother's mind. "You're the heir. You can stop our cousin from— you can save the tenants. We must go back."

"No." Cameron's voice was void of emotion. "I canna make a claim based on one letter. There's nothing remotely official about it . . . and that part about the parents being unmarried at the time of birth. Father married Elinore just after I was born. He was married to her for nearly twenty years."

"The law's the law," Percy said. "I'd venture somewhere in Edinburgh there's a record of your parents' nuptials. Between that and this letter, in the hands of the right barrister, I think you have a strong claim indeed."

"I've no money for a barrister."

"I do," Percy said. "My father—or rather, *I've* got a solicitor in Edinburgh. He can help us find the right man."

"I'd pay you back."

"Of course you will. You'll also invite me to stay in your castle. In a *guestroom*, with a real bed. And windows."

A smile almost sneaked onto Cameron's face at this, but it vanished as soon as it arrived.

He shook his head. "I canna. Even if we *did* succeed . . . I'm no earl. Perhaps if Father had lived, if he'd had a chance to teach me wha—"

"You damn well *will* do it." Tavish had finished reading the letter now and was staring Cameron down. "You have to. For the tenants, and everybody else in Darnalay. They need you."

Cameron met Tavish's gaze, then looked to Percy, then Jane. She gave him a nod, telling him with her eyes what he already knew. Tavish was right. Cameron had to at least attempt to take his place as the Earl of Banton, whether he wanted to or not.

He scrubbed his face with his hands. "Very well, we're to Edinburgh then, not Glasgow." He heaved a sigh. "Let's rest a while. We should still reach an inn by nightfall."

Tavish settled down on the other side of Cameron, and both men stretched out for sleep. Percy reached out an arm in invitation, and Jane curled up next to him, her head on his shoulder. They lay in silence, listening to the buzz of insects, interrupted periodically by the trilling of a lark, the splash of a fish jumping. After a long while, the symphony of nature was joined by the soft snoring of her brother.

Incredible that he could sleep after such news had been delivered, but that was Cam.

"Jane?" Percy's voice was soft in her ear.

"Hmm?"

"You'll have so many options now. You needn't settle for me. I'd understand."

He *was* afraid she'd reject him. She reached her arm across his chest, holding him tight. "Do you love me?"

"Yes, but that doesn't matter. If you—"

"And I love you. That's *all* that matters."

He sighed and nuzzled her ear, pulling her in tighter until she was soaking in his warmth. She would never get enough of the nearness of him.

She was just drifting off when a sudden thought struck her. "Percy. Your guitar. It's still in the castle."

"Mmmm." She'd pulled him from almost-sleep. He reached up to smooth her hair. "Never mind. We'll get it when we return to kick the devil out."

"You really think that will happen?"

"Yes, I do. Now get some rest. We've a long journey ahead. And I've a feeling neither of us will sleep much tonight." She could hear the lazy, seductive smile in his voice. Her wildcat . . . She snuggled in deeper, and they drifted off to sleep to the rhythm of their heartbeats and the soft breeze of early autumn.

TWENTY-SEVEN

IT WAS JUST AFTER nightfall by the time they finally reached an inn. It was acceptable, as Scottish country inns went, offering four very small and somewhat dingy rooms. As tired as he was, Percy was willing to look past a few stains on the counterpane and the lack of a fire in the grate.

They'd requested four hot baths when they arrived, which did nothing but annoy the innkeeper. She shook her head at their gall. There was not a kettle in the world that could heat that much water at once, she'd declared. They would have to take turns. As only one of them had been in the same clothes for eleven—make that twelve—days, without even a basin to splash in, there was no question who would go first. The water was lukewarm and the tub was small, but it was by far the most satisfying bath of Percy's life.

Dinner was nothing more than oat bread, cold mutton and fresh milk, but just like the mediocre inn and the mediocre bath, the mediocre food seemed to Percy to be fit for a king.

Jane's turn was next. Directly after dinner, she took her leave, declaring her exhaustion and bidding the three men goodnight. She hadn't changed out of the boy's clothes she'd worn the night before, and the way the trousers hugged her curves as she walked away, the way her voluptuous backside swayed an invitation he yearned to answer . . .

Damnation. He wanted her.

Yet, he would not go to her tonight, for despite his self-assured comments earlier in the day, Percy was not convinced she would choose him once the reality of her new situation set in. He was even less convinced that she *should*. She could have so much more. If they were to be lovers tonight, or at all, it would be because she chose to come to him of her own volition—for as much as he feared her rejection, it would be exponentially worse if she were to give herself to him only from a sense of obligation.

He stayed up for a bit with Tavish and Cameron, drinking whisky and planning for what lay ahead. According to the innkeeper, one more day's ride would take them to a coaching inn where they could hire a post chaise to Edinburgh. Once there, they'd find a suitable hotel, then call upon the solicitor who was known to Percy's father and begin the work of proving Cameron's claim. Already, Cameron seemed to be donning the persona of a laird. The jovial youth Percy remembered from Glasgow remained, but he'd taken on an air of authority and responsibility—and insecurity, too—that was new. Tavish seemed a good friend, ready to bolster the new Earl of Banton's resolve whenever he faltered. Between the two of them, they would do well for the people of Darnalay.

Percy had yawned three times in the last five minutes. He rose, yawning a fourth time.

"Sommerbell, may I have a word?" Cameron had a strange, tight look about him.

"Of course."

They walked together to the foot of the stairs.

"This is about your sister."

"Aye." Cameron raked his hand through his hair. Percy suspected he'd been rehearsing this moment for quite some time, or at least since he'd realized he was his father's heir. It wouldn't be easy for Jane's good-natured brother to remind him that the grandson of a sheep farmer, even a wealthy one, was not a suitable match for the sister of an earl.

"I know she asked you to marry her. 'Twas brave of her, after your . . . *proposition*." Cameron's brows raised pointedly.

Percy winced. *She'd told him everything.* "Yes. Listen, Stuart . . . I regret that now. I should have just asked for her hand from the—"

"Do you love her?"

"Yes," Percy answered without hesitation.

"And you'll be faithful?"

"Until my dying breath. That is, if she still wants me. I intend to ask her. Again. Now that everything's changed. Give her the chance to change her mind."

"I'd kill you, you know, if you ever hurt her."

"I'd deserve nothing less."

There was a long, uncomfortable silence. Percy eyed the stairs, wanting nothing more than to bolt up them and away from this deucedly awkward conversation.

Finally, Cameron's face broke into a grin. "You have my blessing then. To ask her, I mean . . . Not that you need it. The decision's hers."

"Thank you." Percy heaved an exaggerated sigh of relief. "Well, then. I'm glad that's over." He moved toward the stairs, then paused, and turned back.

Cameron raised his brows in question.

"Good night, Lord Banton." Percy swept into a low bow.

Cameron opened his mouth to object, then closed it again. He grinned. "Good night, Sommerbell."

———◆———

The bath was tepid, too shallow for a real soak, but Jane managed to get herself clean. Every sensation was heightened, anticipating the night to come—the smoothness of her wet skin, the slickness of the soap, the rough towel, the cool whisper of thin cotton as she slipped a shift over her head before burrowing beneath the blankets.

Waiting.

She must have fallen asleep, because she was awakened by the opening and closing of a door. It was the room to the east of hers. Percy's. His footsteps crossed the room, then came the creak of straining ropes as he lay down, then silence.

He was not coming to her, it seemed. So, she would have to go to him.

After an eternity, she heard the opening and closing of the door on the other side. Cameron's. Tavish was in the room beyond that. She waited for her brother to go quiet, counted to five hundred, then rose from the bed and padded to the door, silently passing into the hallway. It was so dark she had to feel along the wall to know when she'd arrived at Percy's door. It wasn't locked. She pushed it open then slipped through, closing it quietly behind her.

The curtain was open, allowing moonlight to filter into the room.

"Jane?" Percy's tenor sounded from the bed. He'd not been sleeping.

"I decided it was too soon for you to be spending time alone in the dark." She'd rehearsed the line over and over in her head as she lay in the room next door. It sounded all wrong now, but he didn't seem to notice.

"You thought right. I can't sleep. *Come here.*"

The command sent a frisson of desire shimmering through her, and she obeyed, glad for the empty room that now stood between Cameron's and this one. The parts of Percy she could see were bare, a play of shadow and light. The smooth contours of his arms, the hard planes of his chest. His eyes were no longer dull. They were smoldering coals, burning into her, threatening to light her on fire.

"'Tis chilly. May I come under the blankets?" All she wanted in the world was to touch him.

He raised one perfect brow, and a wicked smile spread across his face. Once, she'd feared this smile. She'd run from it. But now it pulled her to him as if she were the needle of a compass and he, true north.

"I would never leave my lady out in the cold." He pulled up the blankets, revealing more naked flesh. A shiver ran through her, but it had nothing to do with the chill. She climbed in beside him.

She expected him to pull her close, but without warning, his mood seemed to shift. He just lay there, not touching, staring at the ceiling. A terrible silence ensued.

Was he angry?

She searched her mind for anything she might have done, or said, to displease him. When he finally spoke, his voice was flat and colorless.

"You don't have to do this. You owe me nothing. *Nothing*." He sighed. "I know you only wanted me because you had no other choice. You *do* now."

Relief flooded her. "You're wrong."

He looked at her then, and it was fear, not anger, etched on his face. She reached for him, smoothing the wrinkles from his brow.

"I owe you *everything*."

"No, you don't. What happened in Darnalay—"

"I don't mean for what happened in Darnalay." She paused, searching for the words to explain what she herself barely understood. "Before I met you, it was as if I were doing penance. For Ken. I felt guilty somehow because I survived, I *lived*, and he didn't. I was so sure I didn't deserve love . . ." She threaded her fingers with his. "But then you came, and you were so . . . so *you*. I couldna help it. I loved you. I love you." She kissed his knuckles. "It doesna matter if my parents were married or not. This is *right*. You and me. 'Tis where we belong."

"You've let him go then?"

"Ken?"

He nodded.

"Yes. No. He's still here." She placed his hand on her heart. "He always will be . . . he's part of me. Do you mind? That I still love him?"

Percy smiled. "If he's a part of you, then I love him, too. I love all of you with all that I am."

He *did* pull her close then, and they lay in a tight embrace. Breathing the same air. Listening to one another's heartbeats.

But when he spoke, there was that same fear in his voice. Or was it sadness? "I have a question, and I need you to answer it. Honestly."

"Hmm?"

He drew a breath, his warm exhale tickling against her cheek.

"Will you marry me?"

"Ye—" He put a finger to her lips.

"Don't say yes because you think I need you."

"But I'm n—"

"Or because of what happened in Darnalay. I nearly gave in, you know. I'm no hero."

"Percy, I already—"

"If you say yes, say it only for yourself. Because it's what *you* want. I'll understand, and I'll . . . I won't bother you, or pursue you. You have my word." He turned and held her eyes. "*Truly*."

"Are you finished?"

"Yes."

"Yes. I will marry you."

"You're sure?"

She climbed onto his lap and straddled him, her face just inches from his. It took every bit of will she possessed to keep from leaning in to kiss him. Instead, she placed her hands on either side of his shoulders and let herself fall into his eyes, those bottomless liquid brown eyes she loved so well.

"Trust me."

She held his gaze as she straightened up, reached for the hem of her shift, and pulled it up and over her head. His eyes widened, then a look of wonderment spread over his face as he finally accepted the full weight of her love.

"Make love to me," she murmured. Then her will evaporated and she threaded her fingers through his hair, pulling his face to hers.

⚬

The dam broke.

All the months of pent-up desire, all the lovesick longing, the frustrated lust, the dreams, the hopes, the fantasies . . . They all flowed together into a torrent of passion that slammed into them with such force that Percy did not know which way was up. Where he ended. Where she began. They devoured each other with a powerful savagery that would not be denied—tongues, lips, mouths, hands, skin—licking, tasting, grasping, deeper, more.

He came up for air, then dove back in, cupping her breasts, glorying in the way they filled his palms, the dark nipples, the soft flesh. He took one in his mouth, suckling, nipping, lightly at first, then harder, letting her gasps of pleasure guide him as they explored the blissful edge between pain and pleasure.

He was kneeling over her, and she was leaning back on the bed, bracing herself with her hands. Her head was thrown back, her hair flowing like an auburn river onto the sheet. Her eyes were closed, cheeks flushed, her core grinding against his cock, stroking his desire and hers . . . higher . . . higher . . . faster.

He would spend in seconds at this pace.

With incredible effort, he broke away and gently pushed her onto her back. He came to rest beside her, his head propped on one hand while his fingers traced lazy circles around her navel, figure eights across the pillow soft flesh of her hip. She watched him, eyes wide, pupils dilated.

"Percy, I need—"

"Patience, love." And there was a question he must ask. "Have you . . . Are you a—?"

"A virgin? No. But only once." She looked suddenly nervous, afraid he would be unhappy with her answer.

He kissed her chin, the tip of her nose. "Good. I don't want to hurt you."

He moved the kiss to her mouth. He was in control now, savoring her with his tongue—feeling her lips, her teeth. Tasting her neck, her earlobe. He growled, deep, rough, carnal, and she shuddered beneath him, arching her body toward his.

He had never known what desire was until this moment.

He traced a line with his tongue around each perfect breast, then drew each nipple in turn into his mouth, suckling, then releasing with a popping sound. Their eyes met, and for a moment, they giggled together like children, then turned serious again as his tongue glided over the soft curve of her stomach, her navel. Finally, he arrived at the downy patch of hair guarding her sex. *Heaven.* She opened her legs for him, and he separated her folds with his fingers, marveling at her slick wetness and feeling with his tongue for the jewel that lay hidden in her most secret place. She moaned when he found it—a breathy, low, earthy sound that reverberated through his soul. It was the most beautiful thing he'd ever heard. He played her with his mouth, sucking, licking, swirling, and with his hand, he found her opening. Another growl of pleasure escaped him, this one louder, less controlled.

She was so wet. So smooth, so hot, so unbelievably perfect.

And she was his.

He had to be inside her. Now. But first— "Come for me, love."

She was writhing under him now, panting, lost to her passion as he stroked her jewel with his tongue, fingers slipping in and out of her wet heat. He gave her one last nip—*hard*—then plunged his tongue into her and she came with a muffled shout, gripping him as if he were the only thing tethering her to the ground. He stayed with her. Lapping up every bit of her joy. He would never get enough. She tasted of summer sun, of ripe plums and morning dew.

The tremors of her release subsided, but still she strained against him. Reaching for more. "Percy . . . *Please.*" Her voice was raw with need.

He moved over her, covering her body with his own. He could still feel the ripples of her climax running through her. She opened her legs wide in invitation, and he rubbed his straining cock against her, coating himself in her essence. Their eyes locked, connection sparking between them as he positioned himself at her entrance then slowly, carefully, slid himself into her slick heat.

She accepted all of him. *Him.* The grandson of a sheep farmer. The imperfect heir to an imperfect fortune. She saw him, *knew* him, for what he was, and still she wanted him. Loved him.

Tears were wet on his cheeks. *He was home.*

He found a rhythm, and she joined him, matching him thrust for thrust—a deep, primal beat that belonged only to them. That only they understood. With each thrust, he filled her more deeply, more completely. Faster. Harder. The rhythm became erratic as they wildly reached together for release . . . then, suddenly, they'd arrived. Jane pulled him to her. Frantic. Pressing her mouth to his, and they shouted their pleasure into each other, giving everything of themselves as exquisite release washed over them. He knew not who he was, where he was. There was only her. And love. And her.

They held each other for a long moment, breath mingling, heart to heart, panting from their exertion. Finally, he rolled off her, snaking an arm under her as she snuggled up next to him.

Peace, at long last.

Her voice broke the silence. "'Twas a terrible idea, you know."

His heart stopped.

"Jane, I—"

"You canna cut scion wood in September. It has to be done in spring, before the trees bloom. 'Twould have been dead by the time you got to Glasgow."

Ah.

"And the apples. The apples in my test orchard are late ripening. They won't be worth anything for another month, perhaps more."

"I see."

A long silence, then, "I love you, Percy."

"As I love you." He pulled her closer and smiled into her hair. "For-ever."

For the second time that day, they slipped into contended slumber.

TWENTY-EIGHT

BY NOON, THE CHILL mist of the morning had darkened into a freezing drizzle that was now a pelting rain threatening to turn to snow. More like November or even December than late October.

Jane spent the day working alongside the small, inexperienced staff she and Cameron had pulled together in the three short weeks since their return to the castle. It would take much longer to restore the building and grounds to their rightful state, but for now, she was satisfied. The guest rooms were readied. The great room had been thoroughly cleaned. A cheerful fire burned in the hearth, the big oaken table in the dining room was set and ready for tonight's meal, and Mrs. Brodie, finally back from her sister's house, was cheerfully giving orders to her two new kitchen maids. All was ready, but even so, Jane could not sit, nor could she calm the roiling of her stomach. She wished she could go outside and lose herself for an hour or two in the orchard or the wood, but the weather prevented it, so instead she aimlessly paced the corridors and rooms of the castle.

She found Cameron in the library, sitting at the mahogany desk that had once been Father's. A fire blazed in the hearth. The clock read five, though the gloom outside made it seem at least an hour later.

He was deep in concentration, reading something, and he didn't notice her enter the room. She marveled, again, at how much he resembled Father. Somehow, she hadn't noticed it when they were just two bastards making their way in the world, but now that he was Lord Banton, it was obvious. He had the same warm brown eyes, the same quick smile, the same generous nature. She felt a sudden pang of loss for their mother, that she had not lived to see him thus. How proud she would have been.

Jane would never forget the looks of shock, joy and relief on the faces of the villagers and tenants when she and her brother had made the rounds just after they returned. The tenants had assumed Michael Dunn's sudden exit meant their eviction was imminent, but instead, Cameron, the boy they all knew and loved, had come home. Unsurprisingly, their cousin had allowed the cottages and fields to fall into disrepair. Already, Cam had a list several pages long of repairs that needed to be made before winter set in—a daunting task made less onerous by the arrival of four men from the lowlands, shepherds who'd been promised work on the improved estate. They were disappointed, of course, to find the improvements canceled, but Cameron had offered them generous compensation and they'd agreed to stay on for the winter to help get the farms back in good order.

The two weeks they'd spent in Edinburgh seemed like a faraway dream. The business of proving his claim had taken her brother away for long stretches of time. Tavish had accompanied Cam to court. Percy only had to appear once, to testify about the letter and the kidnapping. Otherwise, she and her love had spent the days together. There'd been hours of delicious love-making—even now, her body responded to the memories—but just as pleasurable were the moments of perfect quiet. The long conversations planning their future. Travels abroad. A new orchard at Grislow Park. They'd puzzled together over what to do about the injustices in the mills. Certainly they'd open a school for millworkers' children, but that didn't seem like enough . . . It solved one problem but left many others intact. Percy still hoped his long-delayed visit to New Lanark would prove helpful, but even still, the mills were a weight that hung heavily in his mind, and even with Jane there to shoulder some of the burden, he seemed haunted by them.

They'd shared a great deal of laughter in those two weeks, a few tears, and even their first small argument, when Percy had attempted to play the gentleman and carry Jane's umbrella in the pouring rain—a task she could perform much more satisfactorily by herself. He'd taken her to a coffeehouse, watching expectantly as she took her first sip, then laughed as she grimaced and sputtered. It really was awful, coffee.

After the case was decided in Cameron's favor, Jane, Cam and Tavish had journeyed north to claim the castle, along with two bodyguards and Mr. Tibbets, an official from the Court of Lord Lyon. They'd hoped to find their cousin still there, so he could be sent to Edinburgh under armed guard to stand trial, but he'd fled by the time they arrived. Aiming to lure him out of hiding, Cameron left the account that Father had set up for his allowance—Michael Dunn's only source of income—open, and hired an investigator in London to help in the search. Now they waited for their cousin to fall into the trap—and hoped he hadn't had the sense to flee the country.

Percy had gone home to Grislow Park. He'd not seen his mother in more than a month, and he wanted to surprise her with the news of his betrothal.

Saying goodbye had nearly broken her.

Cameron still had noticed her. She cleared her throat. "What are you reading?"

He looked up. Blinked. "They've found him."

"Our cousin? Where?"

"London. He tried to draw money from the account. He's to be transported to New South Wales. A seven-year sentence." Cameron was obviously surprised. Kidnapping and usurpation were not small crimes, but seven years hard labor in Botany Bay was an unlikely punishment for a man like Michael Dunn, who had ties to the aristocracy.

"He deserves it." She walked to the window, straining to see past the raindrops.

"Aye. He does. It's just . . . he's the only family we have. 'Tis a shame it had to come to this."

Jane nodded absently, looking out at the rain. Her cousin *did* deserve it. What he'd done to Percy was more than cruel. It was savage. Unforgivable. But even still, there'd been something about him that night in her room . . . He'd been so vulnerable. Real. Certainly he was misguided, but knowing he'd been given such a harsh sentence brought her no joy.

"Any sign of them?" Cameron asked, changing the subject.

"Too dark to see. 'Tis raining hard now. Maybe they'll be delayed."

Her brother smiled. "Sommerbell willna let a wee bit of rain stand in his way. Not today."

Since the moment she woke, her mind had been following the route their carriage would take. If they'd left Inverness at first light as he'd promised, they should be here just about—

A knock sounded on the door. Gregor poked his head in. He was one of the handful of young men Cameron had hired from the village. A footman by title, though his broad smile was decidedly too genuine for his position.

Cameron grinned back at him. "Yes?"

"There's two coaches coming down the drive, my lord. My lady." He nodded to Jane.

The churning of Jane's stomach metamorphosed into a flock of butterflies as she pushed past the footman and flew down the stairs.

The walls were pressing in.

He could not move.

He was suffocating.

Percy pushed away the rising wave of panic with another slow breath, wishing for the millionth time he was back out in the open air next to the driver. Ever since his time in the dungeon, small enclosed spaces had become intolerable. Carriages were the worst. Even the short ride from the hotel in Glasgow to his aunt and uncle's house had caused his pulse to race and little black dots to swim in the periphery of his vision. For most of the long journey from Northumberland to Glasgow, then to Darnalay, he'd avoided the inside of the coach. But a cold hard rain had settled in this afternoon, and he'd had no choice. He sat next to Cybil, eyes closed, breaths slow and steady.

This would not last forever. She would be in his arms tonight.

His mother, sister, and aunt chatted quietly. He didn't try to make sense of the murmuration, just let it blur together into an undulating melody of voices. They probably thought he was asleep.

He felt an elbow in his side. Cybil's. "Is that it?"

He opened his eyes and squinted out the rain-streaked window. His pulse crescendoed. He could hear it pounding in his ears. "Yes. That's it."

"Oh, Percy . . . It's beautiful." He wasn't sure if Mother was more excited about his upcoming nuptials or the prospect of staying in a real castle. Probably it was the combination of the two that enchanted her the most.

Two footmen appeared to greet them, but Percy couldn't wait for formality. He spied an auburn-haired figure standing in the shelter of the portcullis, and before the carriage springs had ceased oscillating, he was out the door, running. Their eyes met and held until he reached her, then their bodies collided with such force that she would have fallen backward had he not swept her off of her feet. His arms enfolded her, holding her close, inhaling her scent, savoring the sure strength of her embrace.

He kissed her, quickly, lightly, then brought his mouth to her ear. "I want you. Here. On the stones. *Now*." He ground his erection against her so she would know he meant it. "But my mother's watching, so we must be good." He pulled back, grinning at the sight of her flushed cheeks and dazed expression.

Jane's eyes darted to the women now descending from the carriage, then to the second coach pulling up behind the first. She nodded to her guests, shooting them an innocent welcoming smile, then she leaned in quickly to whisper in his ear. "Second door from the right. The corridor opposite the library. I'll wait up for you."

He had to pivot himself toward the wall then, and rearrange the front of his too-tight pantaloons, because suddenly they were surrounded by people—his mother and sister and aunt, with their bobbing umbrellas and polite, curious smiles. Then his uncle emerged from the second carriage. Rose Chisholm bounded out after him, streaking toward Jane and nearly knocking her over with a hug around her waist. Cori floated down the steps, bobbing her head to her mistress, eyes wide at the stone edifice in front of her. Will and Nat Chisholm came last, father and son, wearing the same shy smile.

Cameron, Lord Banton strode out of the castle, a wide grin of welcome spread across his face.

"Welcome to Darnalay Castle. Come in. Warm yourselves."

Moments later, they were all in the great room. The musty odor, dust, and desolation that Percy remembered had been transformed into an atmosphere of warmth. Grand, yet cozy. A lively fire danced in the hearth. Hot tea, whisky and scones were served. Introductions were made.

Mother seemed enchanted by Jane, as he knew she would be.

The buzz of conversation and the occasional trill of laughter overflowed the space. Tavish was there, and Mrs. MacPhearson, and an older man Percy didn't recognize but was introduced to as Mr. Mackinnon, the groundskeeper, Kendric's father.

Percy squeezed Jane's hand, then left her and her brother to his mother's questions about the history of the castle. He wandered through the assembled guests, nodding when necessary, letting bits of conversation wash over him. Aunt Cynthia recounting to Mrs. MacPhearson the tale of Jane and his first meeting, and how she just *knew* from the very beginning they were meant to be. Uncle Douglas asking Mr. Mackinnon about the species of pine found in the surrounding woods. Cori nibbling on a scone as she chased the children about the room.

All the while, Will Chisholm held himself back from the crowd, looking uncomfortable. Aunt Cynthia eyed him and murmured something in Cybil's ear. His sister's expression was dubious, but she could not defy her aunt. Percy chuckled to himself as Cybil slowly wound her way to where Chisholm stood and reluctantly drew him into polite conversation.

Looking up, Percy found he'd arrived in front of the portrait of the late Earl of Banton. Jane's father cheerfully surveyed the assembled guests, and Percy felt a sudden stab of grief for this man he would never meet, who had not lived to see this moment.

He gave the Lord a nod. *It's done, my lord.*

—◦—

"I should sleep." Jane smoothed Percy's hair as she spoke, bringing order, albeit temporary, to the chaos. The next two days would be a whirlwind of events, and as both hostess and bride, she would be inordinately busy. She needed to rest . . . and yet, he was here, at last. And though her clock told her it was well past midnight, her body was weighted to the moment, unable to move.

They were stretched out on the settee in her room, half naked, sweaty from exertion. His head rested in her lap, and he cradled his guitar on his bare chest, absently strumming toward the ceiling. She'd kept the instrument in her room during their time apart—having it with her felt like having a part of him—and she'd surprised him with it when he'd crept into her room an hour ago. She'd been half afraid that being reunited with his guitar would overshadow her own reunion with him, but he'd barely glanced at it before pushing her onto the settee and making love to her with a passionate urgency that mirrored her own.

The rain had turned to ice, ticking against the pane. The wind moaned, cold and bleak. But those she loved most were safe within the castle walls, and the sounds only made the embers glowing in the grate feel warmer.

"Seven years," Percy said. She'd just told him about her cousin's sentence.

"Aye," she confirmed. "Not a trifle. It willna be easy for him."

"Nor should it be." Percy sighed. "It's over, anyway."

"Aye." Jane ran her finger over his lips. "Let's not talk of him." She was unwilling to allow Michael Dunn to intrude any further into her happiness.

"Very well." Percy nodded. "You sound more Scottish now than when I met you." He smiled up at her. "I like it."

"I *feel* more Scottish, or at least more . . . *comfortably* Scottish."

"It's like music, your voice . . ."

Percy began to play the guitar in earnest, and Jane recognized the song he'd written the day they'd met. She felt herself sinking into the warmth. The moment. Her eyelids were heavy . . .

He stopped suddenly, as if remembering something.

"Rosehill."

She blinked back to wakefulness. "What of it?"

"I told a friend he could stay there. I hope you don't mind. Since we'll be at Grislow Park, we won't have a need for it."

"Of course. Who is he?"

"Beau. I'm sure I've told you about him. We met at Oxford. He's a painter. A good one. Was with me in Italy . . . and I was *supposed* to go with him to Greece last spring, but then I had to go to Glasgow instead." He raised a brow and shot her a meaningful look.

"Ah." She shook her head sadly. "Such a pity you missed your trip."

He grinned. "I survived." Jane giggled and bent her head down to kiss him. "Beau went without me." He continued. "And it seems he found a love of his own. He's been there all this time, but he has to come home and he needs a place for his lover to stay. Away from prying eyes . . . so I told him they could come to Rosehill."

"Will they be married?" Jane had never yet been to Rosehill, but it seemed the perfect place for a wedding.

"Well . . . no. His lover, Paolo. He's a man."

"Oh." Jane sat stunned for a minute. "That can happen?"

"Yes." Percy nodded. "Beau's always preferred men . . . There are others like him. Plenty of them. I hope you don't mind. He seems happy, and . . . it's not easy for someone like him to find happiness."

Her mind was whirling.

"There were two bachelor farmers, old men when I was a child," she said, speaking slowly. "They lived by the burn just past the village, shared a cottage, and they . . . they always seemed so content. But I never thought . . ." She met his expectant gaze. "It may take some getting used to. But no. I don't mind. I'll be happy to meet them. When do they arrive?"

"Next month."

There was a long, comfortable silence. Jane lightly traced the dark lines of his eyebrows.

"Thank you for bringing the Chisolms," she said. "Darnalay's such a wonderful place to be a child . . . If the weather's better tomorrow, I'll show them the gardens."

"I've offered Chisholm a promotion." Percy said it absently, as if it meant nothing at all. But it did.

"Oh," She breathed. "*Thank you*. He'll make an excellent clerk. I'm sure of it—"

"Not a clerk."

Not a clerk?

"An apprentice then, or . . . a . . . a manager . . . ?" Apparently, she had much to learn about her future husband's affairs. She had no idea what other positions he might hire for.

"I believe I've solved the riddle of my inheritance." Percy grinned up at her. "Or at least I've begun to."

"And it has to do with Mr. Chisholm's promotion?" Jane was confused.

"It does," Percy affirmed. He looked radiantly happy. "You see, I thought I had to be the one to figure everything out, and I was beginning to hate myself because I'm just not that clever." Jane opened her mouth to object, but he cut her off. "Or qualified, if you prefer."

"I do."

"But then, I realized . . ." He strummed a low, expectant tremolo. "I don't. Have to. Do it. Alone. I can spend my time finding the people who *are* the most qualified, then I can put them in the right positions and get out of their way."

He struck a cheerful, resonant chord.

"*If* Chisholm accepts, he'll oversee the factories in Glasgow."

Strum.

"He'll visit New Lanark with me, then institute the reforms to the mills. Devise new ones of his own."

Strum.

"He'll make sure the employees are dealt with fairly."

Strum.

"Make sure things are running efficiently."

Strum

"And he'll keep an eye on the managers, in case they try to skirt the rules."

Strum-Strum-Strum. He concluded with an elaborate flourish.

Laughter and love and elation all bubbled up inside her. She opened her mouth to speak, but instead of words, an uncontrolled squeak of joy escaped her lips. They both laughed.

"He'll be able to provide for the children. Live in a real house," she said.

"And he'll be good at it. Who better to think up improvements to the mills than someone who's witnessed the worst of it?"

"*You*. Are a genius." She leaned down and kissed him. "A generous, free-spirited, musically talented, *clever* genius."

"You forgot devilishly handsome."

Love for him filled her up again, overflowing, and there was only one thing to do.

"Come to bed."

"Lead the way."

She took his hand and led him to her bed, then stripped the dressing gown off him and pushed him down onto the mattress. His shaft was erect and ready. She grasped it, and it was alive to her touch, smooth and warm, yet hard as stone.

He watched, wide-eyed, as she knelt before him, then bent her head to take him in her mouth, kissing, sucking, swirling her tongue. She loved the taste of him, earthy and sweet, music and laughter.

She swallowed up his entire length, then drew back, savoring every inch of him, following her lips with her hands. Then again. He sucked in his breath, and she stopped for a moment to smile up at him through a curtain of hair. Her lips tingled. When she bent her head back down, his hand stilled her.

"I won't last. I want you. With me."

"Aye, my love." She pulled her night rail over her head, then crept up his body. The light friction of her nipples brushing his flesh was more than she could bear.

Finally, he was beneath her, and they both groaned their pleasure as she sank down onto him—a deep, earthy joining that bound them together as surely as a tree was bound to its roots. Then she lifted up, feeling the length of him gliding inside her, then down again, hard, grinding into him with all the force of her body.

"God, Jane. Yes . . . *Yes*." There was no sly wildcat now. All guise was forgotten. He was only a man. She, only a woman, lost in their shared pleasure. She rode him. Hard. Then she lost control of her rhythm, and he grasped her hips, pumping wildly into her, calling her name until they came together in a brilliant burst of light and love and joy and life.

She collapsed onto him, holding him, listening to his heartbeat, breathing in the heady scent of their love. She didn't want to move. Ever. But after a time, she began to feel the chill air on her backside. Reluctantly, she rolled off and pulled the blankets over them both, coming to rest in his arms. There was a long silence, broken only by quiet murmurs of pleasure as they lay together, sated, skin to skin, breath mingling with breath.

She was just beginning to drift off when he spoke. "You'll be sad . . . to leave the castle."

"Sad? No. I'll be your wife."

"But . . . ?"

He was right, there was an uneasiness lurking in the back of her mind, refusing to be banished, no matter how many times she pushed it aside. "'Tis not sadness exactly, more like . . . worry. For Cam. He'll be alone."

"He'll find his way. He's got Tavish. And we'll visit as often as we can."

"I know . . . but he willna—"

"But he won't have you, will he? To take care of him?" Percy sat up a little so he could look her in the eye. "I don't imagine it will be easy for him, but he doesn't *need* you, Jane, not really. I don't need you either. Not like that." He tucked an errant strand of hair behind her ear, his hand lingering on her cheek. "Your life's your own now. I'm just the lucky one you've agreed to spend it with."

Their eyes met, and she felt herself falling into his love. No, she wasn't falling. He was holding her, supporting her, lifting her up, just as she would him. All hesitation evaporated. She took a breath, then melted into his arms.

Slowly, she drifted into dreams of warm oceans and happy children and blooming apple t—

Apple trees. How could she have forgotten?

"I have something for you." She stood up. Goosebumps spread across her naked flesh as she crossed to the small table in front of the window, to the basket that held the handful of apples she'd harvested the day before. One tree. One of the twelve she'd planted all those years ago had borne fruit that defied expectation. The apples had all the characteristics she'd hoped for, inherited from the parent trees, but there was something more. A rich, honeylike flavor that was unlike anything she'd ever tasted. She picked the largest one with the best color—not that he would see it in the dim light—and brought it to him.

"Try it."

He took it, gazing at it in wonder. "It's from one of your trees. One you created?"

She laughed. "Only the soil and the sun can create trees, but it *is* from one I pollinated. The best of them. *Taste it.*"

He closed his eyes and took a bite.

HISTORICAL NOTES

The early nineteenth century was a time of incredible change in the Western world, as the industrial revolution reached its height and unfettered capitalism became the dominant driving force for much of the ruling class—with destructive and often tragic results. This stood in stark contrast to another movement that was gaining popularity at the time: romanticism, with its idealized notion of natural beauty, strong emotion and artistic expression. Like the industrialists, the romantics spun threads that have since been woven into the fabric of our modern lives.

Much of Percy Sommerbell's biography and philosophy is based on that of another Percy—the poet and novelist, Percy Bysshe Shelley. Shelley was as romantic as they came, putting artistic expression, beauty, and emotion above all else. From this vantage point, he sympathized with radical political and abolitionist causes, and, like Percy Sommerbell, he was philosophically opposed to marriage, preferring the doctrine of "free love" instead. Unfortunately, this did not make Shelley the best of husbands to either of his two wives, as he seemed to have a lack of understanding of the realities of life, particularly the lives of women. I found myself wondering, as I researched Shelley's life, just what it might have taken to force him to understand the world in a different way.

And so *Roses in Red Wax* was born.

The Radical War, the week of strikes and unrest that began in Glasgow on April 1, 1820, took place very much as described, though the plot to disable the canal is a figment of my imagination. Historians still disagree on the role of government spies in the uprising, however, most agree that undercover agents working for the Home Office were active in Glasgow at the time. Some even believe a government provocateur may have been the one to pen the anonymous proclamation that was plastered around Glasgow on that Saturday morning, with the intent of drawing radical sympathizers into the open where they could be arrested.

The Highland Clearance, or the removal of tenant farmers to make way for large sheep operations, was a very real and tragic event that spanned the late eighteenth to early nineteenth centuries, in large part caused by an increase in wool prices. Thousands of people were burned out of their homes and forced onto small plots of poor coastal land where survival was nearly impossible. Those who could migrated to Canada and the United States, others went south, to the industrial cities. The vast empty tracts of "natural" land in the modern Highlands are, in part, a result of this forced migration.

Child labor continued to be an issue in Britain (and elsewhere,) until the twentieth century. It wasn't until 1933 that Parliament passed—and enforced—a law prohibiting those under fourteen from being employed in factories and other hard labor. There were, however, mill owners who refused to employ young children, New Lanark, located just outside Glasgow, being the most prominent. People did, indeed, come from far and wide to study the methods of production used in New Lanark, and the example it provided was an important symbol of hope and possibility for advocates of the time.

Interestingly, Robert Owen, the owner of New Lanark, was a friend and frequent visitor to the house of William Godwin—father of Mary

Shelley (the author of *Frankenstein*), and sometimes mentor to her husband Percy Bysshe Shelley—so there was, in fact, a connection between the romantics and the humane industrialists of the time.

Lastly, some readers have reacted with disbelief regarding the way the inheritance laws in Scotland are portrayed in this novel. I, too, found it a bit unbelievable. I drafted *Roses in Red Wax* without really knowing how it would end, and when I came across the legal basis for Cameron's inheritance, it seemed absolutely too good to be true. I double checked. I triple checked. I asked an expert in the field, and yes, dear reader, it's true. Cameron is the rightful Earl of Banton under established—historically accurate—Scottish law.

Acknowledgements

First and foremost, thank you to my husband, Mr. Mayberry, for his unwavering support. He's my alpha reader, my shoulder to cry on, my best friend and my happily ever after. I love you!

I'd also like to thank Annie R. McKewen, who is so much more than just a critique partner, and whose friendship, collaboration and historical expertise were integral to the completion of this book; my editor, Isabelle Felix, who helped me understand what this story is really about; and Sally J. Walker, my teacher, whose kind, yet exacting presence has made me the writer I am today.

Thank you to my beta readers: Mom, Brendon, Cari, Brandy, Patrick, Laura, Katy, Sara, Kate. Your critiques were invaluable. And to my ARC team, for their overwhelming support and encouragement.

Thank you to all the incredible authors whose work inspired me to start writing, particularly KJ Charles, Julie Anne Long, and Joanna Chambers, who not only responded to my fan-girl emails, but took the time to encourage me and give me valuable advice.

And lastly, to my readers. I'm humbled and forever grateful that you've chosen to spend a few hours with Jane and Percy. Thank you!

THANK YOU, READERS!

Thank you for reading this book.

Let's stay in touch!

To stay in the loop on upcoming releases and other goings-on (as well as discounts and freebies!) head over to my website to sign up for my mailing list: www.louisemayberry.com. You can also find me on Instagram and Facebook. My email is louise@louisemayberry.com.

Reviews

If you enjoyed this book, I hope you'll consider sharing your thoughts by posting a review. It may seem like a small thing, but reviews and word of mouth recommendations are incredibly important. It would mean the world to me!

ALSO BY LOUISE MAYBERRY

The Darnalay Castle Series

Book 1: Roses in Red Wax

JANE STUART HAS LOST everything, her betrothed, her ancestral castle in the Highlands, and her life's work—the orchard where she ran her apple tree crossbreeding trials. But after a year of exile in smoke-filled Glasgow, she's gone numb to the loss, indifferent to her lonely, grey future.

Then *he* comes along.

Percy Sommerbell is a musician, a free spirit who holds nothing but disdain for his industrialist father. But when familial duty forces Percy to travel to Scotland to inspect his father's holdings, he's confronted with an uncomfortable truth. His fortune—the money that funds his aimless wandering through all life's pleasures—is generated by the exploitation of people, *children*, in his father's spinning mills.

There's something else in Glasgow, a mysterious Highland beauty whose sad eyes and luscious curves promise temporary distraction from his growing sense of guilt, and inspiration for his music.

Against her better judgement, Jane finds herself falling for this man's charms. But when the mills become the first spark in a violent radical insurgency and old enemies threaten, everything changes. Can Jane and Percy's connection survive as the world catches fire?

Book 2: Swept Into the Storm

Yucatan Peninsula, Mexico, 1824.

Ever since he unexpectedly inherited his father's earldom in the Scottish Highlands, Cameron Dunn's been searching for something, *anything,* to bring meaning to his new life—a search that reaches an abrupt end when he's washed up, alone, on a deserted beach in Mexico.

Or at least the beach *should* be deserted. There's no village for hundreds of miles. So who's that beautiful woman walking toward him over the sand?

Letty Monro has a business to run, a plan for her future. Rescuing a shipwrecked earl wasn't on the agenda. But the man's desperate, so of course she'll bring him to the British Settlement—for fifty pounds. And his signet ring for collateral. She's even prepared to look past the fact he's a peer, part of the system of oppression she despises.

As they begin their journey, sailing south through the Caribbean sea, Cameron finds himself falling for this guarded, stubborn business-woman, and the heat smoldering between them threatens to burst into flame. Keeping her distance from the Earl of Banton will prove one of the greatest challenges Letty has ever faced. Especially when she notices, in the distracting warmth of his brown eyes, the one thing they have in common . . . How lost they both truly are.

Book 3: A Radical Affair

Cybil Bythesea is imprisoned in a marriage that ended ten years ago. That's when she fled the cruelty of her husband, Lord Falstone, and took refuge at her father's estate in Northumberland. Since then, her family's money has kept the villain at bay, and she's been able to pursue her creative passion—writing. But freedom, true freedom, has been beyond her grasp.

Except for her clandestine liaisons with Will.

Will Chisolm is haunted by the past, the tragedy of his family's eviction from their ancestral Highland farm, then his own foolish descent into political radicalism. Even now that he's gained wealth and respectability as the manager of a set of spinning mills in Glasgow, he's burdened with more responsibility and guilt than anyone knows.

But there's something about Cybil—a lightness, a kinship that, at least temporarily, makes all Will's troubles fade away. It's a dangerous game.

Cybil is his employer's sister, the wife of his political enemy and for the last four years, his lover.

She's also with child. Will's child. And their world, their lives, will never be the same.

Available from all major book retailers, or purchase directly from Louise's website: <u>www.louisemayberry.com</u>

Sign up for Louise's newsletter to receive 30% off your first order.

ABOUT THE AUTHOR

Louise Mayberry lives with her family in the Upper Midwest, where she savors the summers and survives the winters. When not writing, she can be found wandering in her garden, attempting to talk her her kids into eating healthy food, or curled up in a pool of sunshine with a cup of tea and a good book.

Made in the USA
Middletown, DE
23 April 2024

53359263R00172